# QUEEN *for a* DAY

# QUEEN *for a* DAY

A NOVEL IN STORIES

# MAXINE ROSALER

DELPHINIUM BOOKS

QUEEN FOR A DAY

Copyright © 2018 by Maxine Rosaler

For information, address DELPHINIUM BOOKS, INC.,
16350 Ventura Boulevard, Suite D
PO Box 803
Encino, CA 91436

Library of Congress Cataloguing-in-Publication Data is available on request.

ISBN 978-1-88-328575-3

18 19 20 21 22  LSC  10 9 8 7 6 5 4 3 2 1

First Edition

*Jacket and interior design by Greg Mortimer*

A shorter version of "Sleepwalking Boy" was published as "The Lost Boy" in the Winter 2015 edition of *Fifth Wednesday*. An excerpt from "Sleepwalking Boy" was published in *Our Lives*, edited by Sarah Shapiro. "Yolanda" was published in the Spring 2018 edition of *Green Mountains Review*. "The Red Cart" was published in the Spring 2016 edition of *Glimmer Train*.

For Benjy

# Contents

# Sleepwalking Boy

O. J. Simpson had just been acquitted of murder the day Jake and I drove from our apartment in Washington Heights for our first therapy session with Stan Shapiro, and that's what we talked about during the entire forty-five-minute ride down the West Side Highway to his office building in the Bowery. We were going to see Stan out of concern for our son, who was three at the time.

Jake had written a long, ruminative essay about Danny, noting his strengths and weaknesses and every possible sign of pathology he could perceive lurking within him, and he presented this fifteen-page, single-spaced document to Stan during our first visit. As we would learn later, Stan thought Jake's essay was rich in clues to my husband's obsessive and fetishistic personality. But Stan seldom used such terms with us. He preferred "That's nutty," "That's just crazy," and other deliberately casual expressions most likely calculated to get us to lighten up.

After a couple of sessions, Stan managed to convince us that whatever problems Danny might or might not have stemmed from the sorry state of his parents' marriage. It wasn't until many months later that I remembered that this was exactly what Stan had told the woman who had recommended him to me.

I was shopping for groceries one day at Key Food, and Sally, an acquaintance of mine from the neighborhood, and I got to talking about our children. Sally had a little girl who never spoke to anyone but her parents—"selective mutism," I've since learned it's called. Sally told me she had gone to see a therapist, who had helped her a lot. The girl still wasn't talking to anyone but them, but Stan had shown her that her daughter wasn't the problem; rather, she and her husband were the problem. Sally gave me Stan's phone number, which I eagerly scribbled onto Key Food's weekly circular.

It came as no surprise to us to hear that Jake and I were to blame for our son's troubling behaviors. We'd been worried for a long time that we had warped Danny's psyche with our constant fighting. We had been fighting since before he was born; indeed, we had been fighting for almost as long as we had been together, since the sudden mysterious expiration of those first six idyllic months of staying in bed all day, talking late into the night and having sex in unusual places. We fought in public and people would stare at us. Strangers on the street, in the subway, on line at the movies would tell us to shut up. Once we had been kicked out of a restaurant and told never to return. Yet after three years of this, we had gotten married, certain that our love was stronger than our hate. We were like those Marvel comic book characters who can smack each other around with trees and houses and still be ready for the next battle: we could take it.

Of course, we knew it would be unreasonable for us to expect our child to be super, too, and we were horrified and remorseful when it turned out that his arrival in our lives did nothing to stop us. We just couldn't restrain ourselves from demanding justice from each other, and we did so at the top of our lungs, with Danny in his high chair at the kitchen table, with Danny lying in his crib a wall away, with Danny in the backseat of the car, with Danny in our arms.

Once, a year before we started therapy, Jake punched the windshield. A tiny crack, hardly noticeable at first, expanded slowly over a period of days, first into a jagged asterisk, and then, after a week, it turned into a sort of spiderweb twenty inches in diameter; this gradual response of the windshield to the injury that had been inflicted on it seemed like a metaphor for the terrible harm we were doing Danny, who never exhibited any sign of being upset by our fights. Maybe that was why we didn't stop; maybe if he had screamed and shrieked like his parents, or if he had cried or run away in terror, we might have tried harder to stop, but he simply ignored our constant fighting; perhaps because this was what he had known all his life.

Danny, who was two at the time, did not seem to notice the cracks Jake had made in the windshield. He was very quiet. There was an old woman we would run into from time to time, one of the dying breed of old German Jews who used to inhabit Washington Heights; once in the supermarket she had reproached a friend of mine for letting her daughter run up and down the fruit and vegetable aisle. A few years later on Fort Washington Avenue, this same woman, noticing

Danny's absolute doll-like stillness in his stroller, had complimented me: "What a well-behaved child," she had said.

It came as a relief to Jake and me to think that Danny's problems could be solved if we could just learn to get along, and we were glad to have someone, a professional who specialized in these matters, step into the ring with us and act as referee.

After each session we would treat ourselves to breakfast at our favorite restaurant, the Kiev, in the East Village. Danny was in nursery school at the time, and eating out together in the middle of the day felt like a healthy, normal thing to be doing; sometimes we thought it was the most effective part of the therapy. Over kielbasa and eggs we would discuss our relationship, but more often, and with much more enthusiasm, we would talk about our relationship with Stan. Jake and I both vied for his approval, and we would have fun debating whom he was being tougher on, and whom he liked more.

In session with him we often felt as though we were playing a subtle and complicated game. It was fun, bantering with Stan, laying all our cute little quirks and oddities out for him to analyze, and although we could never say exactly what it was he was accomplishing with us during those fifty minutes we spent with him each week, we figured that our problems would be taken care of eventually, somehow, someway. We knew that Stan was on the case because he never let us get away with anything. He never took anything we said at face value: he was forcing us to pierce through our illusions about ourselves. We could tell we were getting the real thing and, at the reduced rate he was giving us, more than our money's worth.

It seemed to us that we would get along better on Wednesdays, and we would always have fun going to breakfast at the Kiev afterward, talking about Stan. But on all the days in between, we were fighting as much as ever. Our household was still in a state of chaos, as Stan was so fond of characterizing it, and the level of stress and anxiety was as great as ever. No, it was greater than ever. Something was growing in our emotional lives, something terrible that we couldn't put a name to.

Danny had not spoken until shortly before his second birthday. His language was very primitive for his age, and there was something very odd about the way he used words. He went around the apartment reciting lines from Disney videos and making cryptic comments about them. "Rocks and rocks and gruve." "The candle is afraid of the white clock!"

He seemed to be more interested in the speech of machinery than in the speech of human beings. As if preparing for a life spent in conversation with things instead of people, he reproduced, with uncanny accuracy, the sounds made by the blender, the dishwasher, subway trains, exhaust fans, and vacuum cleaners (after going through a period of being terrified of exhaust fans and vacuum cleaners).

We had heard, years ago, that autistic children were fascinated with machines, and the word "autism" would sometimes occur to us. However, we were afraid to speak it. So we just described Danny's noise obsession to Stan and asked, "What do you think that means? Is that a sign of anything?" Stan shrugged and said, "Maybe when he grows up, he'll be a sound engineer." This was the kind of response we had been hoping for.

We would remind ourselves that our own quirks and oddities were numerous, perhaps as numerous as Danny's, so why should we expect our son to be normal? Besides, even if Danny had not spoken until he was two and even if he did speak strangely now, he had a very large vocabulary. He knew what the words "parallelogram," "paradox" and "equidistant" meant. He also had an interest in the aesthetics of language and had a talent with words. He loved making puns. Once, when we were trying to teach him about safety and we asked him if it would be a good idea to dive into an empty swimming pool, he giggled and said, "Then it would be a dying board." He was great with puzzles. He knew his numbers and his alphabet and was beginning to read. We would try to remember Danny's precocities in these areas whenever we worried about him.

Although Stan didn't think it was necessary, we insisted on bringing Danny to one of our early sessions. We were terrified that he might be retarded—another word Jake and I could barely bring ourselves to utter. Stan observed Danny playing with toys and putting together a puzzle. Reminding us that psychological testing was not his specialty, he said that in his casual but professional opinion, Danny's IQ was probably within the normal range.

We had been hoping he would say that. We were at the stage when whoever said "Boys are like that," or "Kids develop at their own pace," or "He reminds me of Jimmy at that age—wild just like that," was our ally. If anyone seemed to think there was something wrong with Danny, we would feel as though he were being attacked.

Shortly before we started seeing Stan, I enrolled Danny in a nursery school a few blocks away from a Starbucks that had just opened up on 102nd Street and Broadway. My plan was to do my copyediting while Danny was in school, with limited commuting time between the school and Starbucks. Although Danny would often have a temper tantrum when I dropped him off, I assumed it was just a sign of the separation anxiety discussed in the books about child-rearing I never had the patience to read. I didn't think much of it until it was time for the seasonal parent-teacher conference in August. Esther Guy, Danny's teacher, and Pearl Claener, the director of the school, were waiting for me outside the door when I arrived for our early-morning meeting that day. After telling me how adorable my son was, Esther, with a glance at Pearl, excused herself and left.

Pearl sat down behind her big metal desk and I sat in a black wooden chair across from her. I had found that chair in front of a coffee shop on Broadway on my way to pick up Danny one day. The restaurant was in the midst of redecorating and I knew that the school was short on chairs, and together Pearl and I went back to the street to pick up the rest of them.

"Mimi," she said, and after a brief pause, she said that there were a number of problems with Danny's behavior that we needed to talk about. She started tentatively and then the words started pouring out of her so rapidly, I felt as though I were drowning in them.

Danny hardly ever looked anyone in the eye. He ignored the other children. He never answered to his name. He was constantly spinning around in circles—he never got dizzy. He hid in closets. He would often leave the classroom on his own; once he had even left the building. He burrowed himself under the cushions of the sofa. He was always turning the lights on and off. If his teachers scolded him, he would just laugh. It wasn't merely that he flouted authority—he didn't seem to understand that there were such things as rules or that people might get angry if he disobeyed them. He didn't seem to know what anger was.

Pearl said it made her sad to tell me this, but it was clear to her and all the other teachers that Danny required a much higher level of care than anything they could possibly provide. She said I should have him evaluated right away. Testing for developmental disabilities was something that the School District was required by law to do for all children. It wouldn't cost us anything. I had only a vague idea of what the term "developmental disability" meant, but I didn't ask Pearl to define it.

I called Stan as soon as I got home and told him what Pearl had said. Jake and I were afraid, fifty layers of denial ago, of what would happen if some incompetent, literal-minded civil servant tested Danny and put a "label" on him. The label would go into Danny's permanent records, and later on, when his teachers looked at them, they would be prejudiced against him. They would treat him differently. He would be stigmatized.

I asked Stan to call Pearl so that he could hear for himself what she had to say. Four days days later he reported back to me that nothing the school's director had told him had given him any cause for concern. When I asked him whether or not he thought we should get Danny tested, as Pearl (who had called me twice since our meeting) kept on urging me to do, he said "there was no hurry." When I asked him if he thought there was anything wrong with Danny, he told me that he "didn't have anything you could pin a label on."

Afterward, whenever Jake and I worried about Danny, we would remind ourselves that according to Stan Danny didn't have "anything you could pin a label on." We didn't have to get Danny tested. So we let the matter rest: Danny didn't have "anything you could pin a label on." That phrase became our mantra and we would repeat it over and over again to ourselves, to each other and to the occasional friend who would try in vain to sound an alarm.

Danny was too wild to be left in the care of any babysitter, so after he was expelled from nursery school, we would bring him to our therapy sessions. It was clear to us that Stan didn't approve of this: it never seemed to sink into him that Danny couldn't be trusted to walk in the city without his hand being held; that he showed no sense that the street and its cars were to be avoided; that if we didn't watch him constantly when we took him to the park, he might try to fly off the top of the monkey bars like a bird, or leave the playground altogether.

My twin sister, who lived near Stan's office, offered to watch Danny for us in her apartment, but Jake and I felt uneasy about leaving him there. Ruth lived on the thirty-first floor and she had a terrace, and that terrace worried us. Danny climbed on everything: the floor-to-ceiling bookshelves in our office, the kitchen countertops, the piano—anything that looked as though it might be fun to climb on. We also thought Ruth's terrace would present Danny with a temptation to indulge himself in one of his favorite pastimes: observing the different velocities at which things fell from high places. If we left him alone for a minute, we would often find him throwing books, pencils, paperweights, et cetera, out the windows of our sixth-floor apartment. It was his fascination with gravity. That was what Jake and I told each other.

Danny had no fear of heights, and one of his favorite things to do was to try to squeeze himself through the space between the child guards on the windows. Jake, trying to scare him, would say things like, "Don't you know what would happen if you fell out the window? You would be squashed like a tomato!"

"Like a tomato!" Danny would echo happily. "And you'd be dead," Jake would tell him. "Like a tomato!" Danny would answer. He seemed to consider himself just another object whose fall might be interesting to observe.

We weren't sure that my sister would be as vigilant as she had to be. We doubted that anyone could be vigilant enough. But we were especially worried about leaving Danny with Ruth, whose brain had been damaged by a fall from the monkey bars when she was six. We were identical twins: I was three minutes older, yet I had been more like a mother to her than a sister. In Ruth's opinion, I had done a lousy job of it, just as lousy a job, she often pointed out, as I was now doing with my son.

Ruth felt insulted that Jake and I wouldn't leave Danny in her apartment; nevertheless when we came up with the idea of her watching Danny in the tiny vestibule outside Stan's office during our marriage counseling sessions, she agreed. Whenever we returned to the little vestibule after thrashing it out with Stan in his office, she always made a point of telling me that those fifty minutes Danny had spent in her relaxed presence (as opposed to my anxious, toxic one) had been therapeutic for him. She expected that in time her calming influence would help heal the damage caused by the three-and-a-half years he had spent with me.

It was clear to us that Stan felt we were imposing on him by having Ruth babysit for Danny in his tiny waiting room.

No doubt he felt even more imposed upon on days when Ruth was unavailable, and Danny would rush into his office and touch what he had been told not to touch and climb where he had been told not to climb: Stan would observe us in silence as we ran after our son, yelling, "No, Danny, don't do that!" "Danny, stop! Please stop!" "Danny, no! No! No! No!"

When Danny was finished exploring Stan's office, he would sit on the floor, playing with Stan's toys or whatever toys we had brought along. Playing with toys in Danny's case usually meant spilling the pieces out of the boxes and examining them very closely. Only with clay and puzzles did he play in the expected way, making balls and chairs and tables out of the clay, as Jake had taught him to do, and putting the puzzles back together.

Jake would sometimes spell out the words he was saying, and he would get angry at me if I spoke too overtly about delicate matters, such as sex, and so I trained myself to be more discreet. But I did so to appease Jake, not to avoid traumatizing our son. Danny never paid attention to us when we were addressing him directly, so why should he pay attention to us now?

I think that Stan must have suspected that there was something the matter with Danny, something not covered by phrases like "It's a phase," "Kids develop at their own pace," phrases that would make us wag our tails whenever anyone repeated them. But even if he did know what was wrong with our son, his training would never have permitted him to say outright what he thought it was. He would work slowly, with the patient, unhurried techniques of psychoanalysis (he was "eclectic," but in the Freudian tradition) to bring us to insight. Then we would see for ourselves what had been staring us in the face all along. Like Dorothy at the end of *The Wizard of Oz,* after this moral journey we would be ready to know.

A year after Jake and I started seeing Stan, I decided to go to a series of seminars on child discipline that a friend of mine told me about. The idea of seeking advice from someone other than Stan made me feel uneasy at first. I was afraid it might make Stan think I had lost faith in him. But he said I should go: it would be good for me to see that Jake and I weren't the only people in the world who had trouble with their children.

The seminars were sponsored by a large social services agency in the city; they were free and the parents were even given subway fare to attend—at the end of every meeting the moderator would pass around a sign-up sheet and distribute subway tokens. There was always a pot of coffee waiting for us, and a generous assortment of snacks spread out on the table—Entenmann's donuts, Cheese Nips, Oreos and big healthy-looking bunches of fresh green grapes.

As we sat around the chipped Formica table, under the flickering fluorescent lights of that big bare room, we would take turns talking about our children. There was a six-year-old boy who ran up and down the hallway of his apartment at all hours of the day and night; a five-year-old who couldn't bear to have anything touch her body and was always taking off her clothes, at home, at school, in the playground, everywhere; a four-year-old who liked banging his head against the wall and another four-year-old who was always biting people.

After a few sessions I realized that most of the children of the parents attending the seminar were autistic. I decided that I had been sent there by mistake. There was no denying I had a difficult child, but he was nothing like these children.

As time passed, I started feeling more and more uneasy about going to the seminars. Making my way up the stairs, past the larger-than-life-size photographs of children, some of them in wheelchairs, most of them with something visibly wrong with them despite the cheerful smiles they had worn for the camera, I would often have trouble catching my breath. The pictures were faded, and the haircuts and shirts were out of style; it was clear to me that these photos must have been taken a long time ago. These children were all adults now. What had become of them?

I always managed to calm down once I was in the room, entertaining the group with stories about my unruly four-year-old. The parents seemed to enjoy my stories. They thought it was funny, the way my son liked to swing by his arms from the shower rod in the bathroom and was always flushing socks down the toilet and putting silverware, pens and chopsticks into the pencil sharpener. Their generosity, in the face of all the trouble they had with their own children, touched me.

They said that Danny must be very smart; they could tell by the kinds of questions he asked and the observations he made: "Why Play-Doh dries up?" "Why clay doesn't dry up?" "Why is it dark in space?" And his fascination with gravity—the way he was always testing it out by jumping down flights of stairs, jumping off rocks in Fort Tryon Park and throwing things out the window—they thought that was adorable. He sounds like a little scientist, they would say.

\* \* \*

I didn't tell the mothers about the night I walked up and down 181st Street searching for the new kitchen curtains Danny had sent sailing out the bathroom window. It was an excuse for me to escape the havoc of my household, and I fell into a kind of trance as I walked up and down the street, my eyes panning the sidewalks, the gutters, grates and bushes, the flowerpots, the soil that embraced the trees; kneeling on the rough pavement as I looked under the cars parked along the curb, desperate to find my curtains.

After wandering around like this for more than an hour, I found one of the curtains stuck behind the wheel of a blue Chevy Nova parked ten blocks away from our apartment house. I never did find the other one, although I would continue searching, days after Danny had set it free.

I kept on hoping it would turn up, as Danny's sweatshirt had turned up on the sidewalk a day after I lost it. I had dropped it on the walk home from a friend's house one New Year's Eve, and when I went back the next day to search for it, I found it lying in a shiny clump on the sidewalk in front of the candy store where Jake would take Danny for ice cream every Sunday afternoon. It had rained the night before, and the rain had saved Danny's sweatshirt; it had kept it there in one place. It looked so helpless lying in a wet clump on the sidewalk, covered with footprints and sparkling with a thin patina of ice. I loved that sweatshirt; it was violet blue and brought out the blue in Danny's violet blue eyes, and I couldn't wait to bring it home to wash it and dry it and see Danny wear it again.

There was one parent at the seminar who was never amused by my Danny stories. Her name was Mary. She was the mother of a full-grown autistic man. Her husband had disappeared long ago, and she didn't have any friends left. She had spent the past thirty years taking care of her son. She had to engage in hand-to-hand combat with him whenever she left the house—he would block the doorway, all two hundred fifty pounds of him. She had black-and-blue marks all over her arms to prove it, which she wearily displayed for everyone to see. A couple of times Mary turned to me and told me that there was something wrong with my son and that I had to get him evaluated right away.

Whenever Mary spoke to me that way, the familiar terror would grip me, and it wouldn't leave, not even when I was explaining to her that there was nothing wrong with Danny—that a psychologist had assured me he didn't "have anything you could pin a label on."

I was relieved when Mary stopped coming to the meetings, which clearly had nothing to offer her. Everyone else seemed happy to see Mary go, too. She was the only mother of an adult there. All the rest of us were the mothers of young children.

Danny's behavior kept on getting stranger and stranger. He imitated machines more and more often. He still didn't know how to use pronouns properly: he called "hes" and "shes" "its"; he said "you" when he meant "I." He asked questions we had answered a hundred times before. His speech seemed to be an anthology of sentence fragments, many of them his own invention, most of them meaningless, but with occasional bursts of lucidity. The repetitive nature of Danny's attempts at communication (if, indeed, his intention was to communicate—we were never sure) reminded us of the speech of the dolls of our childhood that made one of ten different remarks at random every time you pulled their cords.

He had an average of one tantrum per day, and whenever he was shown a picture of anyone crying—including Thomas the Tank Engine—he would burst into tears himself. For as long as we could remember, Danny seemed to be trying to express a desire to experience new things ("I want to go far away," was part of his limited repertoire of sentences for a long time).

Although there was no end to his curiosity (Danny wanted to know everything about everything), he always wanted things done exactly as they had been done before. When we took him to the playground, he always insisted on traversing the circumference of the park by going from bench to bench, over people when necessary, without his feet touching the ground.

His way of expressing distress or disappointment was very odd. Occasionally in the middle of a tantrum he would say, "I can't talk! I can't talk!" When his grandmother said she wouldn't give him a second helping of noodles because he had made a mess on the floor with his first dish of noodles, he sang the Barney song: "I love you, you love me, we're a happy family." When we wouldn't give him something he wanted, he would sometimes say, "This is a dream. I'm dreaming."

This epoch of our lives came to an abrupt end a year after Pearl Claener urged me to have Danny evaluated for developmental disabilities. It was late August and we had brought Danny along with us to visit Jake's parents in Plainview, Long Island. I had gone off grocery shopping, and as I was getting out of the car, Jake came racing out of the house and down the driveway to meet me. Danny was missing.

Jake's parents' house sat next to a forest. In the other direction, at the bottom of the long country driveway, was a busy road with cars traveling fifty miles an hour. To the right and left were houses with swing sets and lights that would attract Danny when he was in the backyard. We would have to check the backyards, and if we didn't find him, we would have to ask the people in the neighboring houses to help us look for him.

He might also be in the house, an old mansion full of closets he liked to crawl into and lots of high, wide-open windows. After yelling out to my mother-in-law to search the house, I told Jake to go to the neighbors' houses and ask for their help. I reminded him to make sure to explain that the little boy in the white shirt and blue shorts didn't answer to his name. I recall thinking to myself, in the midst of my panic, how difficult it would be for Jake going to strangers and asking them for help, because Jake is very shy. We would always remind each other about his shyness, and his many other strange, isolated ways—the way he would get so completely lost in his thoughts that he wouldn't notice I was talking to him, the way he had always spent so much time alone—to reassure ourselves that there really was nothing wrong with Danny. Like father, like son. That was all.

I rushed back to search the streets of the neighborhood in our car. When I made my way out of the driveway, I was relieved to see that there were no police cars with flashing lights on Waukena Avenue, no ambulance or lineup of cars with their horns honking. There was also no sign of Danny. I traveled up and down the main road and all the nearby side streets, and after fifteen minutes of searching, I drove back to the house and made my way into the forest behind my in-laws' house.

I knew that Danny would never follow a path, so I plunged straight into the woods, stumbling on the uneven ground, one moment sinking into a shallow pit of wet, spongy leaves and the next stepping on dry branches that snapped under my feet. I searched for the blue of the pullover I had dressed Danny in that morning. As I ran through the woods, shouting out the name that meant nothing to him, I could picture Danny amusing himself for hours, crouched among the deadfalls, the roots and the ferns, running his fingers over the moss, peeling bark off trees, tearing leaves off branches and picking away at their green veins, with no fear, no feeling about the strangeness or loneliness or isolation of being lost. It would be nothing new to him. He was alone in a strange place every day of his life.

We searched this way for an hour, and then we called the police. Minutes before they arrived, we found Danny: he had been sitting in Jake's mother's car the entire time. We had forgotten how much he liked to play with the buttons on the dashboard and examine the levers on the steering column. All the yelling and screaming and the search party we had so frantically organized had done nothing to rouse him from his play. The sound of his name being yelled over and over again was no different to Danny from the other sounds that surrounded him: the traffic on the road, the airplane overhead, the birds chirping, a dog barking, a neighbor's lawn mower, our desperate cries—they were all just background noise to him.

It was the end of summer, and we had a vacation planned, and before going away, I scheduled an interview for Danny with a psychologist at a special education school in Riverdale who did evaluations paid for by The District.

The vacation lasted nine days. We rented a cabin in the woods near Lake Taghkanic. On our last day there, when I was going for a walk with Danny on the beach, I ran into a woman who had been in my Lamaze class. Suzanne was a friendly, nice-looking woman. She was very different from the other mothers I knew, maybe because she was from Australia. There had been a period when it looked as though we might become friends, but we never did, and she had moved out of the city a year after her second child was born. Her first child, who was born a day after Danny, was with her now, four-and-a-half years later, building a sandcastle on the beach a few steps away, and when Suzanne told her to come over to meet me, she came over, and when Suzanne introduced us, she said hello, and told me that I was pretty. The contrast was startling. Danny was in my arms, and when I introduced him to Suzanne and her daughter, he ignored them, and when I tried to put him down, he clung on to me like a crab.

I have always been in the habit of blurting out whatever is on my mind, whether I want to or not, and as I watched her little girl trying to interest Danny in helping her build her sandcastle, I found myself telling Suzanne I was worried about my son. I told her we were going to have him tested as soon as we got back to the city. Suzanne asked me what I was worried about, and when I told her, she said with her sunny smile, "Oh yes, I've heard about that. I was just reading a book about that."

I didn't ask her to tell me what this interesting thing she had heard about was. But I asked Jake later on what he thought she meant. "She meant autism," he said, and he blamed me for it. He said I always exaggerated our difficulties with Danny, I always exaggerated his odd behaviors; I never presented a balanced picture. If I had told Suzanne how affectionate Danny was, what a great sense of humor he had, how open he was to new experiences, she would never have thought Autism.

It rained the last day of our vacation and I welcomed the rain, for it was a good excuse to leave that hot little cabin in the woods a day early. It was a record-breaking storm, like nothing anyone on the East Coast had seen in over a decade. There were distinct, white-capped waves on the highway, and our windshield wipers, which under normal conditions were inadequate, were more or less useless, giving me, who was the driver in the family (Jake had let his license expire years ago), only the most meager view of what lay before me on the road. I have always been a fearful driver, and had always especially hated driving in the rain, but now the storm came as a relief to me. It claimed all my attention.

The evaluation was conducted in a large room in the school's basement, which was full of toys. There was a big wooden dollhouse, a plastic barn equipped with a fence and farm animals, a toy washing machine and a toy swing set. Danny started examining the contents of the dollhouse. The psychologist, Ellen Camins, sat in a little children's chair at a little children's table observing him, and I sat in a little chair next to her.

Danny didn't want to leave the dollhouse to take the test, but after a lot of coaxing, he finally agreed to sit down across from Ellen, although his attention kept on drifting back to the dollhouse.

Almost immediately into the test, Ellen turned to me. (Jake had declined her invitation to sit in the room while she administered the exam. He couldn't bear to be there.) She said that it wasn't Danny's fault that he wasn't answering her questions; it wasn't his fault that he didn't know that an elephant was bigger than a mouse—it was "neurological," she said. I had been making excuses for his him. He's very stubborn, I kept on telling her. He's very independent.

"He isn't stubborn," she told me. "It's not in his control."

Jake came back to the school in time for the language evaluation part of it, and Ellen invited him in, but he said he would rather wait outside. He did, however, agree to come in when it was time for Ellen to summarize her preliminary impressions of Danny. The formal scoring of the tests would take a couple of weeks, but she said that she didn't need to see any numbers to know what was the matter with our son.

"It's neurological," I said, turning to Jake.

Danny was inspecting the dollhouse again, and Ellen told Jake to sit down and she proceeded to address us together. She spoke with an enthusiastic, almost congratulatory, smile on her face. She never dropped that smile.

"First of all, he's a delightful child. And he's a very happy little boy. It's a tribute to you as parents. That your son is so happy. Most of these kids aren't happy. He has a wonderful sense of humor, and he's very bright." She said it all pretty much as though she were giving us an award for being the parents of the cutest little boy in the world.

Looking at Jake, she explained, "Often during the testing—as I told Mimi—he would get a hard problem right and then he would fail to answer an easy one."

"He's not very cooperative, I guess," Jake said. "It's hard to know, it's hard to get an accurate assessment with children so young. And especially with a child like Danny, who doesn't answer questions."

Ellen agreed, but she said that she was nevertheless confident of her assessment. She described Danny's problems with language and communication. She said that in order to compensate for his verbal weaknesses, he was a "visual learner," and this was why he had such a precocious understanding of geometry and knew the difference between a parallelogram and a trapezoid, something that was very unusual for a four-year-old.

And there was a term for what he did when he repeated back what people said word for word: it was called echolalia.

Jake said, "Like when he goes around repeating phrases from the Disney videos."

"That's right," said Ellen, and her tone became chatty for a moment. "It's amazing what memories these kids have."

Sitting there in those little chairs, Jake and I felt like the smallest people in the world, and Ellen, who was a tiny, soft-spoken woman, seemed like the most powerful person in the world.

We sat there, abjectly, and questioned her about Danny's future. Would he go to a regular school? Ellen thought that after two years of special education, he could be "mainstreamed." Would he go to college? No reason why he shouldn't. Would he get married? He could get married. Would he have a profession? She looked into her crystal ball and promised us, yes, he could have a career. He could be an architect, or maybe an engineer. He probably wouldn't grow up to be President of the United States. Nor would he ever be the life of the party. But he was smart. He was very smart. Although he had many significant developmental delays.

Then she took out a questionnaire and asked us a long list of questions about Danny, to which she told us to answer "Always," "Sometimes" or "Never." She urged us, whenever possible, to veer on the side of negativity. That is, we should try to show Danny at his worst, not at his best; that way we would have a better chance of getting more services from The District. She spoke with an air of complicity that confused us. The message we seemed to be receiving was that we would have to be very clever—devious, even—in order for Danny to have any chance of The District giving him the help that he needed.

I picked Danny up and held him tightly in my arms. Ellen remarked how attractive he was. Then, her voice reassuming the professional, reflective tone she had maintained throughout the past two hours, she said, "That's good. That will work in his favor. People will want to help him."

In the car, Jake and I speculated about what Ellen could have meant by that strange remark. To begin with, it gave us a glimpse of what we would be up against, what a long journey lay ahead of us. Danny would need a lot of help. And this help would not be forthcoming simply because he needed it. He would have to compete for it, wrest it perhaps from other children who were just as needy, but hopefully less attractive.

Before we left, I asked Ellen to let Danny into her school, and when she explained, still smiling, that she didn't know, all the spaces had been filled, I begged her to make a spot for Danny. Ellen told me not to be so anxious. Everything was going to be just fine.

I asked her what we should do with Danny in the meantime.

"Just relax and enjoy the rest of your summer," she said.

While I made a living copyediting romance novels, Jake wrote technical manuals for a software company. We both spent all our spare time writing fiction and had progressed from youth to middle age confident that sooner or later one or both of us would achieve some kind of literary success, which was why we had crummy freelance jobs that gave us time for writing, but which paid much less than what my father had earned as the advertising manager for an import-export firm and what Jake's father had earned as the owner of a small machine shop when we were growing up.

In the parking lot I told Jake that I was going to drop my novel. I knew he couldn't stop working on his, but would he please work on it at home now, instead of taking his laptop to cafés, as was his habit. He agreed. He said he would go crazy if he abandoned his novel. But yes, of course he would be there; we would work with Danny together.

The idea that we would ever think of putting Danny in a special education school would have been unimaginable to us a few hours ago, but now we were desperate for him to be accepted at this school in Riverdale. One way or another, I would get them to find room for him. I would just have to be persistent.

When I told my friends about Danny, I felt that I was telling them good-bye—not forever, but for now. I was about to go on a long journey, and I didn't expect anyone but Jake to go with me. I wished my friends well, and they wished me well, too.

I wanted to cancel our next appointment with Stan. I never wanted to see him again. But Jake disagreed. He said that what we were going through would be very stressful and he thought that Stan might be able to help us deal with the stress. I had no idea how Jake could think that Stan could be of any use to us. Perhaps it was a symptom of his distress. Whatever the reason, I didn't bother to argue with him about it.

Stan's office was on the nineteenth floor. It wasn't as nice as his previous office, which hadn't been all that nice, and when he had moved there about six months into our therapy, Jake and I had worried that he might not be doing well. Had he moved there for the convenience of his clients, since it was closer to the subway station, as he had claimed, or had he moved there because the rent was cheaper?

My sister was waiting for us outside the building. "Hi, Danny!" she said.

He answered, "Hi, Danny!"

There was a row of elevators in the lobby of Stan's building. Danny would have a tantrum if he didn't get to ride the same elevator he had ridden the first time we brought him here, and I was relieved to see that his favorite elevator was there waiting for us. Once inside, Danny looked up at the mirrored ceiling and said what he always said when he was in Stan's elevator. "Shiny elevator." Jake had to hold his hands to prevent him from pushing all the buttons from 1 to 20.

Trying to push all the buttons was part of Danny's routine, and having Jake stop him was part of Danny's routine, as well; he wanted Jake to grab his hands to stop him just as much as he wanted to push all the buttons. To be at an impasse, to have the same argument over and over and over again and to get nowhere with it, that wasn't a problem from Danny's perspective; it seemed to be precisely what he wanted out of life.

As the numbers lit up, Danny recited them. "One, two, three, four . . ." A woman in a yellow dress smiled and said what a bright boy he was. True, we reminded ourselves. The psychologist who had evaluated him had said he was very smart, although he had many developmental delays.

When we got to the waiting room, Stan was in session with another patient. Danny ran to the door.

"No, Danny, don't go in."

"Because why?"

"Because it's private."

"Because why?"

"It just is, take my word."

"Let me."

"No, Danny."

"Because why?"

"Because I need you to hug me," I said, and picked him up.

"You're confusing him, Mimi!" said Ruth. "It should be what he needs, not what you need!" Then addressing Danny, speaking in a soft, gentle voice, she said, "It's all right, Danny, you don't have to hug your mother if you don't want to. It's up to you who you hug." Usually a dig like this from my sister would have been enough to set off a major fight between us, but I refrained from saying anything.

Jake and I had both noticed that Ruth was good with Danny. My sister had been insisting for a long time that Danny had serious problems. She was more successful than most people at getting his attention. She spoke to him softly and slowly, she waited for him to answer her, and she always insisted on a response.

A grim-looking young woman contemplating the wisdom she had just received from Stan Shapiro came out of the office, and it was time for us to go in.

Danny ran out of the waiting room into Stan's office, where he tried to climb on the windowsills. Jake, as always, ran after him. "No, Danny." Below was the industrial-looking roof of the neighboring building with a much lower elevation, on which stood something that looked like a giant fan whirling. "What's that?" Danny asked as always. "I don't know," Jake said as usual. "What's that?" Danny asked again. "What's that? What's that? What's that?"

Stan had never approved of Jake following Danny around like a "nervous Nellie." What a nervous father. What a couple of nutty parents.

Stan affected a more casual air than usual during that last session. He sat the entire time in his reclining chair, his feet up, the soles of his new shoes staring out at us. Whenever I think about that encounter, I always remember the soles of Stan's shiny new shoes. I remember thinking, irrelevantly, that this must have been the first time he was wearing them since there were many parts where the leather was shiny, clean and unscratched from the dirty concrete sidewalks of the city below. Stan had recently purchased a new wardrobe, a sign, I had speculated, that he might have a new girlfriend. Or boyfriend. This was something that Jake and I would have fun talking about during our after-session breakfasts at the Kiev—whether Stan was gay.

I sat down in the chair nearest the door; I wanted to be as close as possible to Danny, close to where he was waiting with Ruth in the tiny room outside Stan's office. Jake kept on pacing up and down the floor, and when Stan asked him to sit down—he was making him nervous—he sat down on the couch. Jake sat the way he always sits when he is on edge about something, leaning forward with his neck stretched out, his hands on his knees.

He told Stan about the books we had been reading, about our efforts to learn as much as we could about Danny's condition and what could be done to help him. One phrase that kept cropping up was "brain plasticity." Had Stan heard of this? It seemed that the human brain created neurons much more easily in early childhood.

If Stan was paying any attention to Jake's little lesson on brain development, he might have thought that Jake was implying that it was his—Stan Shapiro's—fault that we had wasted a year and a half of our son's precious time. But I knew Jake: it wasn't like him to hint or to insinuate; I knew that he had simply retreated into the realm of reason, his usual refuge in times of stress, and that in his abstracted state of mind he was inviting Stan, that asshole, to join him there.

Jake was the opposite of me that way. I could never distance myself from anything. It was as though I had no skin.

The fact that Jake and I were so different from each other was at the root of many of our problems. I'm not the same as you, he was always telling me. I'm not you and you're not me. It was a concept that was almost impossible for me to grasp.

Jake got up and started pacing back and forth as he spoke about the evaluation. "Why don't you sit down?" Stan said. "You're making me dizzy."

"Well, we're upset, you see," Jake said.

To which Stan responded, "You sound hysterical. There's nothing to be upset about."

That was what he had told me when I called him after the Riverdale evaluation. That I sounded hysterical.

"Oh, I think there's plenty to be upset about," I spat out.

Stan pretty much ignored me and directed most of what he had to say to Jake. He reported that he had called the psychologist who had evaluated Danny, and although she did not yet have the results, from what she said, it sounded to Stan as if Danny had Asperger syndrome. He did not seem to be the slightest bit embarrassed or apologetic.

One thing I had learned, as I traversed the different time zones, calling everyone I could lay my hands on, running our phone bill up into the hundreds of dollars in those days before free long-distance, was that autism was treatable, in some cases even curable, if caught early enough.

My biggest fear was that it was too late for Danny, and one day I got up the nerve to ask the mother of an eight-year-old I had been calling for advice, sometimes as often as two or three times a day. She lived in Ohio and also happened to be named Mimi. Maybe that was why I had become so dependent on her.

Mimi, who had quit her job as a professor of neuroscience to devote herself to taking care of her son, told me about a form of behaviorism recommended in a memoir written by the mother of two autistic children who had been cured. The therapy hadn't cured Mimi's son, but she believed that it was the only one out there that made any sense. It was the only one with any science behind it. In her book the woman cited studies that claimed a nearly 50 percent cure rate. However, in order for that 50 percent cure to be a possibility, the program had to be started before the child turned five. After five, there would be no chance of a 50 percent cure.

"Danny is four and a half," I told her. "Are we too late?"

"You have to get in there right away," Mimi answered. "You have to turn him around. Point him in another direction."

I started to cry.

"This will change you," she told me, saying something I would hear time and time again over the course of the next several weeks. The terrible thing that happened to other people, the thing that changed their lives forever, had happened to Jake and me. And here was this asshole in shiny new shoes claiming that nothing had changed and therefore he had done nothing wrong.

"You knew something was going on before, didn't you?" Stan was saying. "Now you have a label for it, that's all. Don't you think you're attaching too much significance to the label?"

"No, we don't," I said.

"Well, I think you are. Your child is the same child he was before the evaluation."

"But now we know something about him that we didn't know before," Jake said.

"But what you know is just a word that's been applied to him to describe the behavior you've been witnessing all along."

"If I was diagnosed with diabetes, a doctor would prescribe insulin for me and tell me that I should stay away from sweets," said Jake. "So a label does make a difference. It makes a difference in the—"

"This is such bullshit!" I shouted. "There is something wrong with my son's brain, and you're talking semantics!"

"I don't see any reason for you to raise your voice," said Stan.

The conversation went on like that for the rest of the session, with Stan becoming more and more defensive and more and more insistent that it didn't matter when we got Danny evaluated, because there was still plenty of time, and labels didn't matter.

Near the session's end, when we were standing at the door, me with my backpack on my back, Jake with his, Stan said, "I could give both of you labels if I wanted to, but what would it mean?"

"Go on," I said. "Tell us, Stan. What are our labels?"

"Honey, stop," Jake said.

"This is silly," said Stan.

"Go on, tell us our labels."

"Stop, Mimi," Jake repeated.

But I wouldn't stop, and finally Stan said, "Well, all right. Since you insist. If I wanted to give you a label, I would call you a histrionic personality."

"And Jake? What's his label?"

"If I had to give Jake a label, I would call him a schizoid personality."

(A couple of years later, Jake and I were waiting for Danny to come out of the office of a new psychiatrist who had been recommended to us. There was a copy of the *DSM-IV* on the cocktail table. We looked ourselves up and discovered that, in Stan's opinion, Jake was a cold, unemotional loner and I dressed like a whore and demanded a lot of attention.)

Danny was in the vestibule with Ruth, twisting his body into the shapes of letters, a favorite game of his, when we made our exit from Stan's office. I picked him up and hugged him tightly to me, kissing him, and burying my face in his neck and breathing in his sweet and sour smell.

"How's my baby! Did you miss me! Did you miss your mommy!"

Ruth said, "Mimi, stop it! You're overwhelming him!"

After what I had just been through with Stan, I was ready for a fight, but just as I was about to begin my rampage, Danny started to squirm in my arms. The door to Stan's office was still open, and he managed to wriggle his way out of my arms, and to run back into the office.

He headed straight for the couch and started burrowing his way under the cushions. He ignored every effort I made to capture his attention. Stan was standing with his arms folded over his chest, observing the scene with the same detached expression that hadn't left his face during the past fifty minutes.

I looked at him, and then at Danny. All of a sudden, I found myself asking Stan Shapiro, of all people, what we should do about the way Danny never listened. I felt that desperate, and Stan was the only person there.

Stan nodded, acknowledging that, yes, it was hard to be a parent. "You just have to try harder," he said.

As we were walking to the car, which was parked across the street from Stan's office, I said to Jake, "Well, that was a complete waste of time."

"Okay," said Jake. "You were right."

"We don't need any more metaphysical discussions about the meaning of the word 'label,'" I told him.

"Okay."

"I told you I didn't want to come here."

"Yes, you told me. You told me. Okay."

On the way to the car I spotted a short, muscular man with thinning brass-colored hair. He was wearing a well-tailored gray suit and thick aviator glasses that magnified his eyes to twice their size.

"Look. There's Phil," I told Jake.

"Oh God, yes."

"Why 'Oh God'?"

"I don't know."

"Say hello to him."

"Sure, okay."

"What's wrong?"

"What do you think?"

Phil was one of Jake's two friends; Jake has had other friends in his life but there were only two friends he was in contact with now, two he actually spoke to on a regular basis, which for Jake meant every six months. Phil worked near 14th Street and we had run into him once or twice before on the way to Stan's office, which was right across the street from the Outerspace Bookstore, one of Phil's favorite hangouts. That had been bad enough, having to say we were seeing a marriage counselor. This was not a good Jake-Phil topic.

Jake and Phil, both in their forties, usually confined their conversations with each other to the same kinds of subjects they had been talking about, with other conversational partners, since they had been nerdy non-sports-playing adolescents thirty years ago: books, ideas, sex. The question "What are you reading now?" would always come up right away. In a recent conversation Jake had been reading a book about quantum physics for nonscientists and Phil had been reading about the Jacobites. Phil, like Jake, could be witty and amusing if he was in the mood. And, also like Jake, in another mood he could be horribly informative. He could go on about the Jacobites until it seemed—even to someone like Jake— that facts had no purpose and life had no meaning.

Eventually, after their interests of the moment had been explored, one of them, usually Phil, would enter into the part of the conversation set aside for feminine topics: How is Mimi? How is Danny? Jake would ask about Sandy, Phil's wife, whom Jake and I had never met because, according to Phil, she refused to meet any of his friends. Sometimes we would wonder if Sandy could be an invention of Phil's peculiar mind, buit on further thought, we concluded she had to exist since she caused Phil too much trouble not to be real.

Phil and Jake would always be truthful during this small segment of the conversation set aside for personal matters; they would never pretend that things were great if they weren't. But any information they supplied was presented merely as an update. Jake and Phil never turned to each other for advice and support. Up until Danny's diagnosis, Jake thought that this was because he and Phil were men. But after subsequent reading on the subject, he decided that it was probably because he and Phil had Asperger syndrome, which was the diagnosis Ellen Camins gave Danny. Of all the explanations, the genetic explanation was the one we liked best. It seemed to offer the most hope.

Jake hailed Phil, and Phil responded with a distracted smile and a wave and he crossed the street. He said hello to Danny and patted him on the head.

"Danny," I said, "do you know who this is?"

"Who this is?"

"It's Phil, Danny. Do you remember Daddy's friend Phil?"

"It's probably a year since he's seen me. I wouldn't expect him to remember."

"Well, Danny, say hello to Phil."

"Hello to Phil."

Phil laughed, as if this little fragment of our son's "echolalia" had been an intentional joke on Danny's part, like something out of a Burns and Allen routine.

Jake said we were on our way back from our marriage counselor, his throat catching for a moment on the word "counselor," but Phil didn't seem to notice. I remained uncharacteristically silent. It wasn't that I didn't want Phil to know what was happening; it was just too painful to speak of it. Jake asked about Sandy, and we parted soon afterward, with either Jake or Phil mumbling something about getting together sometime soon.

We ate at the Kiev. When we were seated at the table, waiting for our orders to arrive, we asked Danny which was bigger, an elephant or a mouse, and he said an elephant. Good. That was good. He was learning. Already. But other similar questions he answered incorrectly. We asked him how we had gotten to this part of town from our apartment in Washington Heights. He didn't answer, so we supplied him with multiple choices: Did we walk? Did we drive? Did we go by airplane?

"Walk," he said.

"Yes, Danny, we walked from the car to the restaurant, but how did we get from Stan's office to here?"

"Walked," Danny answered.

"Where did we go this morning, Danny? Did we go to Grandma's house, or Stan's office, or to school?"

"Grandma's house."

Outside, the streets thronged with young people who were tattooed all over, with hair in unnatural colors and unusual shapes, teenagers who had taken body piercing beyond what was currently acceptable, people trying, in a world saturated with shocking images, to stand apart, to be, if possible, more bizarre than the advertising. Mingled with all these young people were immigrants and working-class men and women, and even some middle-class people, carrying briefcases and dressed in business suits. Jake and I were in our forties, the age of the immigrants and the office workers, but even when we had been young enough to fit in here, we had never believed the claims the East Village made to freedom and tolerance and alternative ways of being. Now it comforted us to be here with Danny in this carnival-like atmosphere. It comforted us to think that we lived in a world in which differences were welcomed. It made us feel better to think this, even though we didn't believe it.

As we walked from the Kiev back to our car, we pointed

to storefronts and asked Danny what they were. "What kind of place is that, Danny?"

"Indian restaurant," he said.

We looked at the place and then at each other, pleased because he was right about the ethnicity of the restaurant. But whether this was because we had pointed it out to him once before or because somewhere in his mind he knew that carpets hanging from the walls signified an Indian restaurant, we had no idea.

"You're right, Danny. That's an Indian restaurant. How did you know?"

Since he didn't answer, we began, as we did so often that we hardly realized we were doing it, to present a menu of possible responses. "Did we tell you it was an Indian restaurant? Is it because it just looks like an Indian restaurant? Is it the way the letters on the sign look?"

"The candle is afraid of the white clock!" he responded with his magical smile.

We had been planning on taking Danny to the playground in Tompkins Square Park, as we often did on our Stan Shapiro days, but I told Jake I wanted to skip it. We didn't have time for it now.

# The Story of Annie Sullivan

A reporter for *The Chronicle of Jewish Education* once asked Teresa Thompson if she ever wondered what her life would have been like if it she hadn't been the mother of a handicapped child. The question had come up many times before, and Teresa answered in her usual brisk, emphatic manner. "I would have been like all the girls I went to high school with. Once the kids were in school, I would have found myself a part-time job selling lipstick door-to-door for Avon or working behind the cosmetics counter at Macy's. And that would have been fine with me."

The wall behind her was sprinkled with testaments to her success as an advocate for the handicapped children of the Orthodox Jewish community of Sheepshead Bay, Brooklyn. There were pictures of her standing next to rabbis and shaking hands with the head of the Sisterhood, and framed letters from grateful parents. "Every day I thank G-d for you." "Because of you, my Pinny has a future."

After the reporter left, Teresa looked at her son's picture, which stood on her desk in a white wire frame of twisting vines, birds' nests and angels. He was dressed in the three-piece suit he wore every day to his job at The District's beautiful new headquarters in Dyker Heights, where he had been working as a mail clerk for the past eight years. That was quite a coup, getting Nathan that job.

Teresa's thoughts wandered, leading inexorably to Lloyd Kennedy, Louise Kennedy's son. Lloyd had just opened up his third dry-cleaning store—this one in Flatbush; he was the coach of his oldest son's basketball team; every summer he took his family on camping trips to the Adirondacks.

Teresa and Louise had grown up together. They had been bridesmaids at each other's weddings. When their children were babies, Louise, who was a seamstress, made the boys matching overalls. For all these years, Teresa had kept track of Lloyd as though he and Nathan were in a lifelong competition with each other. Would she be willing to trade places with Louise Kennedy? She couldn't say she would. But she couldn't say she wouldn't either.

Nathan had been her first child. He didn't roll over when he was supposed to, and he didn't sit up when he was supposed to either, and at age two he still hadn't started walking. The doctor told her not to worry. Children develop at their own pace, he said.

At two and a half, Nathan was walking, but with such a wobbly gait that once a woman accosted Teresa on the street and accused her of drugging her son. When she asked the pediatrician about Nathan's walking, he reassured her that she didn't have anything to worry about. Finally, Teresa took Nathan to see a neurologist, who diagnosed her son with cerebral palsy, a condition for which there was no medical treatment. Teresa consulted psychics and healers. She went to a laying-on-of-hands ceremony in a Pentecostal church in Teaneck, New Jersey. She took Nathan to see a naturopath in the Bronx, who told her to feed him nothing but white food and green apples. A Tarot card reader on West 42nd Street arranged ten 20-dollar bills in the sign of a cross, to cast off evil spirits.

When it was time for Nathan to go to kindergarten, The District wanted to put him in a class for mentally retarded children. Teresa told the psychologist who had tested him that her son wasn't mentally retarded.

"How do you know?"

"I know. I'm his mother," Teresa said.

"You're going to have to face up to the facts sooner or later, Mrs. Thompson," the psychologist said. "Numbers don't lie. Your son scored fifty on the Wechsler."

"I don't care about your stupid test," Teresa responded. "My son has cerebral palsy! That's why he couldn't do your stupid block designs."

Teresa paid to have Nathan tested privately. He scored out of the mentally retarded range, and The District agreed to place Nathan in a regular class.

For the next two years, Teresa stood by helplessly watching her son flounder. When she heard about a speech and language school that had just opened up in Buffalo, she made an appointment to see it. The principal, a woman with a keen sense of marketing, had TV cameras and a real estate agent waiting for her when she arrived. Teresa was about to put a down payment on a house when a woman she met in the wait-

ing room outside the admissions office told her that the principal was a cold-blooded bureaucrat who made her son wear a
bicycle helmet all day because he had muscular dystrophy and
she was afraid of lawsuits.

She decided to keep Nathan in the public school in Sheepshead Bay and fight. Over the years she managed to see to it that
everything that could be done for Nathan—tutors, summer
programs, occupational therapy, speech therapy, physical therapy—was done. Butting heads with the people who worked
for The District was fun for Teresa, who got a kick out of
knowing that she, with her GED, was so good at fighting the
professionals with all the fancy letters attached to their names.

Word of Teresa Thompson's many triumphs spread
quickly, and it wasn't long before mothers in the neighborhood were appealing to her for help. Teresa had long ago
lost interest in selling cosmetics door-to-door, and she got to
thinking she could make a career for herself advocating for
children whose mothers were too frightened or too timid to
speak up for themselves. Outsmarting The District hacks,
whose degrees in higher education had earned them the right
to deny services to handicapped children, was even more fun
when she was doing it for other people's kids. If she won, she
won, if she lost, she lost; but she liked winning more.

To express their gratitude, the mothers baked her cookies, cakes and pies; presented her with afghans, scarves and
sweaters they had crocheted themselves; and sent her notes
with heartfelt words of appreciation written on Hallmark
cards embossed in gold and silver foil. Within a year, Teresa
had enough homemade goods to open up a combination bakery and crafts store. She decided to go into the educational
advocacy business instead. And so one day in early August,

she hauled all the toys out of the basement, threw out the Ping-Pong table and pinball machine, painted the cement floor periwinkle blue, and using the money she had set aside for Christmas, bought a computer, a small Xerox machine, a secondhand desk and an office chair at a local stationery store's going-out-of-business sale.

Her first client was a mother from a community of Orthodox Jews in a nearby neighborhood, who wanted The District to pay for her son to attend a special education yeshiva in Scarsdale. Mrs. Rabinsky said that a neighbor of hers, a nice Christian woman, had referred her to Teresa. Her neighbor had told her that if anyone could work it out with The District, Mrs. Thompson could.

Teresa called Greg Abrams, the head of The District, with whom she had had many dealings in the past on behalf of Nathan. When she told him that she had a client who wanted The District to fund a yeshiva, Greg said that he didn't see why the taxpayers of New York should have to pay for Abe Rabinsky to learn how to daven.

Without missing a beat, Teresa responded, "You drive a hard bargain, Greg. How about we let Mr. and Mrs. Rabinsky foot the bill for the davening?"

Since religious instruction took up more than half the school day, this would bring the cost of the yeshiva way below what The District usually spent on special education schools. Greg was surprised at what a great deal Teresa Thompson, who was known around the office as The Barracuda, was offering him. But then again, it wasn't her son she was fighting for this time.

Mrs. Rabinsky was delighted when Teresa told her that The District had agreed to fund the secular part of the ye-

shiva in full. It was fine with her when the advocate explained that for schools not recommended by The District,
parents had to pay the tuition up front and then sue for reim-
bursement. Mrs. Rabinsky had a friend who wanted to send
her son to Chaim Akiva, and she referred her to Teresa, and
Mrs. Rabinsky's friend referred a friend of hers to Teresa as
well; and so it went. Her first three weeks in business, Teresa
earned four thousand dollars, almost five times what her husband brought home from his job repairing elevators for Ace
All-Service, Inc., in Queens.

Seven months after Teresa was in business, the yeshiva offered to put her on retainer. That first week Teresa received
calls from six desperate mothers, all of whom complained
that The District refused to cover the cost of Chaim Akiva
just because it was a religious school, and they didn't think
it was fair for their children to be denied a Jewish education
just because they had a few problems. Teresa offered The
District the same deal she had offered Greg Abrams. It was
always the same story, always the same deal.

Within a few years, Teresa had a flourishing business advocating for the disabled children of the Jewish communities
in Brooklyn, the Bronx, Queens, Manhattan and Staten Island. She was on the payroll of four special education yeshivas, and with each new yeshiva, she raised her fee. She had
long ago moved her office from the basement of her house to
a storefront on Nostrand Avenue, the prime business district
of Sheepshead Bay. But when parents started showing up at
her house if they couldn't reach her at the office, she decided
to relocate both her office and her family to Kew Gardens,
Queens.

* * *

Teresa was sitting at her desk eating a pastrami sandwich when Mimi Slavitt came to see her one hot and muggy day at the end of August. Joseph Priskin, the owner of the kosher deli two doors down, sent her the sandwich and a celery soda free of charge every day at one o'clock on the dot—his way of thanking her for getting The District to fund half the cost of a special education yeshiva on Long Island for his youngest son, Yossi. The air conditioner was on full blast, causing the papers covering Teresa's desk to flutter.

Mimi told the advocate that her six-year-old son was going to be attending Chaim Akiva in the fall and that the principal had said Teresa would take care of getting The District to pay for the school.

After Teresa took a sip of celery soda, she asked Mimi if The District had recommended any schools for her son.

"Yes, they did," Mimi replied. "A public school in the Bronx where the average IQ is below borderline. My son is not mentally retarded. He has what they call 'high-functioning autism' or 'Asperger syndrome.' He can tell you everything that goes into making a piano. He knows how to read. He knows the color combinations of every shade on the color spectrum. He can add fractions. He has a very large vocabulary. And except for a few quirks, his grammar is perfect. His problems are mostly social. He certainly doesn't belong in a school for mentally retarded children."

"Before you go on, Mrs. Slavitt," Teresa said.

"Call me Mimi."

"One small point, Mimi. The term is 'cognitive disability.' You don't want to offend people," Teresa said, thinking to herself as she took another bite of her sandwich that this woman, who seemed to think her son was a little Albert Einstein instead of a kid with an incurable neurological disorder, was going to be a real pain in the neck.

"Yeah. Right," Mimi said. "They keep on insisting the school in the Bronx is quote unquote appropriate for my son. When I took Danny to visit the place, there was this beautiful little redheaded boy standing in the corner, flapping his arms. I mentioned to the teacher that I was glad Danny didn't flap his arms like that and she pulled me aside and told me that the boy wasn't doing that when he started there at the end of last year. It was something he picked up from the other kids. She made me swear not to tell anyone, but the little redheaded boy didn't belong there any more than my son did. He was a smart little boy, like Danny. She made me swear again not to tell anyone. She said she was fifty-three years old and no place else was willing to give her a job. This is the school they say is 'appropriate' for my son," the woman concluded.

Teresa smiled. "I'm just curious. Why do you want to send your son to such a religious yeshiva? Chaim Akiva is the *frummest* of the *frum,* you know."

"Yeah, well, none of the schools want my son. Except for the warehouse in the Bronx where that smart little boy with drug addict parents got turned into a bird. Apparently my son is too much for any of them to handle. Isn't that their job? The yeshiva was the only decent school willing to take Danny. When Linda said Danny was in, I had to stop myself from kneeling on the floor and kissing her feet. As for the Judaism, we're not religious but it's okay with me."

"I think I get the picture, Mimi," said Teresa. "Now—"

"My understanding is that The District is obligated to pay for Chaim Akiva, since they have nothing else to offer," the woman interrupted. "As I told Linda, I don't expect to pay for the religious component. We're not Orthodox."

Teresa squeezed the paper bag on which the words JO-
SEPH PRISKIN'S KOSHER DELI were printed and her empty soda
can together so tightly she felt like Superman turning a lump
of coal into a diamond. "Clearly, my dear, you've been very
busy working on behalf of your son," she said as she tossed
the remnants of her lunch into the trashcan across the room.
"From now on, you can leave everything up to me." After
sucking one last surprise strand of pastrami out from between the gap in her front teeth, she launched into the speech
she gave new clients.

"Education is a business like any other, Mimi. Don't waste
your time thinking about what these people should be doing.
Shoulds don't exist in their world. As far as they're concerned,
your kid is a peg they have to fit into a hole. If you have a square-
pegged kid, and all they have are round holes, then they'll try
to stuff your square-pegged kid into one of their round holes.
But not to worry. I've been in this business for over ten years.
I'm on to their tricks. And I have a few of my own."

Wiping her hands on one of the towelettes Joseph always
included with his free lunches, Teresa continued. "Now, as
Charna told you, my fee is nine-fifty." The advocate's usual
fee was six hundred, but this case was going to take a lot more
work than the others. "Did you bring the certified check?"

"I don't understand. Linda Frank told me they had you
on retainer."

"We changed the terms of our agreement two weeks ago.
Charna didn't tell you?"

"No, she didn't."

"I'll have to have a little talk with her about that," Teresa said. "She's been very forgetful lately. The poor girl is in
her ninth month with her ninth kid. Anyway, my dear, you
should know that I'm giving you the deal of a lifetime. No

special ed attorney would let you through the door until you coughed up at least fifteen hundred bucks. And now I hear some of them have started charging extra if they win. My fee is a lot less than theirs to begin with. And that's for everything. Flat rate. Flat fee. I make an honest living."

After pausing for a few seconds, Mimi asked, "Would you be willing to take a regular check? I think I might have one somewhere in my bag."

"Just this once," the advocate said.

Mimi had been running across the same peripatetic check in her many long journeys through the mysterious contents of her backpack, but as she rummaged around for it now, she started having second thoughts, so when her fingertips found the check, which had made its way between the pages of a spiral notebook, she hesitated. She told Teresa it wasn't there and the advocate said she could send her a check in the mail.

"Don't forget to make it certified, my dear," she said with a smile.

There were long delays on the subway for the trip back to Washington Heights, and for the entire two-hour trip home, Mimi conducted a debate with herself about Teresa Thompson. She came to the conclusion that it would be stupid for the advocate to lie about something as easy to prove false as a change in her payment policy. True, she didn't think the advocate was the most soulful person in the world, but there were some things about her that Mimi liked. She liked that Teresa didn't measure every word she uttered, so as not to offend. And she liked how bold she was. She also liked the uninhibited vigor with which she ate her pastrami sandwich.

As for her harsh manner, Mimi decided that Teresa Thompson was a lot like the waitresses at the Meatball Restaurant, where she had once worked as a cashier during a summer break from college. She had liked those brassy women; they were honest, unpretentious and tough.

The most important consideration of all, of course, was whether or not Teresa could win this case, and the advocate seemed confident that she could, just as she had won all the others. Ever since Danny's diagnosis, Mimi had felt like a beggar. Maybe with this gutsy woman in charge, she wouldn't have to be a beggar anymore.

By the time she was on the big escalator that led up to the street at the 181st Street subway station, Mimi was convinced that they should hire Teresa Thompson. Now it would be her husband's turn to be skeptical.

When she got home, she told Jake all about her meeting with the advocate. She told him about the surprise change in the arrangement with the yeshiva regarding the advocate's fee and how she had pretended not to be able to find the check. She told him that Teresa reminded her of the waitresses at the Meatball, tough like them, and that she imagined a lot of people found her intimidating, which was good. She said that she couldn't remember ever having met anyone more sure of herself. Teresa Thompson didn't seem to have a shred of self-doubt and she didn't seem to have a care in the world.

"You can't stand people like that," Jake said. "What about her education?" Mimi said she didn't see what difference that made. The woman had a perfect track record.

Together they went into the office and Googled "Teresa Thompson, Education Advocate." There was an old article about her in a Jewish newspaper.

"That's good. She has a handicapped child," Mimi said.

"Big deal. So she found a way to make money out of her son's disability."

After Mimi had listened to Jake raise every objection he could think of, he agreed with her that they should hire Teresa Thompson, as both of them had known all along he would. The purpose of their debate had been to create the illusion they were making a logical choice when they both knew that, like every decision they had made about Danny since his diagnosis, this one was just another shot in the dark.

The next day, when Mimi called Teresa to report that the certified check was in the mail, the advocate told her to go to Scarsdale to deliver the first year's tuition. There would also be a contract for her to sign.

Teresa was telling Mimi that as soon as she got the check, she would get the ball rolling when Mimi cut in to remind her that her son's grandfather had left him that money for college. "I need you to tell me again. You're sure we will get everything back? I still expect Danny to go to college," she said. And then, speaking more to herself than to Teresa, she repeated, "I still expect Danny to go to college."

"Not to worry, my dear. Your case is a slam-dunk," Teresa responded cheerfully.

On her way back from Chaim Akiva, Mimi decided that going to a yeshiva might be good for Danny. Having been raised according to the conventions of Conservative Judaism, Mimi was very familiar with the Jewish traditions. Mimi's mother had kept kosher, and every Passover she lined the kitchen cabinets and changed the dishes and threw out all the *chametz*; she lit candles to welcome in Shabbos, and Mimi's parents took the family to services every Friday night and on all the High Holy Days.

Although Mimi could never bring herself to believe in any of it, she had always liked being part of this tradition; she thought it was quaint. Then when she was twelve, Mimi decided she was an atheist. As she recalled the day she proclaimed her atheism to her father, it amused, and surprised her, as well, to remember what a precocious and somewhat arrogant little girl she had been.

Her father was driving her home from Hebrew school when she told him that she had come to the conclusion that God didn't exist and that she thought it was a waste of her time to be learning about things she knew weren't true. She announced that she didn't want to go to Friday night services anymore either because she didn't want to be a hypocrite worshipping a God she didn't believe in.

"Remember when we were little and you used to tell us that the moon was following us home in the car every night to keep us safe?" she said to her father. "That's what God is like to me now."

Her father told her that it was okay if she didn't believe in God, but it made him sad to think of her life having no spiritual dimension at all, and the next day he gave her a bunch of books about transcendentalism to read. He told her to write an essay in response to them, and he said that if he thought her arguments were persuasive enough, that is, if she convinced him that there was something she believed in, other than God, she wouldn't have to go to services or Hebrew school anymore.

Mimi's father had told her exactly what he wanted to hear

and she presented it to him in the essay she wrote, which she entitled, "The Flowers, the Trees, the Grass, the Mountaintop and Me." He liked her essay and told her she had convinced him that being an atheist did not necessarily mean she was spiritually bankrupt.

Since Mimi would no longer be going to services, her parents wanted to find something to occupy their daughter while they were gone. Television seemed to offer the perfect solution, but as intellectuals committed to protecting their children from the corrupting influences of popular culture, they had never owned a TV. In the end they decided that their daughter's moral sensibility was strong enough for there to be no harm in buying her a tiny television. Mimi's father told her she couldn't let her brother or sister know about it and that she would have to find a good hiding place for her little ten-by-ten-inch Philco.

Mimi's little black-and-white TV was magic to her. Friday nights, as soon as she heard the car starting up in the driveway, she would take it out of the bottom of her closet, where it had eagerly awaited her all week buried in a laundry basket filled with the clothes she used to wear to play dress-up, and she would spend the next three hours gorging on everything the three networks had to offer.

She would flip from channel to channel, not because she couldn't find anything she liked, but because everything was so wonderful. Soon she was sneaking it out of her closet whenever she could. She decided that Shirley Booth, who played a maid on *Hazel,* was a great actress. She had her first orgasm watching *Dr. Kildare* during an episode in which the handsome doctor fell in love with one of his dying patients, something he apparently had a tendency to do. The weird game show, *Queen for a Day*, which featured three women competing against each other for the pity of the studio audience, repelled and fascinated her. Their descriptions of the lives that afflicted them were beyond anything she could imagine or comprehend. The woman judged to have suffered the most became the winner, thereby turning the other two women into double losers: having already lost the game of life, now they had lost this game show as well. It was so cruel. Every one of these women was in trouble. Why couldn't they all be helped?

The more Mimi thought about it, the more it seemed to her that going to a yeshiva could be good for Danny. Her feelings about religion hadn't changed much since her childhood, but religion had nothing to do with her calculations. People with autism loved rules, and Orthodox Jews lived strictly according to the rules. There was also the fact that Judaism, with its inexhaustible appetite for pronouncing on every possible contingency of every aspect of life, offered someone like Danny, who lacked the ability to think for himself about so many things, a blueprint for living. More important than all other considerations was the fact that Orthodox Jews embraced anyone who was committed to keeping the ancient traditions of Judaism alive.

Mimi's thoughts about Orthodox Judaism evoked for her the early days, soon after she and Jake moved to Washington Heights, long before Danny was born. She would often see a man in a black hat and a black suit walking his son to shul. Back then, Mimi had only the vaguest idea of what autism was, but she could tell by the way the boy walked, shuffling his feet, his head bent to the side, his eyes cast upward toward the sky or at nothing in particular, never straight ahead, that he was autistic. He was in his twenties by now, but his father still had the same worried look on his face and he still always held his son's hand whenever they walked down the street. There was also a teenaged boy with Down syndrome who lived in the small Jewish enclave a few blocks up the hill. Mimi would see his father taking him to services as well. And there was a young boy in a wheelchair; the rabbi of their synagogue gave his father permission to wheel his son to shul every Shabbos.

Mimi decided that if she had to, she would start lighting candles every Friday night and she would keep kosher like her mother had. Or at least she would stop mixing milk with meat. As far as pork was concerned, she had never been able to bring herself to buy pork anyway. It would be up to Danny how kosher they would be. Jake would take him to shul on Saturdays. He would take him to synagogue as often as Danny wanted.

After she and Jake were dead, if Danny wasn't cured by then—a possibility that in her darkest moments Mimi realized she had to take into account—there would be an entire community ready to step in to welcome him with open arms.

The following Monday, Mimi got Danny up at six o'clock in the morning and dressed him in black pants and a white button-down shirt and a yarmulke and *tztizit*, and she waited with him for one of the little yellow school buses that take handicapped children to their special schools.

Standing on the corner with Danny, Mimi thought of the joke she had heard a stand-up comic make about those buses. It was a month after Danny's diagnosis and she and Jake had been lying in bed watching television. Next to movies about serial killers, they liked watching stand-up comedy at the end of each long day. At one point the comic made a joke about someone "riding the short bus." Mimi had often wondered what those little yellow buses were and now she knew. She had her head on Jake's chest, where she always staked a claim, even if they were in the middle of a fight. When they heard the joke, neither of them bothered to say anything about it.

Mimi's landlord, Mr. Gotbaum, did a double take when he saw Danny dressed up like a yeshiva boy. The landlord was a shy, quiet man, with an otherworldly air about him. He served as the sexton for the little synagogue located in the corner of the building. Every Saturday there would be a small parade of elderly European Jews going up and down the corrugated metal steps that led to the *shtiebel*, as tiny synagogues like this one were called. The steps were also a hangout for neighborhood kids, who would sit there and smoke cigarettes, except on Saturdays and during the Jewish holidays, when this small group of Dominicans would respectfully relinquish the steps to the old Jews.

Six years ago, on the day of Danny's *bris*, Mr. Gotbaum had run into the *mohel* in the elevator. They were both members of the corner *shtiebel*, and the *mohel* had invited Mr. Gotbaum to participate in the ancient ritual. It was Mr. Gotbaum who had held Danny during the ritual snipping off of the foreskin, and the experience seemed to have permanently endeared Danny to him.

The day after the *bris*, he had come to their apartment to check the mezuzah. "It's very important for everything to be right with it," he had told Jake. When Jake asked him why, his only response was, "Never mind. Bad things."

Although the scroll inside the mezuzah was intact, there was something about the case in which it was housed that upset Mr. Gotbaum, and the next morning when Mimi was leaving the apartment to go grocery shopping, she found her landlord standing at her front door with a screwdriver in his hand as he went about the task of replacing the bright white plastic cover with one that was a dull brown.

Although Mimi's views about God hadn't changed all that much since she was twelve, she often felt nostalgic about the trappings of Judaism. Oddly enough, she had many close friends who were devout believers in God. Her best friend was an ultra-Orthodox Jew. Giselle contended that Mimi, whether she knew it or not, was, in fact, very religious, and throughout the course of their long friendship she had been on a mission to persuade her to embrace Judaism. It was Giselle who had given her the white mezuzah that Mr. Gotbaum had turned to brown. The day before every Rosh Hashanah, she would slip a piece of paper under her door, listing, in her tiny, meticulous handwriting, all the times the shofar was scheduled to be blown. And every Friday, half an hour before sundown, Giselle would call to remind her to light Shabbos candles. For Mimi's fortieth birthday, her friend had given her forty Shabbos candles, all forty of which still remained unlit.

If anything could have driven Mimi to seek comfort in religion, Danny's diagnosis would have. But it didn't.

Mimi was happy to see how happy Mr. Gotbaum was to see Danny in his yarmulke. She kind of liked seeing her son dressed that way, too. She told her landlord that Danny was starting his first day of yeshiva. She didn't tell him they had decided to become religious, nor did she tell him that the only reason he was going to a special education yeshiva was because no other decent school was willing to accept him.

Danny kept on taking off his yarmulke—he said it tickled his head—and Mimi kept on telling him to put it back on. Mr. Gotbaum told Danny that it was a mitzvah to wear a yarmulke—that it was a symbol of God watching over you.

Mr. Gotbaum had a severely disabled daughter. Mimi didn't think he knew that she knew about Wendy. His wife worked in the management office, and she and Mimi had developed a kind of friendship over the years, because of their children. Sometimes they would talk about their problems with The District. Susan once told her that The District psychologist had justified his decision to reduce their daughter's occupational therapy hours because, according to the occupational therapy report, Wendy had finally learned how to wrap her fingers around a spoon. Susan and Mr. Gotbaum were so upset they had yelled at the psychologist.

"We were very ashamed of ourselves for having been that rude," she told Mimi, explaining that they had never before raised their voices in anger at anyone.

Susan never said exactly what was wrong with her daughter; there didn't seem to be a name for it, but it was so bad that next to Wendy, Danny must have seemed like a regular kid to Mr. Gotbaum.

That first day at Chaim Akiva, Linda Frank called Mimi several times to complain about Danny. During morning prayers he refused to stand up when he was supposed to; he was always taking off his yarmulke and would try to take off the other boys' yarmulkes as well; he made a lanyard out of the fringe on his *tzitzit*; during a lesson on *kashruth*, he announced to everyone that his favorite dish was shrimp lo mein. The phone calls continued over the coming weeks.

After several failed attempts to reason with Danny, Mimi tried bribing him with ice cream, and for a while it seemed to her that it worked because she stopped receiving frantic calls from Linda Frank every day.

Later, Mimi would regret that she had never bothered to consider how Danny might feel about going to a yeshiva. Her son, who always wanted to know the reasons for everything, must have been confused to be learning things that he knew couldn't possibly be true—like a bush burning forever or like a sea splitting in half (which, according to Danny, would have created a "temporary isthmus"). But her son never complained. And even if he felt inclined to complain, he wouldn't, because he didn't know how to express how he felt about anything.

Danny seemed to enjoy learning a new language with an alphabet all its own, and Mimi was grateful for that. He knew all the Hebrew prayers. He knew that fruits that grew on vines required different prayers from those that grew on trees, as did vegetables that grew underground versus those that grew aboveground. Whenever Mr. Gotbaum saw Danny, he would quiz him on one thing or another having to do with the arcane laws of Judaism, and it delighted him that Danny always knew the answers.

In mid-June, near the end of the year, Teresa Thompson called to tell Mimi that The District had agreed to all their terms and that soon they would be sending her a check for thirty thousand dollars. This was the most money the advocate had ever won for a client, and she taped a Xerox of the check to the wall beside her desk next to a photograph of her son standing proudly in the SUPERSTAR MAIL CLERK apron she had bought for him to wear at his job delivering interoffice mail for The District in Dyker Heights.

"See, I told you not to worry," she told Mimi.

"Thank you, Teresa. I knew you would come through for us." And that was true. Still, Mimi had been worried and now she felt very relieved.

Near the end of Danny's first year at the yeshiva, Linda Frank called Mimi to say that Danny would not be allowed to return to Chaim Akiva in the fall unless she hired an aide to go to school with him. "Your son requires nonstop attention," she said and went on to enumerate all the reasons why. Her list included everything that the director of Danny's nursery school had told Mimi when she'd urged her to get her son tested three and a half years before.

Mimi's heart wouldn't stop pounding. Linda hadn't complained to her about Danny for months, and during the parent-teacher conferences, all the teachers ever said was how smart her son was and what a delight he was to have in their classes. Did they think they were doing her a favor, sparing her feelings?

Mimi called Teresa to report that she would have to ask The District to cover the cost of an aide for Danny. The advocate said they would never approve an aide for a school they hadn't recommended.

"But they already approved the school," Mimi said.

Teresa explained that that wasn't the way it worked. The District always made sure to stipulate that in agreeing to fund a particular school, they were by no means giving their stamp of approval for that school. "That's why the documents ratifying their agreements to settle are called 'stipulations,'" she said.

Mimi felt the air being sucked out of her all at once. The fact that she had heard this was the way The District operated didn't matter. Experiencing it now, for herself, gave her the feeling that she had just come face-to-face with evil.

According to everyone she had spoken to, the policy of The District was to scare parents into submission. It made no difference if they had previously agreed to pay for a school; parents still had to pay the tuition up front, then pay a lawyer, or as in the case of Jake and Mimi, an advocate, to represent them, year after year after year. The District knew that most people couldn't afford a lawyer, much less the tuition, or if they could, many would be afraid to take the risk.

It was a game of dare they were playing. And they played this game with the parents of children who couldn't talk, children who couldn't walk, children who couldn't hear, children who couldn't see, children who didn't have long to live, children who would always be children.

"Now, my dear, I have to tell you the aide complicates things for us," Teresa was saying. "The District is going to question how the yeshiva can be appropriate for Danny if he requires this level of support. This time it's going to take a little longer."

Mimi didn't say anything. She was too afraid to ask if that meant they were going to lose.

"You better get used to this," the advocate added.

"I can't afford to pay for an aide on top of the tuition," Mimi replied.

"Not to worry." Teresa told her that she had made a special arrangement with the Hebrew Free Loan Society to lend money to all her clients, interest-free.

Mimi created a flyer advertising for aides to go to school with Danny, and she spent the next two weeks going up and down the streets surrounding universities from the West Village to the Bronx stapling them onto telephone poles and taping them onto the glass enclosures of bus stops near the schools. She wandered the halls of the various departments and asked the professors to tell their students about this "wonderful opportunity." By the time the fall semester was ready to begin, Mimi had hired a fourth-year PhD student in psychology. The girl had finished all her coursework and was in the process of writing her thesis, which coincidentally was about how the school system was failing children with autism.

Teresa Thompson kept on avoiding working on Danny Slavitt's case. She hated it. She hated Mimi Slavitt. And she hated Danny Slavitt, too. Their stupid case was even more complicated than what she had anticipated. It was like nothing she was used to handling, and Mimi Slavitt was nothing like those nice, mild-mannered Orthodox women who were always sending her thank-you notes, babka, rugelach and cherry cheese strudel. She wished she could just forget the whole thing. But she couldn't. This made her resent Mimi Slavitt and her genius son even more.

One day the advocate got a call from Don Swilke, a lawyer for The District, telling her they would agree to settle everything—on the condition that Teresa tell Mimi Slavitt to call off her battalions. The woman doesn't know when to stop! he complained. In addition to precipitating a deluge of phone calls and e-mails from politicians' aides, Mimi Slavitt was constantly clogging up their fax machines with legal briefs and court judgments, articles from law journals and medical journals and voluminous treatises she wrote herself. She always included quotes from autism experts, a couple of whom she had recruited to write letters and make phone calls on her son's behalf.

"I think they'll do anything to get rid of you," Teresa told Mimi when she called her to report the good news. "I told you not to be such a worrywart. I told you I would do it. I told you this one was going to take longer. And believe me, this was no easy peasy. But it's done."

It was the biggest case the advocate had ever won. Although she had done everything she could to avoid it, her aversion to Mimi and her son made any effort she had put into the case feel like hard work and it wasn't long before Teresa was convinced that this was a victory she could claim for herself. She was certain that her conversations with Don Swilke had made all the difference and for a while she basked in the glow of her accomplishment. But then Don reminded her about all the documents she had to send him before he signed off on the case.

"You have to play by the rules just like everyone else, Terry," he said lightheartedly. "No documents, no settlement. I'm giving you three months. Which is more than I would give to anyone else. I'm doing you a huge favor here. It will be a big feather in your cap, winning a case like this. But you miss the deadline, that's it. The offer's off the table. Forever."

Oh shit, Teresa thought to herself. Timesheets and affidavits and attendance records for the aides. Affidavits from the teachers and the principal. All of which had to be notarized. Documentation from a psychiatrist and the boy's pediatrician. And copies of all the checks Mimi Slavitt had ever written to the school. And affidavits from the bank as well. This thing never ended.

She told herself she would e-mail Linda Frank next week. She would ask the principal to take care of most of the paperwork. The woman was in love with her, and like all bureaucrats, she loved dotting *i*'s and crossing *t*'s. But Teresa never got around to asking Linda for help. Her business started to boom, way beyond anything she could ever have imagined: two other special education yeshivas had opened up and they gave all their business to the Christian woman with the golden touch. The advocate pushed Mimi Slavitt's case out of her mind.

Hearing that The District was finally going to settle made Mimi feel weak with relief. Everything was going to be okay. The panic attacks that had been keeping her up at night stopped. But when another year ended, and another one began with still no word from the advocate about the reimbursements she had said would be forthcoming, the panic returned, worse than ever. The only thing that could give Mimi any relief was the voice of Teresa Thompson telling her that everything was going to be okay and that she should stop being such a worrywart.

The last time Mimi had spoken to Teresa, the advocate had told her that if she didn't have the patience to wait, they could bring her case before a judge. "It's up to you, Mimi," Teresa had said, warning that taking a case to court was always very risky since the outcome depended on who you got for a judge, and a lot of the judges were clones of the flunkies at The District. Mimi decided to try to be patient and wait.

\* \* \*

One day when the advocate was working from home—Nathan was sick with the flu, and Teresa always took care of her son when he was sick—she decided that she might as well try to get those old cases of Mimi Slavitt's out of the way once and for all. It had been a couple of years since she had looked at Danny Slavitt's file, and as she started flipping through it, she discovered that it was too late to do anything about any of the cases. The deadline Don Swilke had set for her to produce the necessary documents had expired long ago.

She'd really fucked up big time. And it would have been so easy. Linda Frank would have been fine taking care of the paperwork, but she had forgotten to ask her. There was no telling what Mimi Slavitt would do if she ever found out. It wasn't fair. After all Teresa had done for so many children.

She looked around her office at all the testimonials and awards and the table full of thank-you notes. It took Teresa at least a week to get rid of the unsettling feelings that this oversight of hers had triggered. The advocate was unaccustomed to feeling bad about anything, which made her hate Mimi Slavitt even more. Teresa told herself that there was no point in dwelling on past mistakes.

She decided to pretend that Mimi Slavitt didn't exist. She told her staff that whenever Mrs. Slavitt called, they should say she wasn't in. As a final service to her boss before she went into labor, Charna came up with the idea of posting a big sign on the wall of the common area where the staff worked that said simply: MIMI SLAVITT, enclosed in a circle with a diagonal line through her name.

## MIMI SLAVITT

Mimi had the same e-mail server as Teresa, which she recently discovered made it possible for her to check the status of everything she sent the advocate. When she found out that Teresa was deleting her e-mails without even reading them, she knew she had no choice but to make the journey to the inconveniently located office in Kew Gardens, Queens. There had been a snowstorm the day before and the air was so cold it burned her face, but Mimi couldn't bear to wait a second longer, so after sending Danny off to school on the little yellow school bus, she trudged through the snow and ice that covered the steep hill on 181st Street, to the subway station, to embark on what turned out to be a three-hour trip to Kew Gardens.

By the time she had finished making the long hike from the bus to Teresa's office, her fingers and toes were numb. Gail Seltzer was unlocking the last of the four locks on the front door when she arrived.

"Mrs. Slavitt? What are you doing here?" she said, intent on expressing her annoyance. Gail had always seemed to take pleasure in letting Mimi know how much she disliked her. Another time when Mimi showed up at Teresa's office unannounced, she had told Mimi, who was on the verge of tears, that she played the drama queen well.

Gail was part of the loyal band of Orthodox women who worked for Teresa. They accepted with equanimity their boss's many bold expressions of her Christian faith: the cross she wore around her neck, the picture of the Virgin Mary that hung on the wall between the two windows in her office, the paperweight in the form of a Nativity scene and the Baby Jesus pencil holder she kept on her desk left them completely unfazed. Everything about their boss enchanted these women, who, in strict accordance with the precepts of Orthodox Judaism, covered their hair with wigs and dressed in long skirts, black stockings and long-sleeved shirts, even in the dead heat of summer, and they all did their best to fulfill their obligations to increase the Jewish population.

Every one of them, consciously or unconsciously, had appropriated some aspect of their boss's mannerisms or appearance. Charna, the receptionist, raised her eyebrows in mock consternation the way Teresa did; Helen Schwartzman, the office manager, had her wig styled in Teresa's old-fashioned dark brown page boy and she often dressed in her boss's trademark white Peter Pan blouses and pleated skirts; Lorraine Stahl, her secretary, had taken on Teresa's habit of tapping her fingers on her desk; and Gail Seltzer, Teresa's right-hand woman, had appropriated Teresa's ironic grin, and she was grinning ironically at Mimi now.

"You should know better than to come here without an appointment," Gail repeated.

"I've come to see Teresa," Mimi declared. "I can never get through to *make* an appointment!"

"You can make an appointment now."

"No. I'll wait here until Teresa can see me," Mimi said, and slipping past Gail, through the half-open door, she ran up the steep set of stairs, planted herself in a chair outside Teresa's office and waited.

When Teresa came in an hour later, cheerfully bearing a dozen cherry-cheese strudels from Teitelbaum's Bakery on Parsons Boulevard, a gift from Mrs. Teitelbaum, whose little Moishe was now settled into the third grade at the B'nai Baruch Yeshiva in Huntington, Long Island, Gail rushed into her boss's office and closed the door. After a few minutes, Teresa called out to Mimi and invited her in.

"I'm so glad you dropped by today, my dear. As a matter of fact, I was planning on calling you," she said with a smile. "I have some papers for you to sign. Can you wait a few minutes while Lorraine prints them out for you?"

"You mean they're finally going to come through?" Mimi asked.

"I told you they would, my dear."

"For the entire amount?"

"I explained the situation to them. That with you, things were different."

"And they agreed? For the entire amount?" Mimi asked.

"Don't be such a worrywart, Mimi," Teresa said as she buzzed Gail, who appeared in an instant.

"Do you have the documents ready for Mrs. Slavitt to sign?"

Gail looked confused.

"The papers," Teresa repeated. "The stipulations for Mrs. Slavitt."

"Oh, oh, of course. Mrs. Slavitt's stipulations," Gail said apologetically. "I'll print them out right now."

"Now please excuse me, Mimi. I have an appointment,"

Teresa said as Gail, looking mortified and confused, made way for a short, frightened woman wearing a long skirt and an oversized black beret.

Danny was eleven now and nearing the end of his fourth year at Chaim Akiva. So far Mimi had borrowed more than one hundred fifty thousand dollars from the Hebrew Free Loan Society to pay for the school and the aides (she had hired five so far and was about to hire a sixth). There was still no word from the advocate about the money The District owed her. And Teresa was still not taking her calls. Nevertheless, Mimi continued to cling to the hope she was in the clear. The documents she had signed in Teresa's office were proof that The District was legally bound to come forth with everything they owed her.

Then one night at Chaim Akiva's yearly fund-raiser, Mimi overheard the father of one of Danny's classmates complaining to another father about Teresa Thompson.

"She's very sloppy, very careless," he said in a loud voice. "But go figure it. Her business is booming. There's a lot of self-deception that goes with having a kid with special needs." He said that the lawyer he'd hired to replace Teresa had taken just two weeks to secure the signed stipulation that the advocate had been promising him for the past eleven months.

The man's words took up residence in Mimi's body, and there were many nights she couldn't fall asleep. She would lie awake, too frightened to leave her bed. As she lay there, she would try to calm herself down by listing all the reasons she was overreacting. Which was typical of her, after all. It was true what Teresa was always telling her: she was a worrywart. As for the father who had criticized Teresa at the fund-raiser, Mimi reminded herself that he was always complaining about one thing or another (the air conditioning was too cold; the new math teacher's skirt was too short; the velvet on the mantel of one of the Torahs was showing signs of wear).

True, it was frustrating, to say the least, to have all this time go by with no word from Teresa about anything, but her position was secure. The District had set a precedent by reimbursing her for Danny's first year at Chaim Akiva. There was no reason why the subsequent years should be any different. Even with the added complication of the aide. The advocate's perfect track record offered further consolation. And all those letters from all those grateful parents. The awards that hung on her wall. Her adoring staff, all of whom lived lives based on high ethical standards.

But more than anything else, Mimi's greatest source of reassurance continued to be the stipulations Teresa had given her to sign. She had it all in writing. These were legal documents. The District had no choice but to follow through on their promises.

Lingering always in the background, sometimes going so far as to pole vault its way to the forefront of her rationalizations, was the story of the great teacher of Helen Keller, Annie Sullivan. Mimi had noticed the old newspaper article displayed on a piece of varnished wood, hanging on the wall in Teresa Thompson's reception area the first time she visited the advocate in her office.

The story was about a psychiatrist's inspection of an orphanage in the late 1800s, a time when children like Danny were thrown into institutional hellholes. Walking down the hall, the psychiatrist came across a cleaning woman, who led him down to the basement, where she showed him something that looked like a small prison cell. "That's the cage where they used to keep Annie," she said. Annie Sullivan, as portrayed by Anne Bancroft in *The Miracle Worker*, had had a tough exterior and a brusque manner. Eschewing empty sentiment, committed to what was important, she had been cruel in order to be kind: Teresa was kind of like that, wasn't she? Also, like Annie Sullivan, Teresa Thompson believed in the value of every human being.

At the beginning of Danny's fifth year at Chaim Akiva, the Hebrew Free Loan Society refused to lend Mimi any more money. Honey Moskowitz, the loan officer who had been writing Mimi checks for years, told her that absent signed stipulations from The District, the auditors had forbidden her to make any more loans.

"But Teresa sent you the stipulations," Mimi said.

"The only signatures on those stipulations were yours," Honey told her. "I'm sorry to put it so bluntly, Mimi. I know how hard this has been for you. But according to our auditors, without The District's signatures, those stips aren't worth the paper they were written on." The fear that overtook Mimi was so powerful it robbed her of thought and rendered her incapable of action.

Then, a few weeks into the spring semester, she received a registered letter from a lawyer representing Chaim Akiva, informing her that if she did not pay this year's tuition, her son would not be allowed to return to school. The only option left was to send Danny to the public school up the block.

\* \* \*

When Mr. Gotbaum saw Mimi leaving the house with Danny at seven thirty the following Monday morning, on their way to PS 187, he started to approach them, prepared with the question of the day, but as he got nearer, his crooked smile turned into a baffled frown.

"What, no yarmulke?" he asked.

"They kicked him out," Mimi said.

"What did he do?" Mr. Gotbaum asked.

"*He* didn't do anything," Mimi answered. Mr. Gotbaum looked confused. "*They* were the ones who did something!"

"Who? What? What did they do?"

Mimi was afraid that Mr. Gotbaum's feelings would be hurt if she told him the truth, and she was searching for a judicious way to explain what had happened when Danny darted across the street and jumped into the seat of a gigantic electric toy car that was being driven by a four-year-old.

One day the vice principal of PS 187 called to tell Mimi that during recess one of the monitors caught Danny dancing like a monkey for a crowd of children throwing pennies at him. When Mimi asked about Danny's aide (the "crème de la crème," The District superintendent, a man in a silk suit with manicured nails and a large diamond stud in his ear, had told her when she'd planted herself outside his office in a last-ditch effort to get them to hire the master's student from NYU who had been going to school with Danny for the past year), Mrs. Catallozzi told her Latisha had been on the other side of the schoolyard playing potsy with a group of sixth graders at the time.

He doesn't belong here, the vice principal told her, as she had many times in the past. He needs to be in a special school. She never believed Mimi when she told her that none of the special education schools wanted Danny.

A few weeks after the incident, Mimi's sister told her about a report she had just heard on NPR about a small middle school for "high-functioning" autistic children that had just opened up on Long Island. It wasn't on the list of schools The District funded, but Mimi took Danny to visit it anyway, half hoping she wouldn't like it and half hoping she would.

Years of disappointment with special education should have taught her to be wary, but it wasn't in Mimi's nature to be wary, and the visit to the school left her with a renewed sense of optimism. When she called The District psychologist (a woman she despised) to tell her she had found a school for Danny, Dr. Daisy Hench declared that Danny was doing very well at PS 187.

Mimi contended that the school wasn't "appropriate." She carefully enunciated every syllable of the word that was written into the law giving handicapped children the right to an education. The term was the rope in the never-ending tug-of-war between parents and The District. Mimi said Danny needed a special education school, to which the psychologist responded with a reprimand. "I think you're underestimating your son, Mrs. Slavitt," she said. "He's getting straight A's in the honor class. The consensus among all his teachers is that he's the smartest kid in the school. He even has a best friend."

"Oh. Howard Brodner," Mimi said. "He and Danny aren't friends. They're just the class outcasts. PS 187 is not *appropriate*."

The loathsome woman reminded her that she had the right to call for a hearing.

The only way Danny would be able to go to the school on Long Island was if The District gave Mimi the money they owed her, and having spent the past year exploring every possible option, she decided she would have to go see Teresa Thompson in Kew Gardens and get her to do her job, once and for all. She would threaten to sue the advocate to make her pay back all the promised reimbursements with her own money. She would threaten to sue her for malpractice. She would threaten to tell the newspapers, the parents who worshiped her, every disability organization she could think of, about the advocate's appalling incompetence and egregious neglect. Mimi would see to it that Teresa never had moment of peace until she followed through on all the promises she had made.

When Mimi arrived at the building, the front door was locked. She rang the buzzer. No one answered. Looking up, she noticed something new—a closed-circuit camera, the kind of security device used by drug dealers and movie stars.

Mimi crossed the street to give herself a better vantage point from which to look up at the windows to see if anyone was there. The lights were on, and Teresa was sitting at her desk, talking on the phone. Mimi went back to the building, and looking into the camera, she put her finger on the buzzer and she kept it there, every now and then, when one finger started to get numb, switching to another. Eventually she started beating out different rhythms to express her feelings of rage, humiliation, hatred, frustration and horror.

\* \* \*

Teresa came out of her office and asked, "What's with the racket?"

"It's The Pest," Gail told her. The sound of rhythmic, angry buzzing filled the room.

"After all you've done for her, this is the way she behaves," said Charna. "She called you twenty times yesterday!"

"Well, like I say, the woman's a little cuckoo," Teresa said, making a face that elicited ripples of laughter from her staff.

"What do you want me to do?" Gail asked.

"Just ignore her," Teresa said.

"That buzzing. It's driving me crazy," Charna complained.

"Put on some music," Teresa said.

Gail turned on the radio, which Teresa, who liked seeing how far she could go to get these women to let their hair down, so to speak, had set to the Golden Oldies station. Little Richard's "Good Golly, Miss Molly" was playing. "Come on, girls, let's dance," Teresa said, and the women, following Teresa's lead, tentatively started to move their hips to the furiously happy beat.

Teresa stood there, watching the women dance. She turned the music up louder, and the women danced faster, some of them dislodging their *sheitels* in the process. They looked ridiculous, even more ridiculous than Nathan had looked last week at the church bazaar. He had been sitting on a chair in the corner, looking glum, and when the band started playing "Roll Over Beethoven," Teresa pulled him out of his seat and started to twirl him around on the dance floor. Everyone was staring at them, but she didn't care. Her son was laughing and having fun, and that was all that mattered to her.

# *Yolanda*

Yolanda, the security guard, sat in a tiny chair behind a school desk at the entrance of the rundown building on West 181st Street that served as headquarters for The District offices. An enormous woman with breasts the size of throw pillows straining the coarse blue fabric of her uniform, she wore her hair pulled up on top of her head in a tight bun; the style fit the determined expression carved into the cool black marble of her face. She hated her job, and probably was surly to everyone, but Mimi took it personally, because Mimi took everything personally.

Searching through the various compartments of her backpack, Mimi finally found her driver's license. "Sorry. I'm very disorganized," she said with a nervous laugh.

The security guard's face was a mask of disapproval. After inspecting Mimi's ID, Yolanda told her to sign her name in the log, a child's composition book from which dangled a pencil attached to a frayed piece of dirty twine. Mimi's large, unwieldy signature, made clumsier by her irritation at the unnecessary delay, lapped over the signature of the person above hers and over the empty spaces reserved for the people who would arrive after her.

"You're messing up my book," Yolanda said.

"I'm sorry," Mimi said, "but that's how I sign my name."

"You should sign it different," Yolanda said.

Upstairs on the sixth floor, Mimi found herself in a large room. It was painted hospital green. On the walls were posters, most of them in Spanish, warning pregnant women not to drink alcohol and listing phone numbers for victims of domestic abuse. Lining the walls were a dozen mothers, sitting on plastic chairs of assorted colors, shapes and sizes. The women sat staring into space while their children sat in the corner, playing with a broken-down dollhouse and a scattered assortment of similarly disabled toys laid out for their amusement.

Whenever Mimi brought Danny here, he never showed any interest in the toys. It was only the bathroom with its boarded-up bathtub that captured his attention. Explaining how such a fantastic thing could come to be, Mimi told her son that the office used to be an apartment. This fascinated Danny, who declared his determination to get a sledgehammer and restore the apartment back to its original state, and continued to do so every time he came here.

After signing her name in another notebook, Mimi rushed to the bathroom to adjust her pantyhose, which having begun their descent down her thighs shortly after she left her apartment, had migrated a few inches above her knees. Returning to her seat, she stared at the children and wondered what was wrong with each and every one of them.

An hour later a sad woman with a stooped back and frizzy hair came to deliver her to the conference room, where a group of people sat around a large metal table. Like so many of the children they were supposed to serve, there was something odd-looking about the people who worked in The District office. The head hit man, Dr. Daisy Hench, had large veiny hands and a gigantic jaw, and when she spoke, only her lips moved, reminding Mimi of a character in a cheap animated cartoon. The learning specialist, Fredda Doverspike, had the strangely elongated look of stretched-out Silly Putty. Dr. Hench's ally, backing her every play, was Van Stone. He had some kind of chronic migratory rash on his neck, psoriasis, Mimi supposed, and a bad case of dandruff, which kept him busy brushing white flakes of dead skin off his shoulders.

Today was four weeks before the start of summer and four weeks away from the end of Chaim Akiva's school year. Mimi had come to ask The District to pay for a summer camp for Danny, who was now nine. Dr. Hench, after spending a few seconds flipping through the papers Mimi had given her, said with her dead face, "The documentation does not support your son's need for a summer program."

Mimi felt the familiar pain in her throat, the burning behind her eyes. Before Danny's diagnosis she had never cried in front of strangers; she had never cried in front of friends; she had never cried in front of anyone except her parents and her husband. Now she cried in front of everyone. The District people hated it when she cried. Displays of emotion disgusted them. Still, Mimi had managed to win more battles than she had lost. Lately, however, she seemed to have reached an impasse.

"I don't understand. Please read the documentation," she said.

Why after years of meetings like this did the cruelty and

indifference of these people still hurt so much? Speechless, Mimi pointed to the pile of research studies and journal articles she had assembled; the letters she had carefully crafted for doctors to sign.

Dr. Hench spent another second flipping through the papers and then she said again with her hateful smile, "The documentation does not support your son's need for a summer program."

"What?" Mimi asked in a voice so soft she seemed to be talking to herself.

Addressing the wall above Mimi's head, Dr. Hench said in the slow, even tones of a person gifted with endless patience, "If you disagree with our conclusion, you have the right to a fair hearing." Then she smiled again. They always smiled. They smiled but they hardly ever looked Mimi in the eye. This was something she and Jake had worked so hard to teach their son. For months following Danny's diagnosis, they had sat him down at his baby table and said to him, simply, "Look at me."

Visions of Danny at home for the summer piled up in Mimi's mind: there she was keeping frantic watch over him on the playground, making sure he didn't dive off the top of the monkey bars like a bird; and later, at home, she stood in the doorway of his room, yelling at him for pulling the tassels off the throw cushions on his bed, or carving Jewish stars into the soft pine of his desk with a knife he had taken out of the kitchen drawer.

"But how will my son spend the summer?" Mimi asked.

"He can do the same things that other children do over the summer," the psychologist replied.

"But my son isn't like other children," Mimi said.

Dr. Hench, still with that vile grin, again informed her of her right to bring the matter before a judge. By which time, of course, the summer would be over.

Every time Mimi came to this building, there would always be Yolanda sitting behind the little school desk in the lobby, insisting that she produce her ID. Being forced to prove her identity to the same person over and over again was a source of increasing irritation to Mimi, and the more irritated she became, the more time Yolanda would spend examining her driver's license, copying down each number in her round, childlike handwriting with painstaking precision and care.

As the years passed, Mimi's resentment grew and eventually she was pouring all her frustration out onto the security guard; she hated her and Yolanda hated her in return. Mimi liked hating Yolanda, and Yolanda seemed to like hating Mimi. There was an intimacy to their hatred, a kind of freedom. They scowled and gestured angrily at each other. Muttering under their breath, they called each other names.

Then on a day that happened to be Danny's eleventh birthday, Mimi was signing her name at the front desk and she noticed that Yolanda had changed her hairdo. It was done in a short pixie cut, instead of the severe-looking bun that usually sat on top of her head.

Without thinking about it, Mimi said to the security guard, "You changed your hair! It looks great!"

Mimi was by nature an amiable person. Whenever she noticed that a woman had a new hairdo or that she was wearing a new dress or hat or shoes—she always complimented her, whether she liked the alteration the woman had made in her appearance or not. In fact, the more hideous the change, the more effusive Mimi would be, in an effort hide her embarrassment over what the woman had done to herself.

Although the pixie cut was completely wrong for a woman as big and fat as Yolanda, Mimi liked it because it made the security guard seem less forbidding, maybe even a little vulnerable, innocent even, since Yolanda could have no idea how silly she looked in this ridiculous new hairdo.

Yolanda appeared to be confused by Mimi's compliment, but she seemed to be pleased by it as well.

After going through the usual routine of signing the log, Mimi went to the elevator. As she stood in front of it, keeping careful watch over its suspenseful descent from the eighth floor, she found herself getting lost in a long meditation about hair and the power it had to affect a woman's looks, more than makeup, clothes, jewelry or facials. Mimi's last haircut, five years ago, had left her in such a state of despair she had vowed to never let a hairdresser near her again as long as she lived.

When Mimi and Yolanda met again on opposite sides of the tiny desk in the lobby a few weeks later, the security guard was almost friendly, although she continued to insist that Mimi produce her ID before signing the book.

In February, Mimi brought Danny with her to The District office. He was scheduled to undergo the same useless battery of tests every year. When Mimi arrived at the entrance with him, she greeted Yolanda, and searching his eyes, she put her hands on Danny's shoulders and told her son, "This is Mommy's friend Yolanda. Say hello to Yolanda."

"Hello to Yolanda," Danny said.

"Hello to Danny," Yolanda responded and asked him if he would like to write his name in the ledger. When he did, she complimented him on his handwriting.

"It's a lot neater than your mother's," she added. To which Danny responded by asking, "A phalange is what?"

"A phalange," Yolanda said. "That's a big word. I don't know such big words."

"A phalange is what?"

"Danny," Mimi said. "What did we say about asking rhetorical questions?"

"A phalange is what?" he repeated.

"Why don't you tell me what it is, Danny?" Yolanda said.

"Honey," Mimi said, putting her hands on Danny's shoulders again. "What is a phalange?"

"A phalange is a finger bone or a toe bone," he said. "There are fifty-six phalanges in the human body, fourteen phalanges on each hand and foot. Three phalanges on each finger and toe, except for the thumb and large toe."

"What a smart boy you are," Yolanda said.

"A phalange is what?" Danny asked.

"Danny!" Mimi said.

"It's a finger bone or toe bone," Yolanda said with a wink.

One day Mimi rushed past the security desk, hoping that she would be able to make it to the elevator before Yolanda could catch up with her. She was late; she usually didn't care whether or not she was late; they always kept her waiting forever anyway, but today she was going to be arguing her case before a judge. Mimi had come to ask The District to approve the school on Long Island.

"Where do you think you're going?" Yolanda asked, grabbing Mimi's arm just as she was about to run into the elevator. Now it would be at least another four minutes before she would be able to catch another one up to the eighth floor.

Mimi ran back to the desk and scribbled her name in the register, tearing the paper in the process.

"Your ID."

"I can't believe this," Mimi said.

"Rules is rules," Yolanda said.

Mimi searched her wallet. "I can't find the fucking thing," she said, dumping the entire contents of her backpack onto the little school desk, sending loose coins, hairpins, rubber bands, crumpled-up bits of paper and disconnected Tampax holders flying all over the place.

"Please, give me a break, Yolanda. I was supposed to be here fifteen minutes ago! I have a hearing today. It's important. I finally found a school for Danny."

"Go, just go," Yolanda said, rushing to hold the elevator door open as Mimi scrambled to dump everything back into her bag.

Everyone she'd consulted about this hearing had assured Mimi that The District would approve the school, but she could tell as soon as she entered the room that she didn't have a chance. She could tell by the look on the face of the hearing officer, who was engaged in a spirited conversation with Van Stone and Daisy Hench when she entered the room.

"You're late," the hearing officer said, the previously lively expression on her face turning blank.

"Yes, I know, I'm sorry," Mimi said.

The hearing officer looked at her watch. After dealing with the usual formalities, she asked The District to present its case, which consisted of them stating that Danny was in a perfectly appropriate placement now.

"No," Mimi said. "It is not appropriate."

*  *  *

When it came time for her to present her case for the school, Mimi called the principal. The line was busy. She had phoned his secretary five times yesterday, to make sure he would be available to take her call. Without his testimony, she had no case at all. She redialed his number. The hearing officer exchanged exasperated glances with Daisy Hench as Mimi continued to dial and redial the principal's phone number.

Impatiently, the officer announced: "You have one more chance and that's it."

Mimi dialed again. The line was still busy.

"We have other hearings on the schedule," Dr. Hench said with her frozen smile. "You're not the only mother in the world, Mrs. Slavitt, who thinks she has found the perfect school for her child."

When Mimi started dialing again, Daisy Hench, Van Stone and the hearing officer looked at one another, and all at once, the three of them reached to grab the receiver away from her.

"Please," Mimi said. She held the phone clenched in her fist. "Just one more time."

"We have other hearings on the schedule," Dr. Hench repeated.

Ignoring them, Mimi went back to dialing the phone.

"I told you. That's it," the hearing officer said.

Mimi knew that if she stayed here a second longer, she would either end up begging them to wait until the principal answered his phone or humiliate herself in some other way, like telling them to go fuck themselves. Her eyes cast downward, she gathered up her documents and stuffed them into her backpack. Getting up out of her chair, she left the room without saying a word.

"Where does she think she's going?" the hearing officer asked Dr. Hench, who responded with a frown and a shrug.

Van Stone, brushing the dandruff off his shoulders so vigorously that a few white flakes went flying onto the lapel of Dr. Hench's chocolate brown blazer, responded with a shrug of his own.

Mimi felt like a zombie as she walked down the hall and down the stairs, past Yolanda, who was sitting at her desk in the lobby.

"Mimi! Are you okay?" the security guard called out after her.

Looking back at Yolanda for a second, Mimi started to run down the street. The security guard, leaving her post, ran after her. When she caught up with Mimi, Yolanda pulled her to her breast.

"You're tired, mami," she said. "You need to go home and sleep. You're a good mother. But now you have to go home and sleep. Go home, mami. Go home and sleep. Go to sleep. You need to take care of yourself. You need to sleep."

Mimi decided she would allow herself to stand in the middle of the sidewalk on 181st Street with her cheek pressed against her old enemy's big, soft bosom for another second or two. Then she would go home and get on the phone. There was a woman in a high-level position at The District with whom she had recently established a kind of rapport; maybe she would be able to do something to help, and if she couldn't, perhaps she would know someone who could.

# Two Mothers

Aviva Brodner was putting the finishing touches on the "S" in "Samuels" when the light in the kitchen shifted, turning the shadows her fingers cast on the envelope into talons. She looked up to see the room ablaze with the brightness of the late afternoon. The sun was setting over the George Washington Bridge. She spent a moment admiring the view before getting back to the business of addressing invitations to her son's bar mitzvah.

Reluctantly dipping the nib of her pen in the inkwell that came with her calligraphy set, Aviva wrote "Danny Slavitt" on an envelope. She hated to admit it, but Danny Slavitt was the closest thing to a friend Howard had ever had. As the kids no one picked to join in special projects, the two boys had been thrown together into an unlikely union. Together they had built a lopsided model of the Empire State Building, graphed the entire course of the Nile River in red Play-Doh, mapped a road trip to Singapore and created DNA fingerprints out of each other's saliva.

Despite these and many similarly shared experiences, the distinction of being the class outcasts seemed to be the only thing Danny and Howard had in common. Where Howard was fearful, Danny was fearless; where Howard was quiet and timid, Danny said anything that popped into his mind, no matter how outrageous or ridiculous; and where Howard suffered unbearable shame at the hands of the bullies, Danny never seemed to know that he was an object of scorn, or if he did, it was a matter of complete indifference to him.

Howard was always coming home from school complaining about some outrageous thing Danny Slavitt had said or done. Last week during art class, for example, when everyone else was cutting out snowflakes to decorate the walls of the auditorium for the winter concert, Danny had insisted on cutting out silhouettes of his hands; and the other day when the class was asked to recite the poems they had written in commemoration of September 11th, Danny Slavitt stood up in front of the class and sang his adaptation of "John Brown's Body," beginning with the words "Three thousand bodies lie a-molderin' in the grave," until Mrs. Bolger ordered him to stop. In addition to being stubborn and capricious, the boy was disgusting, and Howard, who himself had a delicate sense of etiquette, disapproved of his classmate's many disgusting habits: Danny picked his nose and was in the habit of passing gas in class, for which he had earned the name "Human Fart Machine." Howard's nickname was Howard the Coward.

Aviva had started planning for Howard's bar mitzvah a year ago. Sitting in her office in Midtown Manhattan, where she was the vice president in charge of marketing for a large cosmetics company, she would flip through the mind-boggling array of floral arrangements and party favors displayed in the catalogs her secretary had ordered, and later on, at home, after dinner, she would surf the Internet for bar mitzvah themes, cuisines and entertainments. She spent two months going from catering place to catering place, sampling foods of different ethnicities and styles.

While Aviva prepared for the party, her son struggled with the ritual aspects of his bar mitzvah. The living room, where his tutor, Jeff Kessler, worked with Howard on his haftorah, was adjacent to the kitchen, where Aviva labored over dinner. She would try to lose herself in her chores, but neither the blender nor the microwave nor the clanking of the silverware could block out her son's cries of frustration; whenever the job of learning his haftorah proved to be too much for him, Howard would run into the kitchen to his mother and wrap his arms tightly around her waist.

"It's too hard, Mommy," he would say through his tears. "Please don't make me do it. I'm stupid! Stupid! Stupid!"

"You must never, ever speak that way about yourself," Aviva would say, resisting the urge to slap her son across the face to knock some sense into him as her heart beat with astonishment and despair. Pulling herself together, she would ask, "Do you remember what it means to be a man?" To which Howard, whose sobs had taken their usual course into a series of never-ending hiccups, would shake his head in assent.

"It means being brave and strong. Don't you want to be brave and strong?"

"Yes, Mommy," he would say when he finally managed to catch his breath.

"Remember what I told you about Rome?" she would ask.

"Yes, Mommy."

"Well, the same is true of your haftorah."

The reminder of the glories that awaited him if he could just learn to recite those twelve lines of Hebrew was usually sufficient to calm him down, and when Howard returned to the living room, he would do so emboldened with a renewed sense of purpose.

As the day of his bar mitzvah approached, Howard's expectations of all the wonderful things that lay in store for him became more and more unrealistic and this worried Aviva. She would often catch him staring at himself in the mirror repeating, "Today I am a man," over and over again. He seemed to attribute an almost magical significance to the words, as though they carried with them the power of some ancient invocation to the gods; for not only did Howard expect to turn into a man, brave and strong, on that day, but he seemed to believe that the Jewish rite of passage would make him taller as well.

Howard's shortness had long been a source of grief for him; the entrance to his bedroom bore scores of pencil marks, many of them, tragically, drawn one on top of the other. It had always been Aviva's hope that Howard would take after her side of the family and not his father's, who with the exception of Frank, himself a passable five foot ten, were on average four inches below average height; but when she took him to visit the top endocrinologist in the city, the bone scan the famous doctor did of Howard's wrist indicated that her son was destined to live out his life as a short man.

When Aviva asked the doctor about growth hormone shots, he told her that they were used for only the most drastic cases. "They can affect anything in the body with a potential for growth—cancer, for example," he told Aviva, who couldn't help thinking that those five extra inches might be worth the risk. There were treatments for many forms of cancer, but for the stigma of being a man of diminutive stature, there were no remedies.

Although she didn't dare tell Howard what the doctor had said, she would try in a roundabout way to prepare him for life as a short man, sometimes out of the blue running down a list of famous short men in history she had found on the Internet. There were dozens of names on the list, including Hitler (but he wouldn't do). "Height isn't everything," Aviva would say. "Character is what matters." She told him that Pablo Picasso, the greatest painter who ever lived, and the great composer Wolfgang Amadeus Mozart were both only five foot four. "And Harry Houdini, a man of enormous strength and the greatest magician of all time—only five five! And Toulouse-Lautrec—remember when you saw his paintings on the class trip to the Metropolitan Museum last year—guess how short he was?"

"Five feet?" Howard said, looking up at his mother expectantly.

"Toulouse-Lautrec was only four foot eleven inches tall! Which is only three inches taller than you are now—and you haven't even had your growth spurt yet!"

Aviva had chosen a Hawaiian theme for the reception. As far as the music was concerned, this was one time she was grateful for Howard's extreme sensitivity to sound—the vacuum cleaner, the steam hissing through the radiator, the buzzing of the microwave still had the power to send him falling to the floor with his hands over his ears. There would be no loud band, the likes of which she had had to endure at the bar mitzvahs of the children of her friends and relatives; instead she had hired a ukulele player, who had promised to learn "Hava Nagila" for the occasion. Everything was working out just as she had planned. Best of all, Howard had finally learned his haftorah.

After weeks of frustration, the tutor decided to give up trying to teach Howard how to read the words in the original Hebrew and had him read a transliterated version of his haftorah instead. Aviva had also supplemented the biweekly tutoring sessions with lessons of her own. In addition, she had made a CD of the tutor singing the haftorah and had programmed it to play continuously by Howard's bed while he slept. Howard knew his haftorah so well he would say it in his dreams. Often, in the morning, he would wake up singing it to himself.

While Aviva couldn't be happier with the way everything was falling into place, the issue of Danny Slavitt preyed on her mind. Whenever she thought of the boy, her right eye would begin to twitch. Some nights when she turned off the lights to go to sleep, the child's face would appear to her, like that of a small, brown-haired monster.

Aviva had met Danny Slavitt once. She and Howard were exiting the subway, on their way back from buying his bar mitzvah suit, when Howard spotted Danny walking up the big hill on 181st Street with his mother. The image Aviva had formed of Danny Slavitt had been that of an obnoxious, willful kid, but she could see right away that this was a child with a serious disability. He was walking lopsidedly, oblivious to everything other than the book he was reading, while his mother guided him up the street like a seeing eye dog. He didn't respond to Howard's greeting, and continued to ignore him throughout most of the encounter.

It horrified Aviva to think of her son being identified with a child who was so clearly impaired. She knew Howard wasn't the most popular kid in the world, but that was just because of his natural timidity, so much of which was changing now. Nothing was wrong with him that a little more work and a little growing up couldn't fix. Certainly he bore no resemblance whatsoever to this strange child.

"My bar mitzvah is going to be in less than two weeks, can you believe it, Danny? Just two more weeks! And today I got a real suit. It has a vest, like a man's vest! It cost two hundred dollars!" Howard exclaimed as Danny settled himself onto the sidewalk with his book.

"And I got real leather shoes, too, not boy's shoes, but man's shoes! And a real tie, not a clip-on tie, but a real man's tie! My father is going to teach me how to tie it when he gets home from work tonight! Do you want to see it, Danny? I could show it to you if you want to see it!"

Danny didn't bother to look up from his book. Fortunately Howard was so caught up in recounting the details of his bar mitzvah that he didn't seem to notice that Danny was ignoring him.

The boy's mother, who had introduced herself as Mimi, gave up trying to get her son to respond to Howard, although it was clear to Aviva that Danny's rudeness distressed her. She just let him sit there on the piss and spit of bums, flipping through the pages of what appeared to be a field guide to rocks and minerals.

"I can't believe it! I can't believe I'm going to be a man! In just two weeks I'm going to be a man!" Howard exclaimed. "Can you believe it, Danny? In just two weeks I'm not going to be a boy anymore. I'm going to be a man. A real live man!"

Suddenly coming to attention, Danny looked up from his book. "That's just an expression," he told Howard. He spoke in a loud, annoying voice. "Thirteen-year-olds aren't men! Some thirteen-year-olds don't even have secondary sex characteristics yet. You're not a man until you're eighteen. Thirteen-year-olds are just boys!"

Aviva looked at her son, whose face had turned red with confusion and doubt. She despised this boy Danny Slavitt and was anxious to get her son home as soon as possible and undo the damage this revolting child had just inflicted on her sensitive son. Holding Howard's chin in her hands, she told him not to pay attention to what Danny Slavitt had just said.

"Well, I have to get home to cook dinner," she said, putting her arm around her son, who stood there, limp with shock, clutching the shopping bag that held the emblems of his impending manhood.

"Your mother's right, Howard," Mimi Slavitt said. "You know the way Danny is. That's just something he says. It has nothing to do with you. It doesn't mean anything, really." Then she turned to address herself to Aviva, who wished she could just tell the woman to shut up.

"Ever since we brought up the subject of a bar mitzvah with him, Danny has been fixated on the idea that technically it would be false to say that he is a man. He has no objection to being bar mitzvahed, per se. But I don't know," she said. She spoke very fast in a loud voice, like her son.

"He simply refuses to say, 'Today I am a man,'" she said, interrupting herself for a moment to reprimand Danny, who had been digging his index finger into his nose and then putting that finger into his mouth. She laughed self-consciously and continued.

"He's quite adamant about it, and when Danny makes up his mind about something, there's never anything anyone can do to change it. I can just see Danny standing there before the congregation saying, 'Today I'm not a man,'" she said. "Danny just likes everything to be true. That's good in some ways," she said, her words trailing off and her eyes beginning to wander. "But I don't suppose it makes much difference anyway—"

Then catching herself, she added, "I don't mean to say that getting bar mitzvahed is insignificant. I just don't think it would be all that significant for Danny. So my husband and I have decided to skip it, at least for the time being. Danny won't turn thirteen for another year anyway. So who knows? Maybe he'll feel different in a year. But I doubt it. One thing about Danny. He never changes. No matter how much we try, he stays stubbornly the same."

Aviva told Mimi Slavitt again that it was getting late and that she had to get started on dinner.

"Yes, it is getting late, isn't it?" Mimi responded. "Come on, darling, time to go home," she said, turning toward her son.

But Danny just sat there, his eyes never leaving his book. He was picking his nose again.

"Stop that! How many times do I have to tell you not to do that?" his mother said, taking hold of his arm. "It's time to go!" But Danny ignored her and continued to read his book. Mimi turned to Aviva and with a fretful smile said, "Danny is really looking forward to Howard's big day."

She bent down to pull her son off the sidewalk. He was small for his age, but it took considerable effort for his mother to get him up. His sneakers were dirty and there was a hole in the knee of his pants. Finally Mimi managed to get her son upright and began leading him down the street. For a moment his face was totally eclipsed by his book, making him look like something out of a painting by Magritte.

One week the class homework assignment was for everyone to write an essay about the happiest day of their lives, and when the teacher asked for volunteers to read their essays out loud, Howard raised his hand. This was the first time in the entire year—indeed, in his entire life—that Howard had ever raised his hand in class; usually he sat in the back of the room, hoping that if he crouched down low enough and avoided making eye contact with the teacher, she wouldn't see him. But today he stood up in front of the class and read his essay. He enunciated every word in a clear voice.

"The happiest day of my life is scheduled to take place in two weeks and three days from tomorrow. Because that's the day I'm going to be bar mitzvahed!" he exclaimed. He told about the party. There was going to be a magician who could bend metal rods with his mind. There would be freeze dancing, scavenger hunts and relay races. His mother had hired a man who was listed in *The Guinness Book of World Records* for making more balloon animals per minute than anyone else in the world. He told about the party favors, which would include digital cameras for every kid and T-shirts with HOWARD'S BAR MITZVAH written in neon letters across the front. At the end of the party there was going to be a raffle and the winner would receive a free iPod. He concluded by reporting that the whole thing was going to cost his parents thirty thousand dollars.

Howard was feeling so happy that afternoon that instead of seeking sanctuary in the nurse's office during lunch, as he usually did, he ate in the cafeteria, and afterward he made his way into the schoolyard for recess. All the other kids were huddled together in groups, and Howard stood by the fence, wondering what to do with himself. He was beginning to feel a headache coming on when he noticed Steve Hartman walking toward him.

Steve was the most popular boy in the seventh grade; the girls wrote his name on the palms of their hands and the boys imitated everything he said and did. When Howard saw him coming toward him, he jerked back in fright: it was Steve Hartman who had dubbed him Howard the Coward.

"Chill, man!" Steve commanded.

Howard looked up at him. How he longed to be back in the nurse's office, lying on her torn plastic couch, a thermometer in his mouth, an ice pack on his head.

"I told you, chill," Steve said, patting him amiably on the back, which made Howard jerk away in terror.

"I'm sorry, but I don't have any money today," Howard said.

"I don't want money. Me and my people want to go to your barmizza."

"You want to come to my bar mitzvah?" Howard asked.

"Ain't that what I just said?"

"Should I ask my mother to send you an invitation?" Howard asked tentatively.

"Yeah. Cool," Steve said. Howard ran all the way home from school. "Could I invite Steve Hartman and his people to my bar mitzvah?" he asked his mother as soon as he stepped through the door. Aviva had come home early from work that afternoon to go over some last-minute preparations with the caterer and the florist.

"Slow down, Howard. I can't understand a word you're saying," she said.

"I can't slow down! I'm too excited!"

"I want you to take three deep breaths. Then you can tell me what you have to say."

After quickly inhaling and exhaling three times, Howard repeated, "Could I invite Steve Hartman and his people to my bar mitzvah, could I? Could I, please?"

"Who's Steve Hartman?" asked Aviva. Howard had always been too ashamed to tell his mother about his persecution at the hands of the charismatic leader, and he was happy now that he hadn't. "And who are 'his people'? That sounds black. Is he black?"

"No, Mommy. He's the captain of the hockey team and he's my new friend," Howard told her. "He asked me to play basketball with him and his people during recess today. I wasn't very good at it but he told me not to stress it! Could I invite him and his people to my bar mitzvah? Please, please, can they come?"

"Of course," Aviva said.

"I can't believe it. Steve Hartman wants to come to my bar mitzvah!"

"And why shouldn't he?" asked Aviva.

After she had helped Howard with his homework and reviewed his haftorah with him, Aviva took her calligraphy set out of her desk drawer and addressed invitations to Steve Hartman and his friends. She would have to order another table and tell the caterer to make enough food for six more people. And she would have to buy six more cameras and maybe add another iPod to the drawing. Now there would parties for Howard to go to and things for him to do on the weekends, instead of moping around the house all the time.

Suddenly the specter of Danny Slavitt rose up before her. If only she could just disinvite him. Aviva was so preoccupied with the problem that she overcooked the string beans and burned the rice. After dinner, when she was in the middle of scrubbing the broiling pan, an idea occurred to her.

She found Danny Slavitt's name in the school directory and picked up the phone and dialed. She hoped his mother wouldn't be home so that she could just make her case to the answering machine. But Mimi Slavitt answered the phone on the second ring.

"Hello, this is Aviva Brodner, Howard Brodner's mother," Aviva said. "I'm calling about Howard's bar mitzvah."

"Oh yes," Mimi said. "Next Saturday at eleven, right? Nine thirty for the synagogue and eleven for the reception, right? It was so nice of you to invite Danny. Didn't you get our RSVP? I sent it to you at least a month ago. I'm sure I sent it to you."

Aviva wished she had just hung up when she heard Mimi Slavitt's voice. She could have waited to call tomorrow during work hours. She had heard Danny Slavitt's mother was a co-pyeditor or something. But now that she had gotten herself into this situation, she had no choice but to press on.

"Yes, we did get your RSVP. But I'm calling about something else."

"Is something wrong?" Mimi asked.

Aviva hesitated.

"No, no, not at all. It's just that . . . The thing is," she started, "I thought it would be only fair to warn you that Steve Hartman and his crowd will be coming to Howard's bar mitzvah." She paused, giving Mimi time to draw her own conclusions.

"Oh yes, I know all about Steve Hartman," Mimi said.

"Yes, well, I just thought it would be only fair to warn you," Aviva said, pausing again.

"Thank you," Mimi said.

"Howard tells me they're not very nice to Danny."

"Oh, don't worry about that," she said. "Danny couldn't care less about those little pricks."

"I just thought it would be only fair to warn you," Aviva said, repeating herself. "That he's coming. To Howard's bar mitzvah."

"That's very considerate of you," Mimi said. "But again, Danny doesn't give a shit about them. And he really loves parties. I don't know why exactly," she said, and after a brief pause that was punctuated with a little laugh, she continued.

"I mean, all he ever does is find himself a corner somewhere and read one of his atlases or field guides. Thanks, anyway, for the warning. But really, you don't have to worry about Danny. He'll be fine. He always is."

Aviva slammed the phone down into its cradle so hard that the crystal paperweight on her desk came crashing down to the floor, splitting into hundreds of pieces. She wept as she got out the broom and began to sweep up the tiny shards of glass.

Howard, who had just come to the kitchen to see when

dinner would be ready, asked his mother what was wrong.

"Nothing, honey. Mommy's just being a big baby, because she broke her favorite paperweight. Don't come in here. I don't want you stepping on glass."

"Mommy," Howard said, "I'm so excited about my bar mitzvah, I can't do my homework. Am I really going to sit at the head of a big table—like a man? In the middle of it?"

"Yes, Howard," Aviva said, holding back her tears as she swept the glass into the dustpan. "It's called a dais. You'll be sitting at the head of the dais."

"And where will your table be, Mommy? Will I be able to see you from where I'll be sitting at my dé . . . dé . . . dé . . .?"

"Dais, honey," Aviva said, hiding her disappointment that her son couldn't pronounce this simple two-syllable word. "And yes, Howard, I'll be sitting with the grown-ups—right next to your big table," she said, the solution to the Danny Slavitt problem dawning on her. It was simple: The reception was going to be held in the basement of the synagogue in a room that was separated by a big dance floor. She could put Danny and his mother on the other side of the room, along with Howard's tutor and his wife, the women from the sisterhood she had felt obliged to invite, and her husband's relatives. Shortly after she and Howard had run into Danny and his mother on the street, Mimi Slavitt had called her up to explain that Danny could not yet go places on his own. It was something they were working on, so Aviva had invited her to accompany her son. If only for once in her life she didn't have to be so fucking polite, then she wouldn't be in this predicament now.

\* \* \*

Howard woke up at five o'clock in the morning, the day of his bar mitzvah, to the strange sight of both the sun and the moon hovering in the early morning sky. When Aviva came into the kitchen to fix breakfast, he was sitting at the table in his bar mitzvah suit.

"Don't you look just like a man?" she said. "But maybe you should take the suit off. We don't want to get it dirty when you eat breakfast."

"I'm too excited to eat, Mommy."

"But you need your strength. You have a big day ahead of you—"

"The biggest day of my life!!"

"Yes, honey, and you need your strength."

"Okay, Mommy. I guess you're right," Howard said and he went into his room and took off his suit, carefully zipping it back into its plastic bag.

When they got to the synagogue, Howard was thrilled to see his name spelled out in big black letters on a billboard outside. His father videotaped him clowning around in front of the sign, pointing at it and then himself and then back at it again. Aviva had arranged for the tutor to meet them and she walked up to the podium with Howard and had him practice reading the transliterated text aloud one last time while she went downstairs to make sure everything was in order with the preparations for the reception.

Howard recited his haftorah without making a single mistake. Afterward he stood and listened while Rabbi Gluck addressed him. "Howard," the rabbi said, "in the Torah portion you read this morning, the words 'Be strong and of good courage' are repeated four different times. The first three times the words are spoken, God tells Joshua that he must bring the people into the land. The fourth time the words 'Be strong and of good courage' are repeated, the people say them to Joshua." Placing his hands on Howard's shoulders, the rabbi continued, "What I want to tell you, Howard, as you stand here beside me on the podium, before all your friends and family, is that you have proven yourself to be, like Joshua, 'strong and of good courage.' I know that your family and all your honored guests join me now in wishing you a great big mazel tov!"

Next it was Aviva and her husband's turn to speak. Addressing Howard, they took turns telling him how proud he had made them. "You really hit the ball out of the park with this one, son," his father said. Aviva stood beside him, tears of pride in her eyes, nearly struck speechless with joy. "I'm so proud of you, Howard. All I can say is today you are a man!"

It was Howard's turn to speak. Resuming his place behind the podium, he said in a voice that to Aviva's ears seemed deeper and richer: "Friends, family, members of the congregation of Temple Emanuel, Rabbi Gluck, I want to thank you all for sharing the most important day of my life with me. I feel like I'm in a dream. The only reason I know it's real is that when I pinch myself, it hurts!" At which point he pinched his arm and winced. The congregation chortled appreciatively. "I want to thank everyone who has helped make this day possible. Rabbi Gluck, my tutor Jeff Kessler, and my parents. I know this is going to be the best bar mitzvah ever!"

Aviva made her way down the back stairs behind the podium to tell the caterer it was time to start serving the hors d'oeuvres while Howard stood with his father, shaking hands with the guests, accepting their congratulations and their gifts. Downstairs, the reception room had been transformed into a Hawaiian luau. The dais where Howard and his new friends would sit was draped in a grass skirt, and at all the place settings were Hawaiian shirts and neon sunglasses and luau hats—bucket hats for Howard's girl cousins and luau baseball hats for his boy cousins and for Steve Hartman and his followers. There were silk flower arrangements on all the tables, and the room was lit up with neon lanterns that were hung from the ceiling with neon strings. On the dance floor, Barry the balloon man was making a flamingo out of a red balloon. Everything looked even better than Aviva had imagined it would, and standing between two cardboard coconut palm trees, she punched the air and murmured out loud to herself, "I did it! I did it! I did it!" It felt so good to be able to breathe again. Taking one long last look at the room, she went into the kitchen to give instructions to the caterer. When she returned, the guests were already swarming down the stairs. Soon she was surrounded by her friends.

"Did you notice?" Aviva said. "He didn't make a single mistake. Not one single mistake."

"And that speech!" declared her best friend Babs Landau.

"He wrote it all by himself. I didn't help him with a word of it. Not a single word! And did you hear how clear his voice was? How clear and strong?" Aviva said.

"Clear and strong as a bell," said her first cousin Barbie Stern.

"So it wasn't my imagination, was it?" Aviva said. Then excusing herself, she went off to find Howard. It was time for him to make the brucha over the challah and the wine. She found him standing next to the life-size cutout of himself in the doorway and two giant bamboo torches. He was surrounded by Steve Hartman and his friends, who were all high-fiving him. There was a look of rapture on his face.

After Howard said the prayer over the challah, Aviva went back into the kitchen to tell the caterer it was time to serve lunch. When she returned to the reception room, she could sense right away that something was wrong. She scanned the room, looking for Howard as she announced that it was time for everyone to take their seats, and soon she spotted him running across the room toward her. He was crying.

"M-m-m-mommy, Mommy," he stammered.

"What is it, honey?" Aviva asked.

"M-m-m-m-ommy," he repeated.

"Take three deep breaths, Howard," she said in a firm, steady voice.

"I-I-I-I-I-I c-c-c-c-c-an't!!!!!!!!"

"Just tell me what happened, darling."

"D-d-d-d-d-d-d-d-d-a-a-a-a-a-a-a-a-n-n-n-n-n-eeeeeeeeeee Sla-sla-sla-sla-sla-sla-sla-sla-v-v-v-v-v-v-v-it, he, h-h-he s-s-s-said—" But he was too overcome with emotion to continue.

Aviva wiped the tears off his cheek with the blue silk scarf she wore around her shoulders. "What happened, Howard? Please tell me what happened."

"D-d-d-d-d-d-d-d-d-a-a-a-a-a-a-a-a-a-neeeeeeeee Sla-sla-sla-sla-sla-sla-sla-v-v-v-v-v-it, he, h-h—he s-s-s-s-s-s-s-ss-s-s-s-said, he, h-h-h-he s-s-s-said th-th-that I'm n-n-not a m-m-m-m-m-m-man!!! B-b-b-b-e-e-e-c-c-c-c-ause I-I-I'm n-n-n-n-ot eigh-eigh-eigh-teen!"

"What? What? What did he say?" Aviva asked.

"H-h-h-h-he said th-th-that I-I-I-I'm n-n-n-n-n-n-ot a m-m-m-m-m-m-an. That I-I d-d-d-d-on't look a day over t-t-t-en!!!"

Aviva held her son's chin and staring into his eyes, she

said, "You are not going to let Danny Slavitt spoil your special day. Do you understand me, Howard? You will not let him spoil your special day. You are a man. You are a proud Jewish man and no one can tell you anything different. You sit down now in this chair and wait for me," she said, signaling to her friend Babs to stay with Howard until she got back. "I'll just be a few minutes, Howard," she told him, and with that, she went off in search of her husband.

Frank buried his face in his hands as his wife commanded him to tell Mimi Slavitt and her son Danny to leave. Not daring to lodge any protest, he followed her obediently as she walked him over to No Man's Land to point out Danny Slavitt, who was busy pulling apart the lei that hung around his neck, while his long-suffering mother tried to stop him.

Aviva watched as Frank approached Mimi Slavitt. He stood before her with his hands thrust in his pockets and an apologetic grin on his face and told her that he was sorry, but he would have to ask her and Danny to leave.

"What?" Mimi asked, confused. "You want us to leave?"

"Yes, I'm sorry. But, you see, Howard is very upset."

"Why? What happened?"

Frank grimaced and looked behind him, where his wife stood with her lips pressed together and her legs planted like tree trunks on the shiny marble floor. "It's something Danny said," Frank said. "Something about Howard not being a man."

"Oh," Mimi said sadly. "I see." Then turning to her son, she wrapped her arms around him protectively and told him they had to go.

"Why?" Danny said. "Why? Why? Why?"

"We'll talk about it later. But right now we have to go."

"I don't want to go. I refuse to go," he shouted. Every eye in the room was on them. "I refuse! I refuse! I refuse!" he kept on shouting.

"We have to leave, Danny. We have to leave," Mimi said.

Danny continued to shout, "I refuse! I refuse! I refuse!"

She bent down and with tremendous effort managed to pick her son up in her arms and carry him out of the room.

When Aviva got back to Howard, he was surrounded by a group of her friends. He wasn't crying anymore, thank God, and he seemed to be listening attentively to everything they were telling him.

"No one can tell you that you're not a man," her friend Mandy Shulman was saying.

"After the way you stood up there and said your haftorah!" Babs Landau said.

"I want you to forget all about Danny Slavitt, Howard," Aviva said. "He's gone. Now why don't you go and watch the balloon maker. Look at all the fun your friends are having. You go over and join them. He can make anything you want. Anything at all."

"Okay, Mommy," Howard said, still slightly stunned, but feeling better. "Am I really still a man, Mommy, even though I'm not eighteen?"

"Of course you're a man, Howard," Aviva said, deciding that when she got back to work on Monday, she would have the art deparment create some kind of certificate of manhood for Howard to hang on his wall. "Just look at you in your suit and tie. And the way you said your haftorah—without a single mistake! And what did the rabbi say?" she said, forgetting in the desperation of the moment that it was she, not the rabbi, who had officially proclaimed her son a man.

"Now go to the balloon maker. Ask him to make you a unicorn. Or a bird. Or a bull. He can make anything you ask him to, in seconds flat. Anything at all."

"Howard's fine," Babs said to Aviva fifteen minutes later. "See how much fun he's having with the balloon man."

Aviva looked over at the dance floor, and there was Howard, grinning in amazement as the balloon man made him a unicorn out of a red-and-blue-striped balloon. More friends came over to congratulate her and gradually she began to relax and enjoy herself.

The dinner was delicious and it was time for dessert. Aviva was telling a waiter she wanted the crème brûlée when she heard a strange popping sound coming from the dance floor. It sounded like artillery fire. Pop. Pop. Pop. Pop. She got out of her chair to investigate. The sounds seemed to be coming from the front of the dance floor, but it was difficult at first to make out what was happening. Weaving her way through a crowd of children, Aviva discovered what the commotion was about: Steve Hartman and his friends were sticking forks into the balloons. The closer she got to them, the louder the sounds became.

Aviva looked for Howard, but he was nowhere to be found. Then finally she saw him in a corner near the stage, crouched in the wreckage of torn, deflated rubber, cupping his hands over both his ears, and pleading over and over again, "Stop it. Please stop it."

Aviva felt paralyzed by a combination of helplessness and despair and some other emotion she couldn't identify. Howard had stopped crying, but his hands were still over his ears, his face frozen with fear. She looked around the room.

Her gaze was drawn to the other side of the dance floor, where she saw Mimi Slavitt standing next to one of the many cardboard cutouts of Howard she had placed around the room. In this one Howard was wearing a baseball cap and holding a bat, in striking position. The photographer had to take many shots before Howard could get the position of the bat right.

Earlier, when Aviva was making her obligatory visit to greet the outcasts in the section of the room she had reserved for them, she had noticed that Danny Slavitt had left his field guide to rocks and minerals on the table; apparently his mother had come back to retrieve it. She wondered if she had been there when Steve Hartman and his disciples were popping the balloons.

The sadness that had been in Mimi's eyes when she carried her son away was still there, but mixed in with it now was something else. Something that Aviva found disturbing. What is it? she asked herself.

Then it came to her. Compassion. It was compassion. The idea that she, Aviva Brodner, could ever be the object of compassion infuriated her.

Then, as though being pulled by the force of an invisible magnet, she found herself locking eyes with Mimi Slavitt. There was almost an air of conspiracy in the way Mimi was looking at her. She seemed to be saying that the two of them, Mimi and Aviva, shared a secret that no one else in this room could possibly understand.

Frightened, Aviva turned away.

As she marched back across the room, she decided that first she would get rid of Steve Hartman and his friends. She would drag them by their arms kicking and screaming out into the street if she had to. Once they were gone, she would attend to Howard. She didn't know exactly what she would say to him just yet, but she knew she would think of something. She always did.

# Queen for a Day

Amy once told me about a time she was standing on the subway platform with her son. Ten feet away a woman carrying a blue suede briefcase was staring at her. Alec, ten at the time, had been pacing back and forth on the platform singing "Baby Beluga" at the top of his lungs, and Amy had been trying to get him to stop. But the woman wasn't looking at Alec; her attention was focused entirely on Amy.

Finally the stranger approached her. She had an autistic son, too, she said. She had left him with his father five years ago when the child was four and she hadn't seen him since. The tears in her eyes were tinted black with mascara as they streaked her cheeks with two symmetrical lines that reminded Amy of spider legs. She told Amy how much she admired her. Alec was still singing.

"What did you say?" I asked.

"I told her not to be so hard on herself," Amy answered. "I told her not to admire me."

We were in a café on the Upper West Side. The original plan had been for us to meet there once a month to commiserate about our children. But Amy was always getting sick and would often cancel or she just wouldn't show up.

Sometimes it was just the flu, or a bad cold, but often her illnesses were rare medical conditions I had never heard of before. Once she had to have an operation on her eyes, which were ironically incapable of producing tears. She had to convalesce in a completely sterile environment and had spent a week blind and alone in a disinfected hotel room. To me the idea of experiencing blindness, wow, what a nightmare. But Amy said it was fine; she had brought along her favorite CDs; it was like being on vacation.

Another time when I called, her husband answered the phone. He said that Amy would be out of town for several weeks. Apparently, every six or seven years her nerves would wrap themselves around her spinal column and the only surgeon who knew how to disentangle them was in Denver, Colorado. When she got back, Amy told me that although recuperation from the operation was painful, the view of the Rocky Mountains from her hospital room was spectacular and the nurses were all very nice.

Amy always seemed to take her illnesses in stride, but when it came to Alec, that was a different story altogether. Her grief would consume her; sometimes for weeks, sometimes for months; once an entire year went by before I heard from her.

Amy's strange disappearances happened so often that I suppose I should have gotten used to them, but I never did;

the only explanation I could ever come up with was that she was dead. Either one of her mysterious illnesses had killed her, or she had been hit by a truck while crossing the street. I once read an article in the *Daily News* about a woman who had been dragged to her death when the belt of her raincoat got caught on the handle of the door of a speeding fire engine. The world was full of strange, unimaginable dangers; autism, apparently, was just one of them.

I met Amy during those critical first weeks following Danny's diagnosis. Frantically crisscrossing the country by phone, I had spoken to Martha Gold, the mother of an autistic twelve-year-old in Madison, Wisconsin, who told me about a boy in Lower Manhattan who was on his way to recovery. His mother was "one of the lucky ones," Martha said in those weary tones I had heard in the voices of so many other mothers. Everyone wanted to talk to Amy, she said. They all wanted her good luck to rub off on them.

Jake and I had chosen the same program for Danny that Amy had chosen for her son. It required him to put in the same forty-hour work week as the men and women I would see walking up and down the hill to and from the subway, whenever I took a break to glance at the world outside my window. Our expectation was that this therapy, which was an intensive form of behaviorism, would cure Danny, just as it was in the process of curing Amy's son.

All Jake and I had to guide us was a manual we had bought off the Internet. We often felt we had no idea what we were doing, trying to fix Danny's brain all by ourselves, and there were several questions I wanted to ask Amy about the program. Most of all, though, I wanted her to tell me that there was still hope for my son, who was just six months short of turning the magical age of five, after which the chances for recovery were greatly diminished.

I had been calling her obsessively, sometimes leaving messages, sometimes not. Martha Gold had told me that she was very hard to reach since parents were constantly calling her (to "touch the hem of her garment," was how Martha had put it), and I was beginning to think that Amy would never pick up the phone until one evening at seven she finally did. The sound of her voice surprised me. It was not the voice of a warrior. It was sweet and soft and very feminine.

I was in our office in front of the computer. The muffled sound of Jake saying "Match" traveled through the wall to my left. I knew the program. Jake was sitting opposite Danny in a little chair in front of a little table before an assortment of blocks. When he said, "Match," Danny was supposed to find another block the same size and shape and then place it next to Jake's block. If Jake's block was round, and Danny picked up a square block, or a triangular block, or a round block of a different size, or if he did nothing at all, Jake would take hold of Danny's hand and direct it to the block that matched his, and then he would say "Good Job!" and reward Danny with a piece of potato chip. Later Jake would reward Danny only if he picked up the right block by himself.

The e-mail friend who had recommended this program to me said that unlike most other therapies for autism, this one did not require parents to abandon all reason. In fact, the major basis for its appeal was reason. There were scientific studies to back it up. It *was* a science. We had to use charts and graphs to track every minute of our children's progress. All of us parents worshipped the mother with the cured kids;

she was the shining example of the therapy's success and she gave us what we needed: Hope. The book she had written was our sacred text. We were members of a secret cult and we were proud of ourselves for having been smart enough to recognize that this was The Answer. We were strictly forbidden to employ any other form of treatment. And that seemed to enhance the therapy's credibility.

What no one realized at the time was that all of us— whatever therapy we happened to choose—were equally desperate; and our desperation turned us into fanatics. We were blinded by the conviction that if only we did what we were told to do, our children would be saved just like the children of the fortunate, intelligent author of our sacred text. Many of us clung to this hope for a lot longer than was logical for us to do so.

The major allure of the therapy for me was the fact that it was so time-consuming and so difficult. I thought that if there was a path to recovery—and there had to be—it would have to entail a kind of primal sacrifice of self; it would call for more hard work than most people—including my four-and-a-half-year-old son—could endure.

The day we were expecting FedEx to deliver the manual to us, I brought Danny's baby table from his playroom to his bedroom in preparation for the start of his therapy. I scrubbed it clean of all the encrusted clay, glue and crayon marks. I poured Comet and bleach on it and sprayed it with Fantastik, and scrubbed and scrubbed and scrubbed, and when, in spite of all my scrubbing, there were still some stains I couldn't manage to get out, I remembered a magical cleanser I had once used to clean the bathtub of our first apartment in Washington Heights, which had been embedded with decades of dirt when we moved into it.

Jake was in the kitchen trying to train Danny to look him in the eye and I called out to him that I was going out to get something. I had to go to three hardware stores before I could find one that carried the cleanser I had in mind, and when I got home, I scrubbed and scrubbed some more and eventually I managed to wipe away all signs that the miniature table had ever been used.

It felt good to be doing something at last. It made me feel less helpless. It made me feel that Jake and I were taking charge. But it also made me feel very sad. In my obsession to make the table as clean as it had been when I bought it for Danny when he was two, I felt as though I were scrubbing away the old Danny, or at least the Danny I had thought he was, the Danny I had imagined he would grow up to be. I was erasing all signs of that Danny. I was making room for this new Danny that Jake and I were in the process of creating from scratch.

Before Amy had the opportunity to say more than hello to me, I went on and on about how relieved I was to have reached her at last. Then I proceeded to do what I always do when I feel uncomfortable—I talked too fast, too loud and too long. I told her about Danny and the nursery school's warnings and the debacle with Stan Shapiro and the confusing diagnosis and how much I hoped that we would be able to achieve the same success with Danny that she had achieved with her son. And of course, I congratulated her. Over and over and over again. It still makes me cringe to remember how much I congratulated her.

"It's been a while since I spoke to Martha," Amy said after I had finished my monologue.

And then she told me what had happened with Alec—she

just gave me the general outlines of it that day. I didn't learn
the details until later, when we became such good friends.

Amy was the eldest of ten siblings and she had had a lot
of experience taking care of babies. This was why she
knew almost from the moment of Alec's birth that there
was something wrong with her newborn son. If he wasn't
with her all the time, he would shriek the kind of blood-
curdling cries that only babies can produce, except Alec's cries
were much louder and altogether more terrifying than any
baby's cry she or the nurses or the doctors had ever heard before. That first night, at three in the morning, when Amy was
sleeping, trying to recover from thirty-two hours of labor, a
nurse brought Alec to her and placed him at her breast. He
couldn't stay in the nursery because he was waking up all the
other babies.

Amy and Steven started taking Alec to see neurologists,
psychiatrists and psychologists when he was two, but they
could never find anyone to tell them what was wrong with
their son. It wasn't until Alec was three and a half that he was
given a diagnosis and the diagnosis was severe autism. The
psychiatrist told them the prognosis was grim. He said they
should "put him away." Another psychiatrist handed them
a brochure for a residential home in Charlotte, North Car-
olina. When Amy told him that she would never consider
sending her son away, he responded: "Are you kidding? You
don't keep a child like this. No one keeps a child like this."

Her friends and parents, the brothers and sisters she had
helped raise, all had the same message. Her father, who was a
pediatrician, said: "You cannot and must not take care of this
child." He insisted that she send him someplace where they
knew what to do with children like this. "His life is ruined,

over before it has begun. But why should your life be ruined, too?"

Her closest friend, a painter with whom she shared studio space in Soho, said, "You have a career that is about to take off. If you keep Alec, you will be throwing everything away. And for what? To what purpose?"

Amy never spoke to her friend again. She packed up her things and found another artist to take over her half of the studio. She was about to embark on a mission that would demand all the strength and courage she possessed, and she could not run the risk of having anything like doubt get in her way. She had to surround herself with believers, people who had faith that Alec could and would be saved. As far as her family was concerned, Amy wasn't willing to cut herself off from her parents and all her brothers and sisters forever, but it would be a long time before she had any contact with them.

When they started doing the therapy, Alec would refuse to sit in the chair and he would throw tantrums, falling to the floor, kicking and screaming. Amy would ignore the tantrums and repeat the instruction and put Alec back in the chair, which was the procedure mandated by the manual: *Be strong! Be firm! Don't weaken! It's for his own good!* And Amy would put Alec back in his chair and repeat the instruction over and over and over again until he was too exhausted to do anything but comply.

Within two months, Alec was mastering the programs rapidly. Once her father-in-law, a New York State Supreme Court judge, came over to their apartment, and observing Amy in action, he pounded the cushions of the sofa where he sat and declared, "You can do this! If anyone can do this, you can! You can cure this child!"

Soon Alec was paying attention to the people around him.

By the time he was four, he knew almost as many words as a four-year-old is supposed to know.

"It was as if a light had been turned on inside him," Amy told me.

She hired graduate students and teachers and trained them to do the program. Some of these young people lasted no more than a day, some no more than a week or two, some no more than a month; some quit, some she fired: she didn't want anyone working with Alec who didn't appreciate the value of what they were doing; eventually she refused to keep anyone who didn't share her fervor for his recovery; and finally she decided to get rid of anyone who didn't love her son.

Her zeal was contagious, and after a year she managed to assemble a small group of devoted tutors, all of whom had the fierce conviction of converts. They were all convinced, as Amy herself was convinced, that it was just a matter of time and hard work before Alec was cured.

Together they celebrated Alec's every triumph, every fleeting glimpse of normalcy they saw in his eyes or in something he said or did, and they faced all difficulties with optimism, courage and grit. It filled them with pride to be participating in this ambitious project of the rebirth of this beautiful child. Most of the people Amy hired were artists of one sort or another, and many of them were thinking that this would be the work they would choose for themselves if their careers as painters or dancers or musicians didn't pan out.

What would Alec be like? Amy wondered. He wouldn't be perfect. She didn't want him to be perfect. He could be selfish or vain; he could have a bad temper or maybe be a little sneaky. (Yes! Please let him be sneaky.) He was entitled to have his share of flaws. Like any other parent, she would just have to deal with problems as they came up.

Still, certain as Amy was that recovery was within reach, she sometimes found it more than she could bear to contemplate. It was too big. Too wonderful.

One morning when Amy went to wake Alec up, he didn't reach out to her, and at breakfast his grip on his spoon was clumsy, and he made the same strange noises that he used to make when he ate. She touched his forehead. She took his temperature. It was normal.

She considered calling off the therapy session for the day, but Alec didn't seem to be sick and today was Maura Conway's day—Maura was Amy's favorite; she was a sweet girl, a graduate student who had responded to the ad Amy had put on craigslist. When Maura arrived, Amy warned her that Alec seemed a little off today.

Maura reminded Amy that Alec had his good days and his bad. Everyone had their good days and their bad.

An hour later when Amy was sitting in the kitchen writing up the week's schedule of programs, Maura came in. She was so overwrought, she couldn't speak at first.

"What is it?" Amy asked. But she knew.

"Amy, we lost him," Maura finally said, tears streaming down her cheeks. "He's gone. His words are gone. His affect is gone. All he wants to do is lie on his bed and stare at the wall." Later that day when Amy took Alec to the park, he refused to do anything but sit in the sandbox, watching the sand running through his fingers over and over and over again.

She allowed herself to hope for a while that what had been taken away for no apparent reason would be restored for no apparent reason and that one morning Alec would wake up whole again. But he never did. She started all over, with the earliest and simplest programs. He's only four and a half, she would tell herself. There was still time.

Maura Conway tutored Alec for a few sessions after that, and then one afternoon after her shift was over, she told Amy she just couldn't do it anymore. "I'm sorry," she said. "I'm not strong like you are."

The panic of those early years sometimes seems so distant to me that every now and then I have trouble recalling exactly what it felt like. There is, however, one incident that has always stayed with me in its entirety.

It was two weeks after our last session with Stan Shapiro and a week before Jake and I decided that we were going to cure Danny with this fantastic new therapy. I was still calling parents across the country day and night. A woman in Chicago told me that jumping up and down on a trampoline helped "organize the brain" of autistic children and I spent two days searching for a trampoline small enough to fit into our apartment. I visited every sports store listed in the Manhattan phone directory while Danny and Jake waited for me in the car. One day I extended my search to the Bronx. It was just Danny and me in our little Honda. I forget why Jake wasn't with us.

I got stuck going in the wrong direction in rush-hour traffic that was at a standstill for over an hour and a half. This was something that usually would have had me cursing myself out for taking the wrong exit. Danny was asleep in his car seat in the back, and there was nothing for me to do but wait. It was the first time since his diagnosis that I wasn't spinning around in circles, doing three things at once.

Sitting there trapped in my car, surrounded by gas fumes and honking horns, I couldn't think of a place in the world I would rather be than stuck on this highway to nowhere. I wished I could stay there forever.

\*\*\*

There was a brief period of three or four weeks when Amy visited me in my apartment every Sunday. She had to get away from her family, she said. Amy lived in Battery Park City, which was at least an hour away by subway from Washington Heights; when the A train was running local or when it stopped running altogether, which it often did on weekends, she could end up riding the subway for as long as an hour and a half. But Amy said she enjoyed having nothing to do but sit and wait and watch the lights of the long dark tunnel passing by. I laughed when she told me that and she laughed when I told her about those moments of peace being trapped in my car during my search for a trampoline. Amy didn't have any trouble understanding why being stuck in traffic, breathing in poison, surrounded by the clangor of outrage, frustration and distress, was my idea of a good time.

If it was lunchtime, I would make Amy scrambled eggs and toast. It was always scrambled eggs and toast since her diet was extremely limited, due to the various medications she took to control her terrible depressions, which were unresponsive to the usual mix of SSRIs and tranquilizers that made life bearable for most of us other mothers.

Fortunately sweets were not off limits for her and I always made sure to bake something when she visited. It made me happy to think that I could do this one small thing for her. Also, baking had always had a calming effect on me—it gave me a wholesome feeling, and I always made too much: cake *and* pie *and* cookies. When she arrived, I would invite her to sit at the kitchen table before my assortment of treats. If her visit extended to twilight, I would move us to the living room in time for Amy to see the sun set over the George Washington Bridge.

A terrible loneliness had settled into me, and Amy was the only person who could offer me any relief from it. It was like a chronic illness, this loneliness of mine; there were occasional remissions, but it was always there; I could feel it when I laughed, a couple of times when I opened my mouth to sing, and once, at a party, when I got up to dance. Jake couldn't understand how I could feel so lonely when he was always within reach—figuratively and literally. Everyone has trouble of one sort or another, he would say to me. Autism just happens to be ours. This is life. But I'm not you, I'm me, I would say in response.

It was comforting for me just to know that Amy was out there, enduring and persevering. I *had* to know she was there. I had to know that I was not alone. We both had suffered from recurrent depressions all our lives, and this thing with our sons tipped us over the edge many times. Neither of us had managed to get past the initial shock and heartbreak of it.

We saw each other very occasionally over the years. There were our infrequent meetings at the café on the Upper West Side, and that brief period of time when Amy visited me at my apartment every Sunday. We would also sometimes run into each other at an autism conference or meeting. One morning we found ourselves in the same elevator on our way to a seminar on sign language. (Amy had told me about the seminar. The idea of trying out a new form of communication with Alec intrigued her.) It was September. Danny was thirteen by now, and Alec was fourteen, and both of our sons were stuck in schools that were all wrong for them because we had been unable to find any viable alternatives. Our depressions had reached new lows. For me, walking down the street felt like I was walking through glue. As for Amy, she spent entire days with her head buried under the covers.

The moment we saw each other in the elevator that morning, we embraced with all our might. Neither of us said a word. I nuzzled my face into Amy's neck, and she nuzzled her face into mine. We stayed locked in each other's arms until the elevator reached the eighteenth floor.

I can't remember exactly when Amy's visits to me in Washington Heights began or when they ended, but my recollection of what they felt like to me is quite vivid. The friends I said good-bye to after Danny's diagnosis would call every now and then to see how I was doing, but talking to them was like talking to the air. None of the other mothers were of any consolation to me either. They all seemed to have moved on—back to their lives, back to themselves. Maybe that was because their children were making progress, whereas Danny remained the same.

The last mother I had spoken to was someone I had befriended at a support group meeting years before when I was on the hunt for playmates for Danny. She reported that her son was now attending a regular school and thriving there. I told her I was happy for her, really I was, and then I burst into tears and hung up the phone.

Since Alec's miraculous recovery when he was four, which was followed by his horrific relapse, he hadn't undergone any dramatic transformations either, but that never stopped Amy from trying to recapture what had been lost.

Her days and nights were spent thinking up new ways to

teach him, and then sitting down with him and teaching him step by patient step by patient step. There were the schedules for the tutors, and the constant back-and-forth dialogues she had to maintain with them, keeping track of Alec's progress and dealing with meltdowns and crises; the endless search for speech therapists and occupational therapists and behaviorists. And then at least two or three times a year, Amy and Steven would hire a car service to take Alec to Maryland, Connecticut, Pennsylvania and New Jersey for consultations with doctors considered to be the leading authorities on autism in the country.

Then, of course, there was always The District, trying to block her every step of the way.

Amy was like a character out of Greek mythology. She was like Prometheus getting his liver eaten every day or Sisyphus rolling that big rock up the mountain. I once mentioned this to her. I wanted to know why she, with all her mysterious illnesses, her intractable depressions and the haunting memory of Alec's horrifying regression never complained about anything, and during one of her visits to me in Washington Heights, I asked her why she was such a stoic.

That was when she told me about her collection of blue and yellow pills, a combination of opioids and benzodiazepines she had been squirreling away over the years. She had two little zip-lock bags, one for Alec, and one for herself.

"Amy," I said. "How serious are you about this?" I didn't know what to do. Should I report her to wherever one goes to report such things?

Smiling the smile that was always accented with a slight undercurrent of pain, she reassured me that she could never go through with it. She was too much of a coward. Still, it comforted her to know that she had the power to put an end to all this if she chose to. She said that she probably enjoyed thinking about her little murder-suicide kit as much as other people liked fantasizing about having superpowers, like being able to fly like a bird or breathe underwater like a fish.

"If I seem like such a stoic to you, that's because of the nuns," she added. "They taught me all about suffering."

Amy told me that she had spent her childhood and early adolescence under the rule of nuns, who'd trained her to sit perfectly still at her desk with her hands clasped together. She had retained the ability to sit for hours at a time without moving a muscle; her husband said it was like a circus trick.

The nuns told her what God did to children when they were bad, and then there were the pictures of slaughtered innocents and martyred saints everywhere, and Jesus hanging on the cross with nails hammered into his hands and feet, and all those scary stab wounds. Amy said that her Catholic upbringing was one reason she had married a Jew. Her husband couldn't understand why she never let him buy a Christmas tree. His family always had one.

Amy's father wanted her to be a doctor like him, and when she was an undergraduate at the University of Nebraska, she had obediently pursued his plan for her. She was a stellar student, completing a rigorous curriculum of science and math in a semester less than the usual allotted time. After she graduated college, she was about to take the MCATs, but right after the monitor had finished handing out the exams, she got out of her chair and left the room without saying a word to anyone and headed straight for the art studio, where she spent the next several months creating a series of paintings that earned her a Fulbright to study art in Paris.

That year Amy spent in France was the happiest of her life. When she returned to America, she had a one-woman show at one of the top galleries in Soho. It was there that she met her husband, Steven Kantor, who bought one of her paintings, a watercolor that in retrospect seemed to eerily predict her future, filled as it was with images of maternal distress, symbolized by broken eggs, a big blotch of cloudy black paint and a woman shot full of jagged holes.

I had never met Steven in person, but I had spoken to him on the phone a couple of times. He always made me feel like an idiot. Amy told me that he had that effect on everyone, including her. This surprised me because I knew how much he adored her. During the one real conversation I ever had with him, I blurted out that I was in awe of Amy. I have never met anyone like her, I told him. She's a saint. I went on like that for quite some time. He didn't say anything for several seconds, and then in a voice free of his characteristic irony, he said that it amazed him how much he loved his wife. That he never thought he could be capable of so much love.

"I want to paint so badly that sometimes I just lie in bed and will myself to sleep just so that I can dream about painting," Amy told me. "That's the only time I paint. In my dreams."

Her face lit up with an almost manic ecstasy as she told me about how much she loved painting. Then she spoke about a recurring fantasy of hers to leave everything and move to the Dende Coast in Bahia, where she had heard you could live for less than four hundred dollars a month.

"That's my dream," she said. "To go there and paint."

I was so intent on coming up with a solution for Amy's problem (it took me forever to realize that this was something she hated), I don't think it even occurred to me that

moving to Bahia meant she would be abandoning her husband and son. I just set my mind to solving the problem the
way I always did.

But how to figure out a move to Bahia had me totally
stumped so I said the first thing that dawned on me, which
was that she should go on *Queen for a Day*. I told her I bet she
would win. "You could win a trip to the destination of your
choice," I continued. "I think that's an option." It made me
nostalgic in a weird sort of way to remember that perverse
game show from the 1950s. I recalled the slightly soiled feeling of watching it on my tiny TV. *Queen for a Day* was on
Saturday morning, and whenever my parents were out of the
house when it was on, I would sneak my little TV out of my
closet and watch it.

"The destination of my choice!" Amy exclaimed.

We went to my computer and there it was on YouTube,
just as we remembered it: the opening parade of leggy dancers dressed up in cardboard boxes advertising the sponsors'
products; the slimy middle-aged MC with his glib responses
to those tales of illness, poverty and despair, and those
wretched, wretched women. Looking at the announcer now,
with his jolly manner and his pencil-thin mustache, the kind
favored by movie villains, Amy and I decided that he must
have been an alcoholic.

At the show's end the woman chosen by the applause
meter to be Queen for a Day sat on a velvet throne, draped in
a velvet cape, wearing a crown and buried under a heaving
bouquet of roses as the MC told her about all the treasures
her life of endless misery and toil had reaped: silver-plated
flatware, toasters, vacuum cleaners, refrigerators, freezers,
washers, dryers and an all-expense-paid vacation for two.

\* \* \*

It was months before I heard from Amy again. She sounded so happy on the phone. The timbre of her voice had changed; it sounded an octave lower, and where there used to be all those shades of darkness, there was only pure bright light.

"Amy. You sound wonderful!" I exclaimed.

She told me that two weeks ago she had spent a weekend in the country, alone at a little bed-and-breakfast in Upstate New York, with her charcoal pencils and sketchpads. The inn was near a Buddhist monastery, and every morning at five before she got to work, she would sit on the front porch and wait for the parade of monks strolling in peaceful silence down the dirt road in their ritual predawn walk.

Since her return she had been spending every minute painting. She painted when she woke up in the morning; she painted into the night until she was so tired that the paintbrush fell out of her hand. There were days when she was so busy painting, she forgot to eat. I wondered what she was doing with Alec all that time, but I didn't dare say anything that might disrupt her happiness.

We made arrangements to meet at our café the following Sunday, but when she arrived, instead of being happy, she seemed more miserable than I had ever seen her before.

She said it was impossible. She had been painting in her bedroom, but last week Steven had developed an allergic reaction to the paint fumes and so she had been trying to create a little spot for herself in the living room. But there was so much clutter. Boxes of notebooks containing all the programs she had created for Alec over the years, boxes of papers documenting the various lawsuits they had brought against the The District, boxes of speech therapy reports, occupational therapy reports, physical therapy reports, psychological re-

ports—all of them useless, but she had to hold on to everything until Alec was twenty-one. Who knows, she might
have to hold on to this shit forever!

"I don't want to go back there. I can't go back there. I
have it in me to be happy. That's one thing I learned at that
little inn. I still have it in me to be happy."

As usual, I tried to come up with solutions for her.

"Why don't you just stuff everything away in a box?" I
told her. "Just dump everything in a box! Clear away a little
corner of the living room for yourself and get one of those
Japanese screens—at Ikea—you could order one online—
and go hide yourself away in a corner! Don't worry about
what's in the boxes! Just paint!"

She smiled at me the way she did whenever I gave her
advice. She was always too polite to do anything but smile.

We arranged to meet at our café the following Sunday and
we met there for the next three Sundays. Amy had calmed
down by then. She was back in her stoical mode. She told me
that everyone has a cross to bear and she was determined to
bear hers with dignity and grace.

Amy and I never spoke on the phone just to talk, but there
was one week when she called me three days in a row. The
first time, I could barely make out what she was saying.
Gulping for air, she told me that she had yelled at Alec. And
then she had slapped him. She had never yelled at him before.
And she certainly had never slapped him! He looked so confused. It broke her heart to see her son like that.

The day after that, she called me again in tears. She said
she thought she was losing her mind. She had spent the last
fifteen minutes sitting in the corner of her bedroom banging

her fists against the wall; she banged so hard that she broke right through the plaster to the bricks.

Then, the day before we were supposed to meet, she called and told me that she couldn't trust herself with Alec anymore. "Remember that collection of pills I told you about, Mimi?" she asked me.

"Yes," I said.

"Well, last night I divided them up: two-thirds for me and a third for Alec. I ground them up with the palette knife I use to mix my paints. And then I put them in two bowls of applesauce. The applesauce turned a light shade of green from the dust of all those blue and yellow p       ills. Alec loves applesauce. And he was so excited to see green applesauce. Green is his favorite color. When I flushed it down the toilet, he had a fit. He really wanted that applesauce. He loves applesauce. He likes it even better than ice cream. And he really loves ice cream. I hated to disappoint him like that, really I did. And I was so proud of him for wanting to try something new."

"Amy, I don't know what to say. I feel I should do something but I don't know what to do. Please tell me what to do."

"You don't have to do anything, Mimi. I'm sorry. I didn't mean to put you on the spot. I could never do it. I see that now. I wish I could but I can't."

I talked it over with Jake. He told me that I had to call Amy's husband right away and that if I didn't call him, he would.

"But she said she could never go through with it! It would be such a betrayal," I said. I reminded myself that I had suicidal thoughts, too. Not as fully articulated as Amy's, but I knew what it felt like to cross the street and be seized with the desire for a truck to come and hit me. I wanted to know what it felt like to be hit by a truck and hurled up into the air and thrown back onto the ground. I just wanted to die for a little while. Probably there is a point in everyone's life where death seems like an attractive option.

"So she says it and that means it's true?" Jake contended.

We went on like that for several rounds and I promised Jake that I would call Amy's husband after nine or ten, which was when he usually got back from work, but when I picked up the phone later on that night, I couldn't go through with it. I had a date to meet Amy in two days. I told myself that I would wait until then to decide whether or not to call Steven.

As usual, I arrived at our little café early enough to be able to secure a table in the corner. After fifteen minutes had passed and Amy had still not shown up, I started to panic and I berated myself for not having taken Jake's warning seriously enough. But then I told myself I was overreacting. Amy was always late, and she sometimes didn't show up at all. I don't know why I waited so long to call her cell phone—habit, I suppose—but when I did finally call her, there was a message saying that the phone was no longer in service. I called her home and her husband answered.

I told Steven that I had a date to meet Amy at twelve and that it was twelve forty-five and she still hadn't shown up. I told him that she was often late, but what really worried me was that when I called her cell phone, I got a message saying it was disconnected.

"Is she there?" I asked, trying to sound calm.

"No," he said.

"Do you know where she is?" I asked.

"No."

"Why is her cell phone disconnected? Do you have any idea where she can be?"

"Yes."

"That's a relief, " I said. "So where is she?"

"She's gone," he said.

"Gone? What do you mean gone?"

"Gone as in gone." He told me that she had left him a note saying that she was going away for good.

"Where did she go?" I asked. "Did she say where she was going?"

"No. She neglected to mention that," he told me. "All she said was that she was going away for good. Oh yeah, and she signed it 'Queen for a Day.' Whatever the fuck that's supposed to mean."

So Amy was taking a little vacation for herself. Good. Let her have her little break. God knows she deserves it, I thought to myself. I knew she would be back and I would wait patiently for her return. I just hoped that she wouldn't stay away for too long. Because without her here, I had only myself to pity.

# This Time Next Year

I arrived a few minutes after the meeting had begun and was scanning the room for an empty seat when a woman with elaborately coiled copper-colored hair motioned to me from across the auditorium. She was wearing lots of makeup, skillfully applied in the manner of the women one sees strolling down Madison Avenue, gold and silver shopping bags dangling from their slender wrists.

Removing her coat from the chair, she whispered, "I'm Karen."

When I sat down, I was surprised to see she was overweight, and wearing an oversized T-shirt, sweatpants and running shoes.

"I'm Mimi," I whispered back.

The principal, a slim woman, fashionably attired in a lime green suit, had just started to speak. As usual, I could barely take in a word that was said. She concluded her speech with a brief film showing an earnest-looking teacher hard at work with a handsome autistic boy.

"They're always so good-looking, aren't they?" the principal said with a sigh after she turned off the projector.

"What the fuck," Karen said to me as the meeting was breaking up. "These people are so full of shit. They're so in love with themselves, it's pathetic. Except the joke's on us. We're the pathetic ones."

The by-now familiar dread started burrowing its way into the pit of my stomach. I had come here to see what lay in store for us once we were ready to send Danny to school. In our mad rush to cure our son before he turned five, Jake and I had been spending forty hours a week doing the program with him at home. Our plan was to keep on working with him by ourselves until we thought he was ready for the next step, which was to go to what was known was a "center-based program," or, "school."

"Do you know what the ratio of applications to openings is?"

"No, I don't," I told Karen. "This is all new to me."

"Fifty to one. For any halfway decent school. They cherry-pick the kids. It's easier for them, and they have better outcomes to show their donors. I have one of the hard ones. And he's dumb as dirt. What about yours?"

Back then I was convinced that it was just a matter of time before Danny would be cured. The experts were always saying how smart he was. I told her that I didn't know.

"How about we go out for coffee and I'll give you a rundown on the whole mess," Karen offered. "There's a great café around the corner. It has the best cheesecake in the city. Do you like cheesecake?"

"Yes," I told her, although the truth is I have never been a big fan of cheesecake.

"Jonathan has been rejected by six schools so far," she told me as we followed the other parents into the elevator.

Everyone was standing together in their private hells as the yellow numbers kept flickering by. Next to the elevator buttons were clusters of tiny raised dots. The Lighthouse for the Blind had offices in this building, and on the fifth floor the door slid open and we all stepped aside to let in two blind men, each one holding on to the harness of a seeing eye dog. Blindness is worse than autism, I thought, although autism was said to be a kind of blindness; "mind-blindness," it was called.

One of the blind men, a big, healthy-looking young man in a bright blue shirt, had the most beautiful green eyes I had ever seen. His large black pupils were surrounded by thin luminescent circles of gold. It took me a few moments to realize that I had been staring at him. It made me feel like a trespasser, staring at the eyes of someone who didn't know he was being looked at and who couldn't look back.

I turned my attention to the flashing yellow numbers and thought about how loaded with significance the mere direction of a glance can be. This was a form of communication not available to someone like Danny and the man with the beautiful green eyes.

A telltale sign of autism is the lack of eye contact, and when Jake and I got home from the evaluation, we looked at old pictures of Danny and watched old videos of him and there he was, his dimples in full bloom, looking into his father's eyes as Jake held him up in the air. And on the desk in our office was a photograph of him, looking up at me with his mouth on my breast. I nursed Danny until he was three and a half but I didn't need a picture to remind me of that moment, or the hundreds of others like it, of him shifting his attention away from my breast to my eyes and back to my breast again.

At some point, Jake and I could never figure out when, Danny stopped looking us in the eye. For Danny, looking at a person's arms, legs or feet was no different from looking him or her in the eye. He seemed to have no feeling, no instinct whatsoever, for the special role that eyes play in human interaction.

The day after Danny's diagnosis Jake decided to teach him how to identify what a person is looking at. First he drew cartoon faces, with the pupils of the eyes set in different positions, and he would ask Danny where the eyes were pointing—up or down, left or right. From there he asked Danny to tell him what the cartoon face was looking at, and finally, Jake (revealing a talent I never knew he possessed) drew various scenarios in which the cartoon face appeared and he would ask Danny if the funny-looking boy in the picture was thinking about the ice cream cone on one side, or the bowl of fruit on the other.

Karen and I found a table in the corner, and she told me she would order for us. She came back ten minutes later, carrying two cappuccinos.

"I sprinkled cinnamon on top. I hope that's okay," she told me.

"Sure. Thanks," I said. When I reached for my wallet, Karen held up a hand in refusal.

"Now for the pièce de résistance," she said, and going back to the counter, she returned with a cake box, tied with thin red string, on which two plates of cheesecake sat balanced.

"This is for you and your family," she said, offering me the box. It was sealed with a turquoise sticker on which THE BEST CHEESECAKE IN THE WORLD was inscribed in gold. Her pleasure in giving me this gift was so palpable that I didn't bother engaging in the usual charade of protest.

"Lots of famous people come here," Karen informed me, running down a list of celebrities she had seen at the Columbus Avenue Bakery. She spoke at such a fast clip that at first I had trouble following what she was saying, but by the time the evening was over, I had grown accustomed to the brisk pace of her speech and the rapid transit of her thought.

"I hate it when they talk to you. They always act as though they're bestowing some great honor on you or something. That's the way William Baldwin was with me last week. He gave me this glittering smile, like we were best friends. He doesn't know me from a hole in the wall. I set him straight about that. He is, by the way, the most gorgeous man I have ever seen. They all have this glow. It's the facials and other forms of extraordinary skin care. I'm actually in the process of developing a skin care business."

She told me that for the past fifteen years she had been working as a personal manager for a string of wealthy people, but she was planning on changing careers. Service wasn't where the money was—goods was where you had to go for the big bucks.

Karen's plan for her son was to visit every school on the "A" list, and once she had identified one she liked and a principal who could be bought—because everyone had a price—she would schedule a meeting and secure a place for Jonathan in that school. There was no point in going through the usual bullshit of applying to these places, she told me. None of them would ever accept a kid as "involved" as her son. Like she said, they picked the easy ones.

It was open house season for special education schools, and Karen told me we should arrange to go to them together. So that's what we did.

At the fourth meeting we attended, at a school called The Learning Foundation, Karen decided she had found what she was looking for. She told me on the subway ride over there that the principal had a reputation for being a tyrant.

"No one knows what she does exactly, but whenever a kid acts up, she takes him into her office, closes the door and, presto, the kid is better," Karen said with the manic laugh that punctuated much of her speech.

"Everyone is terrified of her, especially the parents. The word on the street is that if you want your kid in her school, you have to be willing to drink the Kool-Aid."

"Wouldn't that bother you—not knowing what is going on with your son?" I asked her.

"Are you kidding? What do I know about this stuff?" she said. "As far as I'm concerned, Jonathan is one big fat mystery. And I mean fat. The kid is a blimp." Then, laughing, she added, "If there's some egomaniac out there who wants to take charge of my son, that's fine with me."

The principal, whom everyone addressed by her first name, Cindy, was famous for dressing in short, tight skirts and stiletto heels. She had an upper-class British accent, which the parents said was fake.

"This is good," Karen whispered.

Cindy glared at us from her podium, so Karen jotted down what she wanted to say in the sparkled little girl pad she always brought to these meetings. "She wants to build new gym," she wrote in her hieroglyphic hand. "Have client who needs big tax write-off."

Karen called me a couple of weeks later to tell me that Jonathan was in. She volunteered to cut Danny in on the deal when I was ready to send him to school. I thanked her but told her that I despised the woman and that I knew she would despise me, too. We were natural enemies, I said.

Since neither of our sons had any friends, we thought we should get them together, so one day Danny and I went to visit Karen and Jonathan in their duplex apartment in Chelsea. Jonathan was two years older than Danny. He had a big head and fair skin that was covered with freckles. He didn't bear any resemblance to Karen, except he had her beautiful copper-colored hair. In his excitement to see us, he started making noises that sounded like a baby's squeak toy.

As soon as we got there, Danny ran up the stairs to inspect all the rooms—which was what he did whenever he went to anyone's house. I ran after him. Karen told me not to bother. "Let him get it out of his system. He can break whatever Jonathan hasn't broken already." But I had to go after him. I didn't want him crumpling up Karen's blinds, as he had crumpled up the blinds in my mother's house and in our apartment; or hiding in the closet; also he might decide to engage in his favorite pastime of trying to crawl through the window guards. Besides, he had to learn how to behave.

I had no trouble getting Danny to come back downstairs when I told him there was cake and ice cream waiting for us in the kitchen. After we'd finished eating, the four of us sat on Karen's red velvet sofa and ate popcorn and watched *Pinocchio,* which was Danny's favorite movie at the time. (Jake and

I sometimes wondered if it could have anything do with our relentless efforts to turn him into a real boy.)

About ten minutes into the video, right after the Blue Fairy had made her appearance on the eighty-inch LED screen, Jonathan took me by the hand and led me upstairs to his room to show me his vast collection of stuffed animals. They littered his bed and carpet, they filled his toy chest and closets—this endless assortment of farm animals, zoo animals, dinosaurs and mythical creatures. One by one, he held them up to me and told me their names. It was clearly his intention to introduce me to each and every one of them, but eventually I managed to talk him into going back downstairs to watch the movie.

Jonathan sat next to me on the couch, and before I knew what was happening, he was holding my hand and kissing it, which made me feel a combination of pity, revulsion and guilt.

Karen loved Disney movies—she had never seen any as a child, and she was too engrossed in *Pinocchio* to notice her son's assault on my hand. Jiminy Cricket was about to explain to the little wooden puppet what it meant to have a conscience.

As I forced myself to tolerate Jonathan's caresses, I remembered that Karen had told me she couldn't stand how affectionate Jonathan was. That she herself was not an affectionate person at all.

It had been drummed into our heads that autistic children had to learn how to play with other children, so we had two more playdates, first at my apartment, then at the Bronx Zoo. For one reason or another, we never managed to get the boys together again, and soon after we finished our school tours, Karen and I lost touch with each other. I thought of calling her, but I never did. I would often wonder how she was doing. I hoped that the sexy principal with the huge ego had worked her magic with Jonathan and that Karen had succeeded in getting one of the many businesses she had told me about off the ground.

I didn't think she cared much whether or not we ever spoke to each other again: I had served my purpose for her, and I suppose she had served her purpose for me as well. None of us mothers had time for friends back then.

One day in early spring, eight and a half years after we had first met at that open house, I returned home to find a message from Karen on my answering machine: "This is Karen Renburg. Remember me? Sorry we've been out of touch for so long. But you know how it is. Anyway, I'd love to catch up, so give me a call when you get the chance." She ended by giving me her home number and her cell phone number. "Just in case you lost them," she said. I remembered that Karen never answered her phone, so it was with a sense of futility that I dialed her number, and I was surprised when I heard her voice on the other end.

We spent the first few minutes bringing each other up to date. She told me that Jonathan, who was fifteen now, liked The Learning Foundation. Just like everyone said, the principal kept the parents in the dark about everything. They didn't even have parent-teacher conferences, which was fine with her.

I mentioned the two hearings where I had represented myself, and I told her that I had been completely screwed by my advocate, but it was too painful for me to talk about.

"I've lost the will to fight," I was surprised to hear myself say.

"I know what you mean. There's just so much of this shit we can take. Did you ever think about it—I mean *really* think about it—that all this trouble and misery is caused by just one single child?"

"That's an interesting way to look at it," I replied.

"My psychiatrist tells me that the mothers of children with disabilities have significantly reduced life spans," Karen said. "So let's look at the bright side. Maybe we won't have to deal with this shit too much longer. Anyway, the reason I called was I was hoping you and Danny could come with Jonathan and me to our house in the Catskills. My husband has to be out of town on business. It's supposed to be gorgeous this weekend."

I said that I would love to go with her and thanked her for thinking of me but that I wasn't sure we could make it. I would have to check my schedule and get back to her. I, in fact, had no schedule; every day was exactly the same as the one that preceded it. The truth was, the prospect of spending a weekend away with Danny, without Jake, frightened me.

I told Jake about Karen's invitation. He said I should accept because Danny loved the country, and he hardly ever got to go anywhere. Also, it was not good for me to feel so helpless with my own son, and so dependent on my husband, and it was time for me to go back to having friends.

Karen told me she would pick us up at eight on Saturday morning, and at seven thirty that morning, we kissed Jake good-bye and went to the courtyard to wait for Karen. I was fumbling around in my suitcase, checking to make sure I had remembered to pack our bathing suits while Danny told me in great detail about his plans to settle Antarctica (one of his obsessions at the moment; it bothered him, the idea that an entire continent should be so sparsely populated) when Karen arrived in her gigantic SUV. Jonathan was sitting in the backseat, watching television. He was much fatter than I remembered him. His face seemed to float over his neck, which was shaped like an inflated rubber tube, and he was dressed in the kind of loose-fitting, brightly colored clothes sold in stores that cater to the Big and Tall Man. Jonathan was taller than Karen, who was very tall for a woman; his head was only four or five inches below the car roof.

"Hey there, Danny," Karen said. "Your mom tells me you're a big *Pokémon* fan. Well, guess what? How would you like to watch *Pokémon* right now?" She had asked me what Danny's interests were, the latest and most fanatical of which was *Pokémon,* and apparently she had gone out and bought the entire series.

Danny was thirteen now, and *Pokémon* should have lost its fascination for him long ago. Jake was always telling me that I had to accept the fact that in many ways our son would always be a child of five, but I could never come to terms with it, and it disturbed me that Danny should be so obsessed with a children's TV show. He was always drawing maps and charts and arcane diagrams of the world of *Pokémon*; he knew every episode by heart, and for three Halloweens in a row he had dressed up as his beloved Pikachu.

I had warned Karen that Danny was as antisocial as ever, but she said I had nothing to worry about as far as Jonathan was concerned. He was still as eager to please as ever, and he probably wouldn't even notice that Danny was ignoring him.

"You know how it is with these kids. They don't give a shit about the rights and wrongs of social behavior. I used to think it was a lot of bullshit too."

I had never cared much about social norms, either. Whenever the experts told us that Danny's basic cognitive faculties were intact and that his problems were mostly in the social realm, I would say to myself, Big deal. So he won't be a social butterfly. I had no idea how much these mere "social" problems would impair every aspect of my son's life.

Danny, who had not known it was possible to watch television in a car, would have ignored Jonathan under any circumstances, but I told myself that the excitement of sitting in the back of a big van watching his favorite television show could at least pass as a valid excuse for him climbing over Karen's son as though he were a piece of furniture and buckling himself into his seat without a word or a glance at anyone but Ash, Misty, Brock and Pikachu. According to Jake, the world of *Pokémon*—orderly, rule-bound, finite—seemed to have been created with autism in mind. I had never been able to bear sitting through a single episode of the series.

"Remember Jonathan?" I said to Danny. Silence. Over breakfast that morning I had spent half an hour coaching him to say hello to Jonathan.

"This is Jonathan," I repeated. Silence again.

"Say hello to Jonathan, Danny!" I insisted. To which, after a long pause, Danny responded, his eyes never leaving the tiny television screen, with a robotic "Hello, Jonathan."

As Karen had predicted, Jonathan didn't seem to mind Danny's complete indifference to him. "My mom says you like *Pokémon!*" he exclaimed. "I like *Pokémon* too! She said we could spend the whole weekend watching *Pokémon* if you want! She said whatever you say goes!" Danny responded to Jonathan's friendliness by telling him to be quiet. I turned around to reprimand him, but Karen, putting her hand on my arm, signaled me not to bother.

Karen handed the boys two sets of headphones and Danny spent the rest of the two-hour ride to the Catskills completely ensconced in this cartoon world, which, like some awful computer virus, seemed to have taken over his brain. Danny's incessant talk about *Pokémon* bored and irritated his classmates, and lately, in order to curb his obsession with the TV show, Jake and I had limited his television watching to an hour a day. But I decided that since this weekend was supposed to be a vacation for me, it would also have to be a vacation for Danny.

Karen proceeded to give me an abridged version of the story of her life. "We both come from nothing," she said, explaining that Harold, who had been brought up in the urban poverty of Detroit, was orphaned at age fifteen when both his parents died of cancer within a year of each other, and that she was an army brat whose father left when she was sixteen, but not before raping her, and whose mother kicked her out of the house when she was seventeen. She disclosed the shocking details of her biography in her typically breezy manner.

"What's raping, Mommy?" Jonathan asked from the back. He had taken off his headphones.

"Oh shit," Karen murmured under her breath.

"It's just something grown-ups do," she said in a cheery voice, comically raising her eyebrows and crossing her eyes. "Put your headphones back on, sugar-pie. Go back to watching TV."

We sat there in silence for a moment, and then Karen said

in a low voice, "I never thought I would be glad that his word retention sucks as badly as it does."

She went on with her story. Harold was an orthopedic surgeon, one of the most sought after and expensive in the city. He was a member of that exclusive breed of doctors who refuse to take health insurance.

"I read somewhere—I think it was Carson McCullers—that there are two types of people: lovers and beloveds," she said. "Harold is the lover type. He adores me and he adores Jonathan. He thanks me at least ten times a day for being his wife." Karen added that Harold, who was going to be sixty-eight on his next birthday, was both a mother and father to her, the mother and father she had never had.

"Jonathan was his idea," she whispered. "You should see him with the kid," she said, adding that as far as her husband was concerned, there was nothing wrong with their son.

"He takes him to the country every weekend, to give me a break. Whenever they come home, they're always laughing and singing some silly song they made up. Harold gets right down there in that strange little world of Jonathan's. Just think of it, this hotshot surgeon spending every weekend subjugating himself to the will of an autistic child. That's one reason Jonathan is so fat. If he wants to eat three hot fudge sundaes in a row, Harold has no problem with it. He says it's all just baby fat and that it will melt off after he's done with adolescence. And the guy's a doctor. His love for his son blinds him.

"Harold is a real gem," Karen continued. "I hate to think of where I would be if it weren't for him. He put me through college when I was in my late twenties. I aced all my courses. And then he sent me through grad school. MBA with honors from NYU. He told me he thought having a career of my own would be good for my self-esteem, which believe me was gravely damaged by that worthless piece of shit mother of mine—she could care less that she has a grandson. I never heard back from her when I wrote to tell her that I had a baby. That she, theoretically, was a grandmother. She has an unlisted number, you see, so I had to sit down and write her an actual letter.

"Anyway, Harold wanted me to know that I was a person in my own right. And I'm proud to say I've made quite a success of myself. I make over two hundred thousand dollars a year managing the lives of people who are too rich to be bothered counting their money or their houses. I don't know if you remember—I think I told you about it. That was over eight years ago. Shit! Eight years! Eight fucking wasted years! Anyway, I think I told you that I was planning on getting out of the consulting business.

"I'm getting into a whole different kind of thing. Two rooms of our country house are filled with all the junk I've bought off the Internet. Various lines of product packages. I'm going to start with skin care. I've assembled selections of products from all over the world for every type of skin. All very high-end stuff, although between you and me, it's all a crock of shit—nothing beats honey and lemon juice and a good night's sleep."

Then glancing at the rearview mirror, she said, "The problem is Jonathan—the kid's a major pain in the ass. He's so fucking needy! I've hired nannies to be with him—but he's always running into my office. With him underfoot all the time, I don't have the focus to get my business off the ground. That's why I decided"—she glanced in the rearview mirror again at her son, who continued to seem as engrossed in the show as Danny was—"I'll tell you about that later," Karen concluded, at which point Jonathan appeared from out of his apparent immersion in the world of *Pokémon* to ask, "Are you talking about me, Mommy?" His headphones were off again. "What are you saying about me, Mommy?"

"What could I possibly say about you?" Karen said, reaching back and squeezing her son's leg. "Except that you're the most wonderful boy in the whole wide world."

"You love me, Mommy?" Jonathan said.

"Do I love you?" Karen asked him. "Is the sky blue? Is the grass green? Did God invent little green apples with his little green apple inventing machine?"

"You're funny, Mommy," Jonathan said with a laugh, at which point Danny ordered everyone to stop talking.

"Danny is right," Karen said with a whisper. "Go back to watching *Pokémon*."

"So tell me about The Learning Foundation," I said after Jonathan had put his headphones back on.

Flashing me a somewhat guarded look, she whispered, "I'll tell you all about it later." Then changing the subject, she said, "I like old people and old music. Do you like the jazz singers from the forties and fifties?"

I told her I did, and with that, she put a CD into the slot in her futuristic dashboard. Then turning to Jonathan, she told him that Mommy wanted to listen to some music and that she didn't want to disturb him and Danny so she was going to bring the glass wall down.

"No!" Jonathan said in a plaintive voice. "Please don't, Mommy!"

"Mommy will be right here," she told him, blowing him a kiss. "Okay?"

"Don't go away. Mommy! Please don't go away!"

"Where would I go? Do you think I'm a bird? Do you think I can fly? That would be fun! I wish I could fly! Don't you wish you could fly?" she said, and blowing him another kiss, she told him to say, "Okay, Mommy."

Reluctantly Jonathan said it was okay.

"He hates when I do this," she said, and pressing a button, she brought a glass wall down between the kids and us. We spent the rest of the trip listening to the music of my parents' generation, which has always been more familiar to me than the music of my own.

"I love this crap," Karen said. "It makes me remember what it was like to be young and stupid. I cry when I hear these songs. It's fun to cry about this stuff. It makes you forget all the heavy shit we have to deal with all the time."

I told her I was happy that these songs still got to me. "It shows me I haven't been broken yet," I added.

"Broken?" Karen said. "I could tell you about broken."

When the voice of Billie Holiday emerged from the van's surround sound speakers, singing with greater clarity than I had ever heard her sing before, I told Karen that Billie Holiday and I were born on the same day.

"Every April seventh, WKCR plays Billie Holiday for twenty-four hours. That's how I celebrate my birthday. Listening to Billie Holiday on the radio."

"I never celebrate my birthday. I don't want to have anything to do with the cunt that spawned me. Do you know what she named me? Cinnamon! I swear that woman hated me before I was born. I changed it after she kicked me out of the house. As soon as I turned eighteen."

Karen was so easy to be with, I didn't feel my usual compulsive need to make conversation. It felt good having nothing to do but look at the signs marking the highway and the digitized white lights that kept reassuring us that traffic was moving smoothly for miles ahead. The nearby trees whizzed swiftly by as the mountains drifted slowly toward us and drifted slowly away.

Whenever Jake and I took Danny on a car trip to visit my mother in Oceanside, or Jake's mother in Plainview, or to try out a new doctor who was developing a reputation for helping children with this thing that no one seemed to know much about, or for an occasional excursion across the George Washington Bridge to go hiking when we felt Danny could afford to take a break from the rigors of the behavior program we had such high hopes for, Jake would look out the window and describe the sights to me. Danny would sit in the back, looking out the window, too, asking, "What's that? What's that? What's that?" This was something he had done for years whenever we went anywhere, until one day we noticed that he had stopped—we have no idea why or when; he just stopped.

We were well out of the city by now. The faces pasted on the billboards belonged to DJs and politicians I had never heard of. A monstrous trailer-truck with a dozen cars heaped precariously on its back cut in front of us. I hated driving anywhere near trucks; they were all bullies. Whenever I managed to find the nerve to pass one on the highway, my little Honda Civic would sway helplessly from side to side as I fought my way through the wind tunnel that had been created because I had finally forced myself to make my getaway from the hulk that had held me in thrall for miles. The car carriers completely unnerved me. I was always certain that at any minute the cars would tumble loose and bury my little

Honda in an avalanche of twisted metal. But Karen seemed fine driving behind it.

When the trailer turned off at the exit, the stuffed animal that must have been attached to its front fender came flying onto the road; it was crushed beyond recognition by the time we drove past it from the middle lane.

At the end of the exit ramp, slumped against the sign post, there was a hitchhiker dressed in dirty, baggy jeans, a dingy white T-shirt and a sports jacket that was three sizes too big for him; he wasn't wearing any shoes and he was very skinny. From the distance, it looked as though he had enormous bruises or birthmarks on his cheeks and forehead, but as we approached him, I saw that his entire face was covered with tattoos. Underneath all that, he couldn't have been more than eighteen years old.

I told Karen that I felt sorry for the boy's mother.

"His mother? What kind of mother do you think he had?" Karen scoffed. "He probably did it to spite her."

The town of Catskill announced its arrival with a succession of hand-painted welcome signs. It wasn't long before we were in farmland, with cows and barns and bales of hay scattered around the cropped fields, wrapped in white plastic, which made them look like gigantic marshmallows. Karen opened the windows and the sweet grassy smell of the sun in springtime filled the car.

I sensed a tiny glimmer of the kind of peace and comfort the country used to give me when I was still capable of experiencing the full range of human emotions. Jake was always telling me to stop blaming everything on the autism. He said that no one our age reacts to the glories of the world with the same kind of intensity they experienced when they were young.

My usual response to the first sight of a cow or a barn or a grain silo was to make sure that Danny saw it. I tapped on the glass to try to get his attention, but his eyes stayed glued to the television screen. Jonathan acknowledged my tap with an eager grin and an even more eager wave. I waved back.

I felt the same about Jonathan as I had during those play-dates eight and a half years ago: I felt sorry for him but his insatiable hunger for affection repelled me. Beholding it made me feel grateful for Danny's total lack of interest in anyone who wasn't his mother or his father; yet if Danny had waved at Karen as Jonathan had waved at me just now, I would have called Jake right away to rejoice with him about it.

For years we had been wishing that Danny would show some interest in humanoids for reasons other than how tall they were, how much they weighed, the color and texture of their skin and the year and date of their birth. Nevertheless, we couldn't help feeling that maybe Danny was lucky to be so emotionally self-sufficient, to be so irrevocably himself. We liked to believe that this was because somewhere in that peculiar brain of his he knew he was loved.

Danny's complete lack of self-consciousness, vanity, shame, jealousy and pride; his utter disregard for what other people thought about him; and his freedom from the emotional burdens that plague most humans created the illusion of strength. I wanted to believe it was strength. But I knew it wasn't. I knew it was a terrible weakness.

Sometimes, when Jake and I thought about what would really happen if our happy son ever made that big breakthrough we had been working so hard for him to achieve, we would wonder if we were doing the right thing with Danny. What would happen if he ever woke up completely? If one day he discovered a need that he had never known existed. Jake and I wouldn't be enough for him anymore and his next discovery would be that he was lonely.

We were waiting at a stop sign at the end of a country cemetery now. Off in the distance I saw a woman in a blue dress banging her head against one of the tombstones.

At last Karen turned into a long circular driveway at the end of which was an old farmhouse and a red barn and a vast stretch of lawn.

"We wanted to find a place away from everything. When Harold is ready to retire—sometime in the next five years— we're going to move here and say good-bye to the city and all its bullshit forever."

She had told me there was a forest on one side of the house, and there it was. On the other side were some twisted old apple trees, and on the front lawn, slung between the trunks of two colossal maples, was a purple, red and orange polka dot hammock.

As I stepped out of the van, I felt enveloped by the sudden silence. Then I felt a thread of something very delicate touch my forehead and mouth, and as I waved my hands in front of my face to wipe it away, a slender strand of a silk-like substance became visible in a stray shaft of light, and I looked up and saw an inchworm dangling from the droopy leaves of the big weeping willow.

"We're here, Danny," I called out, knocking on his window. "We're in the country. Look, an inchworm," I said. Danny loved bugs, especially if they had interesting names: stick insects, pill bugs, dung beetles, inchworms. I opened the door to his side of the van. He sat there, bleary-eyed from three straight hours of *Pokémon*. Then, without warning, he jumped out the door and started crawling in the grass. Soon, he was standing up with a four-leaf clover in his hand. It was the fourteenth he had found in the past three years.

At the entrance to the house was a hand-painted wooden sign that said, WELCOME TO OUR HAPPY, HAPPY HOME. Karen had once mentioned that arts and crafts were a hobby of hers. Everything she had told me about her childhood infused the block of wood with yearning and heartbreak.

I had mentioned to Karen that Danny liked swimming, and hiking in the woods and eating out at restaurants, and before taking the boys upstairs to set them up in front of the television, she assured me that she had a bunch of fun activities planned. "But we'll also need to spend time recuperating from our little outings, because, let's face it, it's hard work being with these kids."

Karen left me in her elaborately decorated living room while she took the boys upstairs to Jonathan's room. There were champagne satin drapes slung over tasseled braided ropes and crystal chandeliers and gold satin sofas and Oriental rugs and vases, and original Victorian-looking oil paintings hanging on the walls. Still, ornate as the decorations were, the room didn't have that patina of invulnerability that the rooms of the wealthy usually have. For one thing, it was very messy. A flannel shirt hung over the back of one brocade armchair, and there was what appeared to be an oil stain on one of the satin sofas. Newspapers and pieces of unopened mail lay scattered on the floor, and the toe of a worn-out pair of running shoes was stuck beneath the foot of a china cabinet.

The Persian rug was scattered with sooty footprints made from the ashes that had spilled out of the fireplace. A collection of framed pictures sat on the mantelpiece and I went to look at them. There was a photograph of baby Jonathan sitting on the shoulders of an older man, whom I assumed was Harold. I had already formed a picture of Harold in my mind—he would be stocky and jovial, with a balding head, and the face that looked back at me from the picture frame bore a remarkable resemblance to the face I had imagined. Next to it was a picture of Harold with his arm draped around a beautiful young woman who was dressed provocatively in high-top boots and a tight-fitting, low-cut red dress.

"Is this Harold's daughter?" I asked Karen when she came downstairs. "She's gorgeous. I didn't know he was married before."

Karen laughed. "That's a picture of us on our honeymoon."

"That's *you?*" I asked, not bothering to try to hide my astonishment.

"That *was* me," she said.

"Wow. You're quite the trophy wife."

"Harold's not the one who got the trophy. I'm the one who got the trophy. I really don't deserve him. But he's mine."

"What a lovely thing to say, Karen."

"It's a pretty funny story. Can you keep a secret?"

And then, not bothering to wait for me to respond, she went on to tell me how she and Harold met. She was living as a high-priced call girl in Los Angeles at the time, and Harold was one of her clients, she informed me in the same offhand way she said everything.

"I was his favorite hooker. And soon I was his only hooker." On their tenth assignation, Harold showed up with a nine-carat emerald-cut diamond ring. He decided they would move to New York City, to get a fresh start.

"He said we would just put it all behind us. He concocted

a story about how we met. That I had come to him with a broken leg after a water-skiing accident. He's been the only man in my life ever since. Not that anyone would want me like this," she said, pulling up her sweatshirt and grabbing hold of a big hunk of belly fat.

"I have Jonathan to thank for this. Harold put me on a diet of three-thousand-calorie protein shakes when I was pregnant. He wanted to make sure we had a healthy baby. What a joke that turned out to be. I suppose I could lose the weight easily enough. Bulimia used to be a specialty of mine. But to tell you the truth, it's a relief being able to walk down the street without men hitting on me all the time. Except I have to say people are not very nice to us fatties."

"What about Harold?" I asked.

"Harold?" She laughed. "Harold just says there's more of me to love. Even if it was my body that got me to him to begin with, he says it's my soul he loves. To tell you the truth, I think he might prefer me this way. The guy's a gem. But like I told you, he's a lot older than I am, and who knows how much more time we have left to be together. That's another reason I came up with my plan."

It was then that Karen told me that she had decided to send Jonathan away to a residential school.

She said that it took her a while to get Harold on board with it. He was so madly in love with the kid. But she had finally managed to convince him that living away from home would be the best thing for Jonathan. How else would he ever learn how to be independent?

"This is the hope all of us fools cling to, isn't it? It's so pathetic," Karen said. "I don't buy it. I never did. Not for most of the kids I know, and certainly not for Jonathan. But Harold's head is so stuck in the clouds when it comes to Jonathan, that's what changed his mind about sending him away. The idea that Jonathan could learn how to be independent.

"I had to look at seven schools until I found one that would be acceptable to Harold—and acceptable to me, too—because I really do love the little fucker," she said.

When Karen called to make arrangements for this trip, she told me she had lost all faith in the willingness or the ability of any educational institution to do what it took to help a child like her son. She said that Jonathan's speech therapist used to have him play video games during what were supposed to be his speech therapy sessions. And the job development counselor stuck the kids in the dark basement of some department store stamping shoeboxes all day. Yet now here she was telling me that she had decided to institutionalize her son.

I had little hope of influencing her decision. Nevertheless, that was my intention when I told her about a trip Jake and I once made to Boston with Danny to see a residential school that The District wanted us to visit. We had no intention of ever sending Danny away, but we knew that it would work against us if we didn't take him to see the school.

The city paid for a limousine to drive us there. The principal seemed to be very proud of how neatly the children—all of whom were dressed in uniforms, the boys with crew cuts, the girls with the same short haircuts—marched in single file to class ("like little soldiers"). In order to maintain discipline and keep them in "tip-top shape," the students were required to jog around the campus for an hour every morning before breakfast and for an hour every evening before dinner.

On the way out of the school, I saw a mother in the parking lot bent over the hood of her car. I went over to her and asked if there was anything I could do to help. I put my arms around her and she told me that last week the police had carted her eight-year-old son away in handcuffs. When I asked her why, she told me that he had talked back to the principal.

"Maybe he yelled at him," she said, explaining that he did that sometimes when he couldn't find the words to express what he wanted to say.

"So I guess you're going to take him out of here," I said.

"No. I can't," she responded. And looking at me with eyes that were too bereft for anger, she told me that all the other residential schools were even worse than this one.

I asked Karen where the school they had in mind for Jonathan was located and she told me it was in a beautiful rural area in Phoenix, Arizona. Right near the Phoenix Mountains. They took the kids hiking every weekend. It was called The Miracle School.

"Harold fell in love with the place," she told me. "Jonathan seemed to like it, too. He was ecstatic about the TV, which has a screen the size of a movie theater screen. And the indoor swimming pool. And the petting farm. It's part of the 'therapy,' they say.

"Of course, he has no idea he's going there. Anyway, when we got back, I set everything in motion. We should be getting the acceptance letter in a couple of weeks. I figure the kid should be settled there by the time the spring semester rolls around."

I was shocked to hear that the school she had in mind for Jonathan was over two thousand miles away. How could she think of doing this to a child who was so desperately in need of her love that he was afraid a glass wall would make her disappear?

"We're taking him to Disneyland during the break. As a kind of bon voyage present. I've never been to Disneyland. For me, Disneyland has always been the supreme symbol of childhood. Going there would be a way for me to reclaim my childhood that never was. That's what my therapist says.

"I know you probably hate that shit," said Karen, who apparently had more insight into me than I thought. "But I love it. And I won't have to worry about the lines. They have these disability passes. Ours came in the mail today."

I could think of a number of reasons why Karen would want to send Jonathan away. Her childhood had been a nightmare. Harold was the closest thing to a mother or a father she had ever had. She had never wanted to be a mother in the first place. The idea of being a mother to a child who would need a mother for the rest of his life frightened her. I came up with half a dozen other justifications for her decision. I didn't want to judge her. Nevertheless I couldn't stop myself from judging her.

It wasn't vacation season yet and all the lakes were closed for swimming, the lifeguard chairs were empty and the snack bars were shuttered. This was a tremendous disappointment for Danny. But he was happy when we found a place that rented bicycles, even though we were confined to riding in an area that was under construction and cordoned off with orange plastic fencing.

We also went hiking. The hikes had to be easy for Jonathan's sake.

After the trail passed through a meadow and we entered the woods again, Danny found a millipede (so he informed me after I asked him three times in a row what he was holding in his hand). The millipede was occupying all his attention, and after ten or fifteen minutes, I convinced him to set it free to spend the rest of its short life wandering the woods on its thousand legs.

"Millipedes don't have a thousand legs," he informed me. "The most they have is seven hundred fifty legs. That's the species called *Illacme plenipes.*"

"Isn't Danny smart?" Karen asked Jonathan. "Yes, Mommy," he answered.

It made me feel ashamed to be proud that my son was smarter than another handicapped child.

We ate all our meals out, and always went out for ice cream afterward. Karen insisted on paying for everything. After each outing, Karen would send the boys upstairs to watch *Pokémon* and she and I would spend a couple of hours lying side by side on chaise lounges, relaxing on her deck. Karen, who was a recovered alcholic, told me that it wouldn't bother her at all if I drank. Harold drank in front of her all the time.

I had brought along a manuscript to copyedit. Karen lay beside me, reading a paperback edition of *Nicholas Nickleby*, which she held in one hand, bent at the spine. She loved reading and told me she was working her way through Dickens for the second time. I had never read *Nicholas Nickleby*, but I remembered from the PBS miniseries that Nicholas gets a job in a horrible boarding school for children whose parents just want to get rid of them. I wondered what in the world Karen could be thinking about, reading that book.

After my third beer I couldn't focus on my copyediting so I put the manuscript back in its envelope. The view from the deck was magnificent, and it was entertainment enough for me to watch the dark blobs of cloud shadows migrating ponderously across the green mountains like the bubbles in a lava lamp.

Once, I heard Karen mutter to herself, "It will be good for him."

On Sunday, when Karen dropped Danny and me off in Washington Heights, she and I told each other that we would meet for lunch sometime soon, but we never did.

Seven months after that weekend in the Catskills, I was waiting for the legendary M4 bus on 116th Street and Broadway. A couple of girls were sitting in two of the bus shelter's metal seats; the third seat was taken up by their Trader Joe's shopping bags. I wanted to sit down, but asking them to move their bags required more social interaction than I had the energy for at the moment.

I had spent the last twenty-five minutes peering down Broadway looking for signs of the phantom Number 4, trying to summon it with the power of my impatience. Two had already come and gone, each one sadistically flashing its NOT IN SERVICE sign just as it approached where I was standing. I thought I saw one stopped at a red light three blocks away. But I wouldn't be certain for another block, whether it was the Number 4, or a Number 104, three of which had stopped and dutifully picked up passengers since I had been standing here.

Right after I determined that yes, indeed, there was only one digit on the bus's digital display, and not three, I noticed a woman staring at me.

It was Aviva Brodner. Her hair was cut short, and she was dressed in jeans and a white tailored shirt. Her jeans were pressed, and she was wearing pearls. She was in the process of unbuttoning her cashmere coat, because the weather was unseasonably warm for late November. It was a Monday, and as I recalled, Aviva was an executive at L'Oréal. I had seen her only twice before—that first time in front of the subway station on 181st Street when Danny was sitting on the sidewalk reading his field manual, ignoring Howard's thrilling account of the suit and the real man's tie his mother had just bought him, and the second, when Aviva had ordered her husband to kick Danny out of Howard's bar mitzvah.

"Mimi Slavitt?" she said. I was surprised that she seemed happy to see me. "I've wanted to apologize to you for a year."

Was it possible that only a year had passed since Howard's disastrous bar mitzvah? Was Danny really thirteen now? According to the Talmud, he was already a man.

"There's nothing to apologize for," I said.

"Well, I wanted to apologize."

"It's hard," I said, without thinking.

"Yes. It's hard," she responded. And after a long pause, she continued.

"You know, we have a friend in common. Karen Renburg. Johnny and Howard are in the same class at The Learning Foundation. It's a small world, isn't it?"

"Yes it is. I haven't heard from Karen in a long time. How is she?"

"Well, that's quite a story," she said. "Last time I spoke to her, she sounded like she was on the verge of a nervous breakdown."

Just then the Number 4 bus rolled up to the curb.

"I better get that," I told Aviva. She hugged me good-bye, and I hugged her back. We hugged each other with sincerity and compassion, even though it was clear to both of us that we could never be friends.

\* \* \*

The first thing I did when I got home was call Karen. I left a message on her voice mail, telling her about my brief encounter with Aviva Brodner.

She called me back a couple of hours later, and after a few preliminaries she said that before Jonathan went away to the school in Arizona, she'd arranged a trip with him and Harold to Disneyland. "Did Aviva tell you that Harold couldn't go with us? The day we were supposed to leave, he got a phone call from one of his most famous patients—a halfback for the Dallas Cowboys. A real pain in the ass. He always gives Harold season tickets and club seats.

"Usually it's the guy's knees. He'll end up in a wheelchair before he hits fifty. This time it was his arm. He's a big baby. Always insists that Harold be on call for him. No other doctor will do. And then Harold always has to hang around for the post-op."

"God," I said, "that must have been tough."

"To put it mildly. Jonathan freaked out as soon as we got there. The sight of Mickey Mouse walking around in the flesh, so to speak, scared the hell out of him."

Karen told me that she had decided on their second day in Disneyland that the only way she would ever be able to make it through the week would be to get herself a bottle of scotch, and after the week was up, she had polished off four bottles. She told herself that when she got home, she would go back to AA and get sober again. With Jonathan away at school, she would have so much less stress. That was what kept her going that whole week—the thought that soon Jonathan would be gone—that and the scotch. Whenever things got so bad that she felt on the brink of killing herself and/or her son, she would say to herself, "This time next year."

Every night, when Harold called, at nine on the dot, in time to tuck Jonathan into bed from afar, Karen would tell him in a perfectly sober-sounding voice that everything was great, that they were having a wonderful time.

"We old drunks are very good at covering up for ourselves," she told me.

The only thing that interested Jonathan was the food and the gift shop, and that's where they spent a lot of their time, when they weren't hanging around their hotel room eating junk food and watching videos—Disney videos, of course.

"So much for reclaiming my lost childhood," Karen said, clicking her tongue. "That was tough on me. I really go in for all the razzle-dazzle, you know. One day I hired a babysitter and I spent the entire day going on all the rides and stuff and seeing a couple of the shows. I had a blast. I was tempted to spend the rest of the time like that, but I couldn't do that to Jonathan. This was, after all, supposed to be his bon voyage present."

Karen said that she ended up getting so many things for Jonathan at the gift shop—mostly stuffed animals, of course—that she had to buy a separate suitcase to bring all the presents back to New York.

As soon as they got home, Karen sent Jonathan to his room with the suitcase filled with the stuffed animals. Harold wasn't due back from the conference until later that evening—and she sat at the dining room table, searching through the pile of mail the concierge had given her, and set herself up with a big glass of scotch on the rocks—to celebrate—it would be her last, she promised herself—she had even dumped the bottle down the garbage chute before she started looking through the mail.

She felt so happy when she saw the return address from the school in Arizona with Jonathan's name hand-printed on the letter that in her excitement to open up the envelope, she ended up tearing the letter in half. Piecing it together, she read: *We are sorry to inform you that we don't have an appropriate spot for your child, but we know that you will find the perfect placement for him.*

It took a few moments for the whole thing to sink in, but when it did, she let out a howl so loud it sent Jonathan running from his stuffed animals to see what was wrong. He went over to Karen and started stroking her arm. She was sitting there, banging her head on her huge mahogany table, screaming, "NO, NO, NO," the tears running down her cheeks. Then she started hitting herself in the face and scratching her arms so hard that she drew blood.

Jonathan stood there, trying to calm his mother down, taking her hands in his, kissing her on both cheeks, telling her how much he loved her. Karen just sat there, with her head on the table again, not banging it anymore, just laying it there, wondering how she could go on. And hating the kid and loving him at the same time.

"Because you know I really do love the little fucker," she told me.

Then Jonathan went back to his room and brought her his twenty-four-inch Dumbo, who Karen said happened to be her favorite Disney character, even though she couldn't help being jealous of him for having had such a wonderful mother.

"Oh, Karen," I said.

"Don't worry. I worked everything out weeks ago. Jonathan will be going there in a month. Right after spring break is over," she told me. "It's like I always say. Everyone has a price."

After I got off the phone, I went down to the lobby to see if the thief who had been stealing packages left there had stolen my shipment of vitamins yet. My neighbors had been taping notes to the elevator door pleading with whoever took their package ("by mistake") to please return it. Lately, the notes had become more dramatic. There's a thief in our midst! Who could stoop so low to steal from their neighbors? Some of the notes were translated into Google Translate Spanish. The elevator was broken, and as I was climbing back up the stairs to my apartment, my box of vitamins cradled in my arms, it occurred to me that before Karen told me that she had worked everything out, I might have said something like, "Well, maybe it's just as well. Now maybe you'll be able to find a place closer to home."

But I knew I wouldn't have said anything to her, even if it had occurred to me at the time. Her mind was made up. And if she ever had any doubts about what she was doing, she would have talked herself out of them long ago. Besides, I have always hated people who impose their moral judgments on others. I never feel I have the right to presume to tell anyone (except Jake) that I think what they're doing or what they're thinking of doing or what they have done is wrong.

The image of Jonathan bringing Karen his precious stuffed Dumbo was as clear to me as though I had actually witnessed the scene of poor, lonely Jonathan trying so hard to comfort his poor, orphaned mother. I thought about Dumbo and his mother, and how she was put in prison just for trying to defend her funny-looking child. I knew the movie by heart. When Danny was five years old, he had watched it so many times, the tape snapped. I thought about the scene where Dumbo had been teased and poked by kids in the circus audience, and the way his mother had stood up on her hind legs, trumpeting and bellowing, and that she had been put in a cage with a sign that said, MAD ELEPHANT. She suffered because her child suffered, and then all her unhappiness disappeared when the nice little mouse brought Dumbo to visit her. It makes me happy to remember the delirious smile on Dumbo's face when his mother reached out from between the bars of her prison and swung her funny-looking child back and forth on her trunk, all his unhappiness wiped away in an instant, and his mother's unhappiness wiped away, too, because her child was happy now, and they were together again, and I thought about how their love was all they needed to sustain themselves in the cruel world, from which they emerged triumphant, in the end, when Dumbo learned how to fly.

# Route 94

When Danny came into her room that morning, Mimi ignored him at first, roaming the bordertowns of sleep, where dream and reality lie down together, mysteriously intertwined.

"Wake up, wake up," he was saying.

Then she remembered. Today they were going apple picking. Mimi had been dreading this day almost as much as Danny had been looking forward to it: there would be the hayride with children less than half his age, the mothers of those children, the apples and pumpkins that cost twice as much as those sold at the bodega up the street, the animals Danny would want to pet, the tractors he would want to drive, the haystacks he would want to pull apart, the trees he would want to climb. And to top it all off, this year, Bernice Weinstock.

Mimi had hoped that, by thirteen, Danny would have

outgrown the annual apple-picking excursion, but Danny never outgrew anything, so when Bernice offered to take her and Danny apple picking in the North Fork of Long Island, Mimi had accepted. Putting up with Bernice just seemed easier than renting a car.

"Wake up, wake up," her son kept on saying as he tugged at her sheet.

"We don't have to leave for another two hours," Mimi said. "Bernice won't be there to pick us up if we leave now."

"*Ri-ise and shi-ine and give God your glory glory*," Danny started to sing, tugging at her quilt. Through half-open eyes, Mimi saw that he had dressed himself. His shirt was buttoned crookedly and his fly was unzipped. But he was dressed.

"It's six in the morning." Mimi was wide awake now. "Let me sleep."

"I can't wait. I hate to wait. I can't bear to wait. I refuse to wait."

"I told you, Bernice won't be there to pick us up if we leave now. You don't want to take the train to the station and have no one there to pick us up, do you? Now go back to your room and let me sleep. Please, just let me sleep."

Mimi sidled up to Jake. Resting her head on his chest, she wrapped herself around him, savoring his skunk-like scent; his inexplicable tranquility. How could he be in love with the same bewildering child and not let his life turn into one gigantic tragedy, too?

Bernice lived on Long Island, forty miles away from the city. Mimi had met her at an autism conference five years before. She hadn't seen her since then, but she would hear from her constantly, sometimes as often as five times a day. Bernice, whose life consisted of one crisis after another, had appointed Mimi her personal advisor. It was something she tried out on everyone, but Mimi was the only one who was enough of a sucker to respond to her incessant cries for help.

"It's Ber—niiiice," she would say whenever she called, turning the syllables of her name into half apology, half lament: she had bad news to report, some crisis that required Mimi's immediate attention. "I have to run something by you. It will just take a minute. I promise."

Bernice's astonishing self-involvement had become a running joke with her and Jake. He would stand with the phone pressed against his chest and tell Mimi, "It's Ber—niiiice." Once, Bernice reported with bitter incomprehension that her best friend had cut her off without a word of explanation. "I don't understand how she could do that to me," she said, going on at some length about how much she had enriched her friend's life by sharing her "complex, multidimensional perspective."

A few years earlier, Mimi would never have put up with anyone like Bernice; back then there had been no time for anything except Danny. But when Bernice arrived on the scene, except for Mimi's endless fight to get The District to pay back the money they owed her, the major battles were all pretty much over. The war to save Danny had been fought and lost.

Bernice had been working on a PhD in psychology for five years, and her unfinished thesis was her major topic of conversation. She was a single mother; her house was a mess; her son was driving her crazy; her deadbeat ex-husband had stopped paying child support; her professor was refusing to grant her another extension. How would she ever be able to find the time to get her dissertation finished? Was she such an awful person that people should treat her this way?

After Bernice finally finished her thesis and got her PhD (she had written about women and narcissism, a subject on which she had un-ironically told Mimi she was an expert), she complained that she would never be able to find a job; she was too old. Mimi told her to have faith in herself. Bernice, whose thesis had been published by a major academic press, was incapable of writing a coherent sentence, and she would call for help with her letters of application. Mimi would dictate paragraphs over the phone, and when Bernice found a job at a small college in Queens, Mimi helped write her lesson plans and her course synopses.

Sometimes Mimi wondered why she bothered having anything to do with this woman for whom she had no real affection or sympathy. Maybe advising her was just an easy way to pass the time as she went about her household chores or while she lay in bed, exhausted from the day's travails. Also, with Bernice, she had found herself falling into a familiar role. It was comforting to be doing something she had always done, something she was good at; perhaps accepting the role of Bernice's advisor was her way of trying to reclaim part of herself.

On the A train to Penn Station, Danny squeezed himself into the seat between two women who were blocking his view of the subway map. He could draw the New York City Subway map by heart, along with all the street grids of Manhattan, Brooklyn, the Bronx and Queens. It was the first thing he did when he came home from school. He would head straight for the office, take paper out of the printer and go to his room, where he would lie down on the floor and draw maps. Every now and then Mimi would collect the looseleaf pages of the maps Danny was always leaving scattered around the apartment and put them in a folder. He could tell you how to get anywhere in the five boroughs by public transportation—still, whenever he was in the subway he always had to look at the maps displayed under glass on the walls of the subway cars.

The women glowered at him at first, but after doing a double take, they whispered to each other and smiled at Mimi sympathetically. It was only when they were out in public that Mimi realized how obvious it was to everyone that Danny was a child with a serious handicap. Mimi hated the pity more than she hated the intolerance.

She told Danny to apologize to the women. Apologizing to people was something that Danny had picked up very quickly. Probably because she was always yelling at him. Embracing her son, she kissed him on the top of his head and said in a quiet voice that he could look at his subway map at home, or they could pick one up at the station in Mineola. At the next stop, a giantess who had been occupying two seats got up to leave, and Mimi, noticing that the woman had been sitting in front of another subway map, took Danny's hand and she told him he could go look at that one instead.

The plan was for Bernice to pick Danny and Mimi up at the train station in Mineola, and from there drive two hours to a farm where Bernice's food coop was holding its annual potluck picnic; after that, they would go apple picking. When they got off the train, Bernice was there waiting for them in her SUV. She had lost thirty pounds since Mimi had seen her and she looked terrific. Bernice was always bragging about what a knockout she used to be, but Mimi had never believed her. Beholding her transformation into a beauty had the effect of making Mimi actually happy to see her. However, when she went over to kiss her hello, Bernice stiffened.

The other day, when they were talking on the phone, she had sensed a negative turn in Bernice's attitude toward her. In a display of the excessive gratitude that Mimi could never manage to restrain herself from expressing, she had been saying for the tenth time how much she and Danny were looking forward to the trip and Bernice had interrupted her to point out that she sounded obsequious. She went on for quite some time lecturing her about the deleterious effects of projecting a negative self-image. When Mimi told her she didn't have a negative self-image and that she didn't like being told that she did, nor did she need anyone to tell her how to behave, Bernice said she was only trying to help. She told Mimi she understood, because she, too, suffered from low self-esteem.

There had been a brief period of time right after Bernice got her teaching job when Mimi thought Bernice might actually turn out to be a friend. One night when they were on the phone, Bernice stopped what she was saying and asked, "So, how are you?" She had never before asked Mimi anything about herself, and at first, Mimi thought it was a mistake, the result, perhaps, of a misfiring of some cortical neurons. But over the course of the next several conversations, Bernice continued to ask her about herself, and after a while, Mimi started talking to her about Danny. Bernice always had something useful to say. A couple of times they had even had conversations about something other than their children (and other than Bernice). Once they talked about politics. Recently they had talked about Virginia Woolf, who was one of Bernice's favorite writers.

Now, at the Mineola train station, Bernice was saying, "Andy has a cold. I don't know if you want to expose Danny to him. Maybe you shouldn't come."

Astounded that Bernice could suggest this after she and Danny had made the two-hour-long trip from the city to meet her, Mimi assumed a casual tone and responded, "Oh, don't worry about that. Danny never gets sick." She wished she could tell Bernice to go fuck herself and take the next train back to Penn Station, but Danny had to go apple picking today. It was the end of October and next weekend all the apple orchards would be closed.

"So how is your trigeminal neuropathy?" Mimi asked, steering Bernice onto one of her favorite subjects. She would spend the entire trip listening to Bernice's problems, Danny would go apple picking, and then after Bernice dropped them off at the Mineola train station, Mimi would be done with her once and for all.

When Bernice had exhausted the subject of how she spent every day in unbearable pain, Mimi asked her about her job. Bernice complained about the heavy course load. She didn't know how she was going to do it. She was so disorganized. She hadn't taught in five years and was afraid she had forgotten how.

"Of course you can do it," Mimi told her. "How many single mothers in their late forties can get a PhD? With honors, no less."

"That's only because I'm so gifted," Bernice said. "You don't know what I've had to overcome to get this far. I have serious ADHD. It takes me forever to focus. You can't imagine how much I suffer."

Mimi was trying to think of a suitable response when Danny, who had been looking out the window in silence until now, started talking to Andy about *Pokémon*.

"Your son talks very loud," Bernice said to Mimi.

"We're working on it," Mimi said.

"He should have been trained out of it by now," Bernice said.

"We're working on it," Mimi repeated, biting the inside of her lip so hard she could taste blood.

"Please tell him to lower his voice. He's giving me a headache."

Mimi turned around, and placing her hand on Danny's chest, she told him to speak with his "inside voice."

Addressing herself to Bernice's son, she said that she hoped Danny wasn't bothering him, to which Andy, a sweet boy, responded that he wasn't; he was interested in *Pokémon*, too.

She had noticed it right away, as soon as they got off the train, how good Andy looked, how normal. There didn't seem to be anything wrong with him.

"It's all Danny talks about these days," Mimi told Bernice. "It's so nice of Andy to listen."

"Andy is very good with special needs kids," Bernice responded.

"What?" Mimi said, at a complete loss for words.

"All his teachers say he's very gifted."

"He looks great," said Mimi, regaining her composure.

"Thank God he takes after my side of the family and not his father's."

"So it looks like you don't have anything to worry about

in the height department either," Mimi said. Her son's height had been another source of worry for Bernice, and Mimi was surprised to see how tall Andy was.

"They say he's going to be five foot nine. He lost a couple of inches because of the Ritalin," Bernice told her.

"Five nine is a good height for a man," Mimi said.

"Everyone in Marco's family is tall," Bernice said. "Luckily that's the only thing Andy inherited from his idiot father."

"And the Tourette's?"

"That's been gone for a while. It often clears up with adolescence."

"Looks like you got lucky," Mimi said.

"It wasn't luck," Bernice said. "I've put a lot of work into him, you know."

"So I suppose the autism went away, too," Mimi said.

"There's a lot of misdiagnosis going around," Bernice said. "Apparently he never had it."

"So he's fine," Mimi said. So many of the other children had gotten better.

"Yeah, he's a good kid. Like I told you. His teachers all say he's very gifted."

Mimi looked out the window.

They had left the highway and were in Suffolk County now. A used car lot gave way to half a mile of pine forest. They passed a broad stretch of recently cleared land, where yellow bulldozers and backhoes were scattered haphazardly among heaps of brown earth.

Eventually they were in farmland, where all there was to see on either side of the road were trees bursting with flame-tinted leaves and houses with front porches and wreaths made of twigs hanging on doors. Mimi had grown up on Long Island, and she had never associated it with anything but shopping malls and housing developments and other forms of nothingness, and she was surprised to find herself in such a lovely setting. She had been so preoccupied with the apple picking that she had forgotten about the leaves and she sought refuge in them now.

For years, all the seasons had been the same to her. All that existed were the letters she had to write and the phone calls she had to make and the struggles with The District and looking for schools for Danny and, once she had found one, trying to get them to do what they were supposed to do; the meetings with all the various doctors and therapists and lawyers and the politicians she would beg for help, and the conferences and workshops and the endless succession of tutors she hired to teach Danny the sorts of things that other children learn on their own. Worst of all was the appalling treachery of Teresa Thompson. The rampant anxiety ate away at Mimi like leprosy. Added to that was all the time and energy she spent trying to get the advocate to do her job and then trying to do the advocate's job by herself, which, hard as she tried, was impossible. On visits to The District's main office, a security guard would accompany Mimi to meetings with officials.

There were, however, those occasional moments of relief. The time the lilac bush on 181st Street was in full bloom and Mimi stopped to breathe in its sweet scent. Or she would be walking down a street and an old man dressed in ragged clothes and sitting on a stool held together by duct tape would be playing an old jazz tune she loved on a saxophone; or waiting on the subway platform there would be a young soprano, dressed in a lilac tutu with fairy wings attached to her back, singing an aria a cappella in the most beautiful voice Mimi had ever heard. Mimi would stop and listen, and for those few moments, everything else in the battlefield of her existence would disappear and the only thing that would exist for her was all this beauty.

Bernice's abrasive voice broke through Mimi's thoughts. "We're at the potluck," she said as she pulled into a parking lot full of cars. "We can't stay too long. It's freezing out and all I have is this sweatshirt."

"I brought an extra sweater, just in case. Here," Mimi said, and taking it out of her backpack, she offered it to Bernice.

"I don't want it," Bernice said. "We have to make this brief! I'm telling you, I can't stand the cold."

"So take the sweater," Mimi said.

"I told you, I don't want it. We'll have to be out of here in ten minutes."

"Okay," Mimi said. On the train, she had told Danny that they were going to a real farm with real cows and chickens and turkeys and she was sorry they would have to leave before he had the opportunity to see them, but he was so intent on the apple picking, she didn't think he would mind.

There was a line of people waiting at a long table laden with food. Everyone had been very generous with their contributions. Mimi let go of Danny's hand and told him to wait in the line while she went to place the bread she had baked for the occasion on one of the tables, but when she got back, he had disappeared. She found him scraping the icing off a masterfully crafted carrot cake with his fingers.

"You must behave. You must behave," Mimi said, pulling him angrily by the arm. "How can I take you anywhere if you don't behave?" Everyone was looking at them now.

"I'm sorry," Danny said.

"That's what you always say," Mimi said. "I don't believe you."

"Believe me. Believe me. Believe me. With a cherry on top."

"Go sit on that bench over there," Mimi said. "I don't want you to move an inch. Promise?"

"I promise."

"I'll get you some soup and some cake and cookies, okay? But I don't want you to move an inch. Promise me you won't move."

"I promise."

"Tell me I can trust you not to move from this spot," Mimi said.

Danny stared back at her blankly.

"Say, 'You can trust me, Mommy.'"

"You can trust me, Mommy," he said after a delay of four seconds.

"Good. That's good. That's a good boy."

Just when Mimi was about to ladle some chicken soup into a paper cup, she saw Bernice running toward her. There was a desperate, angry look on her face.

"We've got to leave!" she exclaimed. Her arms were wrapped around her shoulders and she was shivering dramatically. "I'm going back to the car. Meet me there right away."

"I'll go get Danny," Mimi said.

He wasn't on the bench where she had left him. It had been so long since she had been out with her son that she had gotten out of the habit of holding his hand every minute. Mimi ran around the grounds frantically calling his name. Finally she found him sitting on the ground near the barn pulling a haystack apart.

"I'm looking for a needle in a haystack," he exclaimed with his wonderful smile. His hair and everything he was wearing was covered with hay. Mimi looked at her son look-

ing up at her and she was reminded of what a happy child he
was. She and Jake were always telling each other what a good
thing it was that Danny was happy; their job was to see to it
that he would always be happy.

Instead of scolding him, Mimi took hold of her son's hand
and said, "Let's go. Apple picking here we come!"

"You're late," Bernice said when they got back to the car.
"I have to make a stop at the organic egg farm."

When they arrived at the egg farm, Bernice told Mimi
to stay in the car, but Mimi said she wanted to come along.
Last week on the phone, she had offered to research what
apple orchards would still be open for picking, it being late
in the season, but Bernice had told her not to bother. There
would be signs posted everywhere. There always were. But
all the signs they had passed so far had said the orchards
were closed for picking and Mimi was getting worried. She
hoped that one of the locals would know of a place that was
still open.

"Andy, would you watch Danny while I go out?" she
asked. "Make sure he doesn't leave the car, okay?"

Then turning to Danny, she put her hands on his shoulders, sought out his eyes, and told him, "I'll be back in a minute. I want to find out where we can go apple picking. I don't
want you to leave this car. Do you hear me?"

"Yes."

"Tell me you won't leave the car."

Danny was looking out the window. He didn't respond.

"Tell me you won't leave the car," Mimi repeated.

After several seconds of silence he said, "I won't leave the
car."

"Good boy," she said, noting with satisfaction that Danny

had reversed his pronouns correctly; this had been something she and Jake had been working on for ages.

"I can lock the doors," offered Andy, who was two years younger than Danny.

"Good idea. Please do that," Mimi said, and she was off.

When Bernice went to the back room where the eggs were kept, Mimi asked the woman behind the cash register about the apple orchards. She told her that Carter's Farm on Cherry Blossom Lane was the only orchard in the area still open for picking. It was about a quarter mile up Route 94.

"But all they have left are Macouns and Empires," she said.

"That's okay," Mimi told her. "As long as there are trees for picking. That's all my son cares about. He has his heart set on apple picking, and once he has his heart set on something, there are no ifs, ands or buts about it."

"Yes, the young kids love it."

"I guess so."

"How old is he?"

"Six," Mimi said, wishing it were true.

"I have a six-year-old, too, so I know what you're talking about. They can be very stubborn at that age. Wait until you see what's coming," she said with a knowing look. "But they grow out of it. My fourteen-year-old is a perfect little gentleman now, but you should have seen him at six."

"That's good to know," Mimi said, and after thanking the woman, she went back to the car. Danny was talking to Andy about *Pokémon*.

"I hope you don't mind, Andy," she said. And again the perfect specimen of a child told her that it was fine, he was interested in *Pokémon*, too.

When Bernice returned to the car, Mimi told her that the woman in the egg store had said an apple orchard off Route 94, on Cherry Blossom Lane, was the only one in the area that was still open for picking. "I was getting worried," Mimi said. "Did you notice all the signs that said CLOSED FOR PICKING?"

"I'm warning you," Bernice said with a frown. "We can't spend too much time there. I have a ton of work to do. I should never have gone on this trip in the first place."

Mimi looked out the window, searching for Cherry Blossom Lane and Carter's Farm. They had traveled a lot farther than the quarter mile the woman at the farm stand had said they would have to go, and Mimi still hadn't seen any signs for the orchard or the road.

"Apparently we missed it," Mimi told Bernice. "I guess we'll have to turn back. The woman at the egg store said that it's the only apple orchard still open for picking. She said Cherry Blossom Lane was less than a quarter of a mile away from her store."

"You told me that already," Bernice said.

"Yes, well, Danny has been looking forward to this for weeks," Mimi said. "This is a big treat for him."

"I can't turn back," Bernice replied. "I told you, I have a lot of work to do. I'm very backed up. I don't know how I'll ever be able to get any of it done in time. I'm a single mother. My ex hasn't given me a cent in months. I have to get home as soon as possible. I can't waste any more time."

"Please, Bernice," Mimi said, lowering her voice to a whisper. "You have no idea how much this means to Danny. He'll be devastated if he can't go apple picking."

"I told you I can't do it. I have too much work to do. My

back is killing me. I've had four spinal surgeries in the past three years. I should be home in bed. We can't go. Don't ask me anymore. I'm not going to change my mind."

At this point Danny came to attention. "Where's the apple orchard?" he asked.

"I'm sorry, honey. There's been a change in plans. We're going to go apple picking tomorrow instead."

"Tomorrow?"

"Yes, darling, tomorrow."

"Tomorrow and not today?"

"Yes, darling. Tomorrow. But not today."

"Not today?"

"Yes, darling, I'm sorry. Not today. But tomorrow. I promise, we'll go apple picking tomorrow."

"Noooooooooooooooooo! I want to go Todayyyyyyyyyyyy!" Danny howled at the top of his lungs.

"Danny, please, don't scream. I promise we'll go tomorrow. We just can't go now."

"Noooooooooooooooooooooooooooo! I want to go Todayyyyyyyyy! Not tomorrow but Todayyyyyyyyyyyyyyyyyyy!"

"That screaming! I can't stand it! Tell your son to stop screaming!"

"Danny, please, honey, I beg of you, stop screaming. I told you, we'll go apple picking tomorrow. Daddy and I will rent a car and we'll go apple picking tomorrow."

"Noooooooooooooooooooo! I want to go apple picking Todayyyyyyyyyyyyyyy!"

Turning around, Mimi ordered Danny to stop screaming, at which point her son lurched forward and covered her mouth with his hand. Mimi bit him.

"You bit me! Why why why?"

"I'm sorry, darling. I'm so sorry," Mimi said, the tears welling up in her eyes.

"I want to go apple picking."

"Danny, we can't go apple picking now. I told you. She won't take us."

"Take us. Take us," Danny started screaming. "Pretty please, with a cherry on top!"

"Tell him not to ask me," Bernice responded. "I told you I have work to do!."

"Nooooooooooooooooooooooooooooooooooooooooooooooo!"

"I can't stand this," Bernice said. "He's giving me a migraine. My head is splitting in two."

"Danny, you must stop screaming!"

"I want to go apple picking Nowwwwwwwwwwwwwwwww!"

"I told you. Daddy and I will take you apple picking tomorrow."

"I want to go Todayyyyyyyyyyyyyyy! Not tomorrow. Todayyyyyyyyyyyyyyyy!"

"I can't stand this screaming," Bernice said.

"Shut up, Danny!" Mimi said, turning around and angrily grabbing hold of his arm. "Shut the fuck up!"

"I can't have that kind of language in front of Andy," Bernice said.

"I want to go apple picking Todaaaaayyyyyyyyyyyyyyy yyyyyyyy!" Danny shouted out at the top of his lungs. "Not tomorrow. Todaaaaayyyyyyyyyyyyyyyyyyyyyyyyyyyy!!!!"

"I can't stand this anymore. I'm going to have to drop you off at the nearest train station," Bernice said.

"What?" Mimi said.

"Your son is giving me a migraine. I can't listen to this anymore. I'm taking you to the nearest train station."

"You can't do that! We're in the middle of fucking nowhere! There won't be another train for God knows how long."

"I want to go apple picking Nowwwwwwwwwwwwww-wwwwwww!"

"I have work to do. I'm very behind. Your son's scream-ing is disturbing my equilibrium. I'm a single mother. I can't afford to lose this job. I'm going to have to drop you off at the nearest train station," she repeated.

"Danny. You must stop this instant," Mimi said, turning around again. "She's going to kick us out of this fucking car if you don't stop. Please stop. I beg of you."

"I want to go apple picking Nowwwwwwwwwwwwww-wwww!!!!!!!!" Danny said, tears streaming down his face. Mimi couldn't remember the last time she had seen her son cry. Even when he split his chin open on the playground when he was five, he hadn't shed a tear.

"Tomorrow, we'll go apple picking tomorrow. I promise. We'll rent a car and go to Upstate New York like we did last year. I promise. Remember how much you liked it? We'll go on hayrides and we'll go the country store and you can have as many cinnamon donuts as you like."

"I want to go apple picking Todayyyyyyyyyyyyyyyyyyyyy yyyyyyyyyyy! Not Tomorrrrrrrrrrrrrrooooooooooowwwww-wwwwwwwww! Todayyyyyyyyyyyyyyyyyy!"

"That's it," Bernice said. "I've had it. I'm taking you to the train station. There's one right at the next intersection."

"Stop the car," Mimi said. "I want to talk to Danny alone."

Bernice brought her car to a screeching halt by the side of the road. "Okay. But I'm warning you. I'm just giving you a couple minutes. I have to get back to my work."

Mimi pulled Danny out of the car. His face red and blotchy and wet with tears, he started jumping up and down.

"I want to go apple picking Nowwwwwwwwwww!!!!" he yelled out at the top of his lungs.

"Please calm down, Danny, I beg of you," she said. "You must calm down. We'll go apple picking tomorrow, I promise."

"Not tomorrow, Todayyyyyyyyyyyyyyyyyyyyyyyyyyyyyyyy yyy!!!!!!!!!!!" he said.

"Danny, I'm telling you, you have to stop this right now! That fucking bitch is going to leave us in the middle of fucking nowhere and then where will we be? If you don't stop screaming, I won't take you apple picking tomorrow. I won't take you apple picking ever again!"

"I want to go apple picking Todayyyyyyyyyyyyyyyyyyyy! Not tomorrow! Todayyyyyyyyyyyyyyyyyyyyyyy!!!!!!!!!!!!!!!!!!!!!!!!!!!!"

"I told you. That fucking narcissistic bitch won't take us! You must stop this instant! Please, I beg of you, Danny," said Mimi. "We'll go apple picking in Mineola, okay? How about that? As soon as we get to the train station, we'll go apple picking in Mineola. We'll pick apples off the apple trees of Mineola."

"In Mineola?" Danny, who had a comprehensive understanding of geography, asked. "But Mineola isn't the country. It's a suburb," he said with a look filled with confusion and hope.

"No, Mineola is different. There are apple orchards in Mineola. There are! There are! There are!" Mimi told him. "And then we'll go apple picking tomorrow, too. Mommy and Daddy will rent a car and we'll drive to the apple orchard in Yorktown Heights, the one with the baby goats. And you'll go apple picking and we'll go on a hayride and we'll get a pumpkin and Daddy will carve the face of Pikachu on it.

Won't you like that? Just think of it. You'll go apple picking twice this year, instead of just once. As a bonus for being such a good boy. Okay?"

"Okay, Mommy," Danny, in the blindness of his innocence and trust, consented.

"Now remember. Not a peep out of you until we get to Mineola. Promise?"

Danny looked back at her blankly.

"Please say, 'I promise, Mommy.' Please say, 'I promise. Not a peep.'"

Mimi waited until Danny recited the words, "I promise, Mommy. Not a peep."

"Good boy. You're my good, wonderful boy," she said. Mimi took Danny in her arms and she held him so tightly she felt as though she were trying to absorb him back into her body. She buried her face in his neck and submerged herself in the peace that only holding Danny could give her. Then taking his hand, Mimi walked with her son back to the SUV.

"Everything's settled now," Mimi told Bernice as she sat down in the front seat.

"I'm warning you, Mimi. My nerves can't take another second of your son's screaming. Another word out of him about apple picking and I'm taking you to the nearest train station."

"I think it's better not to say anything about that particular subject right now, okay?" Mimi said, reaching back and taking Danny's hand in hers. "Just take us back to Mineola." Mimi looked out the window. The leaves were saturated with the last gasp of the sun's brightness.

They were two hours away from Mineola. Mimi would have to distract Bernice until they got to the train station. She decided she would start with Bernice's much-reviled ex-husband. Bernice loved complaining about him. When the topic of her idiot ex began to dry up, Mimi struck up a conversation about the female urge to procreate. This led to the issue of abortion. Bernice herself had had five.

As they entered the more developed areas of Long Island, Mimi shifted the topic to demographics. Bernice was in the middle of a disquisition on the recent socioeconomic changes in Mineola when they reached the train depot, at which point Mimi jumped from her seat, and grabbing Danny by the hand, she unbuckled his seat belt, pulled him out of the SUV and carried him to the tracks, where, as luck would have it, a train had just pulled into the station. She was happy that she had had the presence of mind to remember to say good-bye to Andy, who really was a great kid. She didn't say good-bye to Bernice, or even look at her when she left the SUV, although she caught a glimpse of her out of the corner of her eye. She was gazing at Mimi in bewilderment, perplexed to behold yet another person betraying her trust, her generosity and her goodwill.

## The Bike Path

Jake left the apartment to take Danny bike riding at 9:00 in the morning. He had promised to check in with Mimi at 10:00, and when the clock struck 10:05 with still no call from Jake, Mimi felt the familiar dread creeping up on her. By 10:08, she was dialing and redialing his cell phone. Ten minutes passed, with still no call from her husband, just four rings followed by the eerily posthumous sound of his recorded voice. Mimi had imagined it hundreds of times before: the inconsolable grief, the unbearable loneliness, the inconceivable misery of life without Jake. And what about Danny? What would she do about Danny? She could never take care of Danny on her own.

Finally at 10:14, Jake answered the phone. "Where the hell are you?" she said, relief giving way to anger.

"Stop it," Jake said. Now he was the one who was angry, and his anger always outstripped hers. Mimi retreated.

"I'm sorry, but please try to understand how worried I get."

"Stop being so irrational."

"Maybe if you thought about how you are about heights."

"You mean the way you are about everyfuckingthing else."

Mimi laughed. Her husband had come back from the dead.

"I couldn't call you. The signals were out," he explained.

"Where are you?"

Jake told her they were on the bike path, which he had just found out about this morning. As soon as they left the apartment house, Danny had blown out his front tire, running over a nail, and they had gone to the bike shop on Bennett Avenue to get the flat fixed. Their neighbor, whose father owned the shop, had told him about the bike path, which ran along the banks of the Hudson down the entire length of Manhattan.

"You mean Hector?" Mimi asked.

"I don't know his name. He's the kid who's always doing wheelies in the courtyard."

"Hector. His name is Hector." About five years ago, Mimi had hired the boy to play with Danny. And for a few weeks, every Sunday he and Danny would sit at the dining room table, where Mimi could keep an eye on them, and play battleship. Danny was very good at games and he always won. Mimi didn't think that was why Hector stopped coming over. She knew it was his mother, who had called to tell her that Hector was too busy with schoolwork to come over and play with Danny anymore. After that, the woman always avoided looking at Mimi whenever she encountered her in the laundry room, or in the lobby, or in the elevator, or on the street.

"What's it like? The bike path?" she asked. Then interrupting herself, she said, "Are you riding? Don't talk to me if you're riding." Jake could get so lost in his thoughts that the physical world would cease to exist for him. Two years ago he had almost walked straight into the path of an ambulance that was racing down 49th Street. He said he had been trying to remember a line from "Tithonus" at the time. She didn't respond when he quipped that his last thought in his life on earth would have been "Here at the quiet limit of the world" if a young man in army fatigues hadn't pulled him out of the way.

Her husband hadn't changed much since the first time she had seen him, in his cousin's house in Upstate New York, where they were attending the same college. She had gone to the house to borrow a book from a girl in her Romantic poetry class, and that was when she first saw Jake. He was sitting at the kitchen table reading a paperback and eating a turkey leg (which, Jake told her years later, his mother had sent via his cousin, who had just come back from a visit home). The image of him sitting there so completely ensconced in his contented little world was as vivid to her now as it had been twenty-five years ago.

Mimi loved seeing this boy, so immersed in his simple pleasures. She could never imagine herself ever feeling that content. It was something she wanted to know, something she had always wanted Jake to teach her.

At the time, Mimi was sharing an apartment with a nasty girl, a film major with delusions of grandeur, like so many of the film majors she knew, and when a friend of hers moved out of the rooms she was renting in a house at the edge of town, Mimi moved there, and one day when she was hitchhiking to school, she ran into Jake, who turned out to be living across the street from her. She would visit him in the crummy apartment he shared with a friend of his from high school. They took LSD together once, and wandered around the hideous Binghamton College campus, which seemed to them to be as glorious as the Emerald City of Oz. They made out on a nearby hill, and later spent the night lying in his loft bed reading to each other from the *Norton Anthology of Poetry*. The words came out of their mouths in colors, and the ceiling above them kept changing shape, expanding and contracting and moving up and down; at one point she could feel the weight of it covering her like a blanket. They didn't sleep together that night. The next day they sat on the bank of a nearby creek, and Jake, with his antiquated sense of honor, told her that he had not wanted to take advantage of her in her drugged state. They had sex right after their talk, and when Mimi, who spent her entire college career moving from apartment to apartment and college to college, decided to change apartments yet again (this time to a converted funeral parlor in another part of town), they had sex a few more times, the way people did in those days, casually and on the spur of the moment.

At the end of the semester, they both transferred to different colleges, and they didn't see each other again until they were both standing in line waiting for a table to open up at the Odessa restaurant in the East Village. Mimi, addressing the boy standing in front of her, asked him if he was waiting for a table, and he turned around and looked at her rather rudely, she thought, and nodded his head yes. Then Mimi said, "Jake?" and Jake said, "Mimi."

They started living together right after they met.

Mimi had always hoped some of Jake's eternal calm would rub off on her, but quite the opposite turned out to be true. There was too much Jake in Jake for there to be any room left for Mimi to appropriate any of that inner peace for herself. Someone had to do the worrying. And the worries kept piling up. Ever since the incident with the fire engine, Mimi would worry about Jake every time he left the house. It had gotten to the point where she was afraid for him to go across the street by himself to get a quart of milk. He was absentminded—like Danny. Or rather, Danny was like him. Only more so. Tragically more so.

"We're off our bikes now," Jake said, explaining that Danny had stopped to pick a bed of dandelion puffballs he had seen growing in a field by the river. He wouldn't be satisfied until he had picked every last puffball and until he had watched every last filament scatter in the air under the force of his breath. Mimi could see him methodically clearing the field of all the dandelions while Jake stood by, patiently watching. Her husband took such pleasure in Danny's innocent appreciation of the things of the world; he got a kick out of "his little idiosyncrasies," as he called them. She used to get a kick out of them, too, but they were just a conglomeration of symptoms to her now.

"I feel as though we've discovered a secret passageway to a whole other world," Jake told her. "I can't believe this has been here all this time and we didn't know about it," he said, describing the sights they had passed so far—the tennis courts and the river and the bridge and the stretches of green grass and the old railroad tracks that reminded him of the rundown towns in Upstate New York they used to visit before Danny was born.

"Maybe we could go hiking in New Paltz next weekend. Danny would like that. I've been thinking it's time to start living our lives again. We can't let autism rule us forever, you know." Then he went back to telling her about the bike path. "I wish you were here with us. We've got to get you a bike."

The following Monday, when Jake was coming home from working on his novel at the Starbucks that had just opened up at the top of the hill, their next-door neighbor Manny was sitting on a milk crate in the corner of the hallway that served as his workshop, repairing a bike he had found on the street. Manny was a tiny man with a glass eye and a talent for fixing things. He had been a car mechanic in Ecuador and he always wore blue denim overalls with EMANUEL MECÁNICO embroidered in big red letters across the front. Retired now, Manny occupied himself picking things up off the street and fixing them—a typewriter, a paper shredder, a high chair, a fax machine, a computer desk. The small studio apartment he shared with his wife, Amada, was piled high from floor to ceiling with things he'd found on the street. Once or twice a year they packed up all their little treasures and sent them to Ecuador, to be distributed among the various members of their extended family.

Manny didn't speak English, although Mimi knew he liked American movies. The sound of his television traveled through the thin wall that separated their two apartments. Once when the tenant in 5D forgot about a pan of oil she had left on the burner and it caught fire, filling the hallways with smoke, the building had been evacuated by the fire department at one in the morning, and they found themselves standing next to each other in the elevator. Manny had looked at Jake, and nodding his head enthusiastically, he told his wife, "*Como Paul New-*

*man en la película.*" Jake was wearing a sleeveless undershirt, like the one Paul Newman wore in *The Sting*. Mimi always thought Jake looked great in sleeveless undershirts. He was past forty, but his body was firm and strong.

Jake managed to convey to Manny that he wanted to buy the bicycle—and after some negotiation, which consisted of Manny saying that Jake could have the bike for *treinta dólares* and Jake, who didn't want to take advantage of Manny's ignorance of the cost of things in America, offering him *cincuenta dólares*, Mimi had a bike, and the next day she went out with him and Danny on the bike path.

Riding along the banks of the Hudson, the George Washington Bridge rising like an optical illusion out of the sky, Mimi could see that the bike path was indeed a wondrous thing but she was too worried about Danny to enjoy it. He was so impulsive. He had no sense of danger. There was no telling what he would do from one minute to the next. Once, when he was five, she had woken up to find him hanging halfway out the window between the child guards. It was incomprehensible to her how so completely in control of herself she had been, that with the force of her will she had managed to make time stand still as she got up out of bed and pulled her son into her arms.

"Just ride ahead of us. I'll take care of Danny. Try to enjoy yourself, goddammit," Jake told her. He said she was spoiling everyone's fun, yelling at Danny to watch out at every turn. "Give him space," he said. "How can he learn with you breathing down his neck every second?"

Shortly after she took the lead, just as they were going down a steep hill, Danny cut in front of her, causing her to lose her balance and fall down, scraping layers of flesh off her arm. Danny was delighted to be able to observe firsthand the different stages of healing he had read about in his medical textbooks. The first thing he did every day when he came home from school was to check her arm; he seemed completely oblivious to her suffering; perhaps because he wasn't particularly sensitive to pain himself. The doctors called it "hyposensitivity."

After Mimi's arm got better, Jake kept on trying to convince her to go out on the bike path with them again. "Danny has learned his lesson," he told her.

Since when does Danny ever learn his lesson? Mimi wanted to ask him. But Jake hated when she talked that way.

Ever since the accident, the thought of Jake and Danny going out bike riding terrified Mimi. For reasons that were clearly irrational to her, it was now only Jake she worried about, never Danny. She wished she could go out with them so that she could protect her husband from harm. Once or twice she had gotten as far as the door. But she could never bring herself to go with them. Every weekend the days were sunny and bright. Sometimes it felt as though the sun, the sky and God were all conspiring against her. Soon it would be November, and Mimi tallied up the number of weekends before winter arrived, when it would be too cold for bike riding. Jake could take Danny to the Museum of Natural History on the weekends, and the movies. Maybe Mimi would go with them. She would force herself to go out with them.

Jake didn't say good-bye when he left for the bike path that morning. He didn't want to wake her. But Mimi wasn't sleeping. She was lying in bed listening to him get Danny ready to go out. She used to be the one to set the household in motion in the morning, rising before the sun, anxious to start the day. There was always so much to do. But lately she could barely bring herself to get out of bed. It was Jake who woke Danny every morning and made sure he combed his hair and brushed his teeth; it was Jake who checked to see that his shoes were tied and that his fly was zipped and his shirt was tucked in. It was Jake who made him breakfast and packed up his lunch. It was Jake who walked him to the school up the block, where Danny spent the day being led around like a puppet by an aide who had never been trained to work with him.

Mimi listened as Jake told Danny how to release the bike from the lift in the ceiling. He was so gentle with their son; his patience reminded her of how impatient with Danny she had become.

Lately, when she got angry at Danny, she would remember the mother she had met at an autism seminar on advocacy a few years ago. The woman had come from Vietnam to New York City on her own, because she had heard that services for handicapped children were better here. Her son, who was eighteen, weighed almost three hundred pounds. He couldn't talk, was incapable of dressing himself and was constantly leaving his semen everywhere. Mimi had asked her, What do you do when you get angry at him? The woman had told her, I love him so much, so much. When I am angry, I tell him, Hug Mommy, and everything go away.

Mimi couldn't be like that woman. The other day when she caught Danny cutting the fringe off the Oriental rug in the foyer, she slapped him in the face. She hadn't hit him very hard, but she had hit him. "Why did you hit me? Why? Why? Why?" he kept on asking her as she embraced him and tried to kiss away the red mark she had left on his cheek.

"No, not that way, Danny," Jake was saying. "That's better. Easy does it. Now try again. That's it, my sunny son son."

The bike lift hung over the arch outside the bathroom, and for a long time, Mimi would be haunted by visions of it crashing down on them. Weeks after Jake had installed the contraption, she kept on nagging him to take it down. They could go back to storing the bikes in the vestibule. So what if they tripped over them occasionally?

It wasn't until she heard the rattle of Jake's key in the door that Mimi got out of bed. Her bladder had been close to bursting for the past half hour but she wanted to avoid witnessing the morning turmoil of getting Danny ready to go out.

Mimi went back to bed. She studied the crack in the ceiling. It had been years since their apartment had been painted, and the walls and ceiling were a mess, with paint and plaster peeling off everywhere. When Danny was little, she would lie down with him and together they would talk about what the cracks in the ceiling looked like. Eventually they decided on a white dachshund running through white clouds in a white night sky. Once, before Danny's diagnosis, Mimi was in the kitchen doing the dishes, and she heard a crash coming from her bedroom, and when she rushed to see what had happened, she found Danny standing in the middle of the room, surrounded by big chunks of broken plaster. He was laughing and repeating over and over again, "The ceiling is falling! The ceiling is falling! The ceiling, not the sky! The ceiling, not the sky!" Mimi was relieved that Danny was unharmed, and relieved also to see that the section of the ceiling that housed the white dachshund was still there, and that he was still prancing happily around in the white night sky.

The early summer air, with its comforting heaviness, its gelatinous quiet, drifted in through the window. Soon it would be hot, and they didn't have an air conditioner in their bedroom. To cool off on hot summer days, she and Jake would take lots of baths and lie around naked under the window fans and take turns complaining about the heat. They made a game of it. But Danny was getting older now and she couldn't walk around naked anymore. Lately, he had become preoccupied with her breasts. He was always trying to touch them and asking to look at them. Jake said it was just adolescence. It was easy to forget that on top of everything else, Danny was also going through puberty. But Mimi didn't think his sudden interest in her breasts had anything to do with hormones. It had to do with the distance that had been growing between them; it was the gulf she had created and this was how Danny was trying to navigate his way across it.

Mimi had nursed Danny until he was three and a half; it often seemed to her that nursing was the only part of motherhood she had been any good at, and lately she had been wishing that she had never weaned Danny. She missed the lazy peacefulness of lying in bed with her son in her arms. Most of all she missed the easy access it gave her to this child who seemed to be drifting farther and farther away from her with each passing day.

Three and a half years of nursing had wrecked her breasts, but Mimi didn't care. To her, the stretch marks that now ran up and down them like the tributaries of two big fat round rivers were proud emblems, irrefutable proof, of what now seemed to be her dubious claim to motherhood.

She could still vividly recall the comforting heaviness of

the ducts filling up with milk. Occasionally, without warning, they would erupt, saturating her clothes with that wonderful sweet and sour scent. Sometimes when she nuzzled her face in Danny's hair, she thought she could still detect a ghost of the smell lingering on him like a phantom of her former self.

Mimi lay in bed and listened to the traffic on the George Washington Bridge. And the chirping of birds. There was something soothing about the steady whirr of the wheels on the pavement. The cars sounded happy. But the birds sounded miserable. They sounded frantic. They sounded desperate to be released from the prison of the city sky.

The voice of a policeman talking in staccato rhythms into a microphone interrupted Mimi's thoughts. He was telling a car to turn off the street: "Pull over to the side of the road." She would occasionally hear these words coming from 181st Street at random hours of the day and night. It had taken her years to figure out that the strange sounds, which made it seem as though the city had fallen victim to a fascist takeover, just came from a policeman enforcing the rules of the road.

At the end of last winter, their car had been towed away. Mimi had neglected to pay hundreds of dollars' worth of parking tickets, and when she went to retrieve it, the city refused to release it because she had forgotten to pay her car insurance for an entire year. Danny missed having a car. Every day he pleaded, "Get a car. I want a car. I need a car. I can't live without a car." "Maybe later," she would say to appease him. But Mimi was relieved to be rid of the headache of having to keep track of the parking rules in Manhattan and worrying about vandals breaking her windshield and removing her headlights to sell to chop shops in the Bronx.

*  *  *

Jake called at ten o'clock to report that they had arrived safely at their first destination of the day—the Barnes & Noble on West 82nd Street. Although at home Danny would spend hours reading field guides about rocks and minerals, fish, birds, insects and botany; science textbooks, encyclopedias, dictionaries, atlases, music magazines and a variety of shopping catalogs for everything from camping equipment to element coin collections; books about medicine, etymology, biology, chemistry, gardening, human anatomy, nutrition, and two new interests of his, American slang and the North Pole, the only thing he ever wanted to do at Barnes & Noble was look at the pop-up books. He would gather a pile of them in his arms—they were always the same books. He would bring them to a corner—always the same corner—and play with them. He never tired of pulling the cardboard flaps in and out over and over again. Jake and Mimi knew that anyone looking at him would think there was something weird about a thirteen-year-old in playing with baby books, and this bothered them. But since they were always forcing their son to do things he did not like doing, it didn't seem fair to be denying Danny a simple pleasure like this.

Jake said they would stay at Barnes & Noble for another half hour. After that he would take Danny out for lunch. They should be getting back on their bikes around three.

Mimi told him to promise not to ride in the street, but Jake refused. Lately he had been growing more and more intolerant of her constant worrying.

"Besides, it's illegal to ride on the sidewalk," he told her.

"But you promised," Mimi said.

"'The coward dies a thousand deaths,'" he declaimed.

"Ha. Ha. Ha," Mimi said. Then she heard Jake giving the phone to Danny, telling him to say hello to her.

The telephone confused Danny. Although he knew how it worked from a technical perspective, it flustered him to use it.

"Go on, honey. Talk to your mommy," Jake said.

"I love you," he shouted into the phone.

"I love you, too, Danny," she said.

"How much?" he asked. It was a game they used to play. Every night before he went to sleep, she would lie in bed with Danny and tell him how much she loved him. That was how she came to teach him about infinity. He was only four but he understood what she was talking about right away; he had been pondering it on his own for a long time. "The sky goes on forever. But the sidewalk ends. And numbers don't stop counting." This was something he had discovered by himself when he was three.

That was also the night she told him about death. They were talking about how some things never end, and Danny asked her about flowers and animals and insects and birds and people. He was inconsolable when she told him that every living thing had to die sooner or later. But there could never be enough room in the world to hold all those living things, Mimi tried to explain. What about the moon? Danny asked. And all the other planets? What about the universe? He calmed down finally when she told him that when he grew up, maybe he would discover a cure for death.

Mimi decided to spend the day sorting through Danny's clothes and getting rid of the ones he had outgrown. Throwing away all the little T-shirts and little pants and little socks, Mimi felt as though she were betraying Danny, as though by throwing away his old clothes, she were throwing away all hope for the future. If only he could stay thirteen forever. Or twelve. Or ten.

When they stood back to back now, the top of his head was less than three inches below the top of hers; last June she discovered a delicate dusting of hair covering the pale skin above his upper lip. As soon as she noticed the mustache, she whisked him into the bathroom to shave it off. "The time has come for you to have your first shave, I'm afraid," she told him.

"Just make believe," he told her, remembering, probably, how Jake used to take him into the bathroom and spray shaving cream on his face, and pretend to shave him with the back side of the razor.

"No, I'm afraid it's for real this time," Mimi told him. But Danny insisted that there was just a very little bit and that he wasn't going to go through puberty for a couple of years, at least. He was merely prepubescent, he said. He looked uncharacteristically solemn as she covered his upper lip with shaving cream and got rid of the offending hairs.

It was two the next time Jake called her. They were about to head back on the bike path.

"What's wrong?" he asked. He could always tell whenever something was bothering her.

She told him that she had been spending the day sorting through Danny's old clothes. "When did he get so big?" she said, choking back the tears.

"Forget about the clothes," he told her. "Why don't you just read a book? Or watch television. Look for something stupid. Be stupid. It's fun to be stupid. We'll be home in an hour."

Ten minutes later the phone rang again. It was Jake, reminding her to turn on the television. She went obediently to their bedroom and turned on the TV. A little box in the lower-right-hand corner of the screen said that the show was called *The Bachelor*. From what Mimi could gather, it was a reality show about the real-life quest for love and romance—played out for the television audience to see.

Apparently, the bachelor, a generic-looking young man, with vacant eyes and a perpetual grin, had spent the last several weeks sifting through a pile of women and now he had finally whittled his choice of a soul mate down to two candidates. He was presently on the horns of a dilemma, trying to decide which of them to choose. "I think I love them both," he said with a wholesome grin, bred of his incredible stupidity, Mimi supposed. "They're both so awesome. They're both the women of my dreams. I've never felt this way before, really."

Mimi sat down on the bed, fascinated. Jake was right. This was fun. Later, when they went to bed, she would utter those words to him, or some such version. I think I love you. I mean I adore you. I can't believe the way you make me feel. I think you're the man of my dreams. You're so awesome. I'm in awe. You're the awesomest man in the world. She would go on and on like that, and Jake would keep on telling her to shut up, but she wouldn't stop until he had wrestled her to the floor. They had fun, didn't they? Despite everything, they still had fun.

Jake called at four to report that Danny was fishing in the river. On the way home, he had hopped off his bike and run over to a man who was sitting on a rock by the river fishing. Now the fisherman was teaching Danny how to cast his rod.

"But you said you would be home by five," Mimi said.

"You know how much Danny wants to go fishing," Jake told her. "I can't take him away now." Last spring Mimi had gotten him a fishing rod and a tackle box, and every night before Danny went to sleep, he would dump the contents of his tackle box onto his bed. He would run his fingers up and down the ridges of the silver scaling knife, unwind and rewind the spools of fishing lines and examine his collection of lures, turning them over and over again in his hands and putting them close to his nose and sniffing them, as though he could detect the scent of the sea lingering on the pristine pieces of metal and plastic. Danny had made a list of places within a thirty-mile radius of their apartment where they could go fishing, but they had never gotten around to taking him to any of them. Whenever Danny was asked to fill out one of the questionnaires designed to diagnose what was wrong with him, he always listed fishing as one of his three favorite hobbies. It didn't seem relevant to him that he had never actually gone fishing.

Jake told her that the fisherman was impressed with how curious Danny was, and how much he knew about fish and the sport of fishing. And he didn't seem to mind answering all his questions.

"Please, Jake," Mimi said. "I can't bear to wait any longer."

"Stop it, Mimi," Jake said impatiently. "You can't really expect me to take Danny away now, can you? This is a dream come true for him."

"What can you do with a fish you catch in the polluted waters of the Hudson?" she argued. Knowing that her fears were unjustified never made them any less real to her.

"You know that's not the point, Mimi," he said.

She paced back and forth on the floor and tried to comfort herself with the thought that they had already made it through the most perilous part of the journey—the part where the bike path broke off into the crowded city streets. Now there was only that hill a quarter mile before the river to worry about, the one where Danny had cut in front of her. But Jake said Danny hadn't done anything like that since the accident. Maybe he really was learning.

She went back to watching television. While she had been on the phone with Jake, the bachelor had made up his mind about which supplicant was really the one and only girl of his dreams. Now the time had come for the girls to find out which of them had been judged to be the most awesomest. Mimi watched as they combed their long straight hair, and dressed their perfect bodies in shiny evening gowns, carefully preparing themselves for the moron's verdict. After the commercial, the camera showed a stretch limousine pulling up to the curb. The blonde smiled bravely as she climbed out of it, and proceeded to walk up the long stone path to where the bachelor stood waiting in a gazebo. Mimi kind of liked the blonde. She felt a little sorry for her too. There was something sad about the girl. And insecure, as well. Like after she told the bachelor that her parents were Buddhists. She knew the bachelor would probably think it was strange, but it was true, so she had said it.

The sun was about to set, and for several seconds the television screen was burning with the colors of twilight. The bachelor was standing next to a little table on which lay a single red rose. The blonde stood there in a state of suspended animation as he went on and on about how wonderful she was and how amazing she made him feel and how terrific

and awesome and beautiful she was, her eyes constantly shifting to the rose (chosen by the writers to be the symbol of true
love). When the bachelor failed to pick it up, a look of trepi-
dation passed over the young woman's face. After listening to
him say again how incredible and beautiful and amazing she
was, she walked stoically back down the path alone. Next the
camera flashed to her in the car. She was crying.

"Why does this always happen to me? I'm thirty years
old. What's wrong with me? Why doesn't anyone ever want
me?" she said.

Looking at this beautiful young woman crying in the back
of a limousine, Mimi could almost understand what had
driven the girl to look for love on a reality TV show. When
she was two weeks away from her thirtieth birthday, Mimi
had started searching for Jake in the Manhattan telephone
directory, calling people named Wiesenthal, which for reasons neither of them could ever figure out she had thought
was Jake's last name.

Next it was the brunette's turn to get out of the limousine,
walk up the path and stand there in front of the gazebo while
the bachelor told her how beautiful and awesome she was
and how fantastic she made him feel.

Mimi shut off the TV. She decided to do the laundry,
but when she got down to the basement, all the washing
machines were taken. The Dominican woman who lived
with her two children and her mother and father and three
brothers and her pregnant niece in a one-bedroom apartment
on the fourth floor was using all three of them. One of her
neighbors, part of the new crop of tenants who had moved
into the building since the housing boom had hit Washington
Heights, causing rents to triple and the Dominicans to leave,

told her that she suspected the family was using the building's three washing machines to run a laundry business out of the basement. The woman announced that as soon as she had proof, she was going to report them to the landlord. "Nine people in a one-bedroom apartment. I don't understand how these people live, do you?"

Mimi wouldn't be surprised if it was true that Yvonne was operating a laundry business out of the basement. The woman across the hall ran a bed-and-breakfast; there was always a constant stream of people from all over the world coming in and out of her apartment, all of whom she claimed were her relatives. The man in 6A sold wine. The woman below her cut hair for twenty dollars a head. And Mimi's next-door neighbor ran a day care center. The windows of their kitchens were directly across from each other and Mimi often heard Norma singing to herself in Spanish. She was a tiresomely cheerful woman who took good care of her invalid husband, and seemed to really like the children, whom she would greet with great enthusiasm when their parents delivered them to her door. She was always telling them how much she loved them.

When Danny was three, Mimi had asked Norma if she would watch him a few hours a day. She wanted to block out some time for herself to do her copyediting. She had originally thought that she would be able to work while Danny napped, but Danny never napped; he hardly slept at all. Norma had refused. "No, mami. Sorry, mami. All full. All full." It wasn't until several years later that Mimi figured out that Norma had lied to her about not having enough space. It wasn't just the new, ever-expanding crop of children in their bright orange strollers that clued her in; it was the look of pity she would see in Norma's eyes whenever she ran into her. Mimi hated Norma and her pity; most of all she hated her for knowing all along that there was something wrong with Danny. How long had she known? Mimi wondered.

When Mimi got back to the apartment, Jake's voice was on the answering machine saying that they were heading back home. She got to the phone just before he was about to hang up.

She asked him where he was.

"We'll be home soon," he said. "Danny wants to tell you something."

There was a pause, during which she could hear Jake prompting their son to talk to his mother.

Danny finally said, "I caught a fish."

"That's wonderful, honey," said Mimi. "Does that mean we are going to have fish for dinner?"

After another three-second wait, he said, "I threw it back." And after another pause, during which she knew Jake was prompting him to tell her why, he said, "It was toxic. Because of PCBs."

"But it's great anyway, that you caught a fish," said Mimi. "I'm so proud of you. I once caught a fish but I was too afraid to reel it in. Did you reel it in?"

There was another long pause. This was the longest telephone conversation they had ever had. But Danny didn't respond.

"I'm so proud of you, darling. Mommy loves you so much! I'm so happy that you caught a fish!"

"Hi, honey. It's me. Well, that was a record! I'm glad Danny got to go fishing at last. Of course I had to tell him to say thank you to the fisherman. And of course I had to thank the guy, too. You can imagine how pleasant the whole experience was for me. We really do have to take him fishing."

"Okay, now it's time for you come home," Mimi said.

\* \* \*

Mimi was setting the table when the phone rang. That was Jake. He always called when he was at the door. She would answer the phone, and when she opened the door, there he would be, and they would look at each other and continue talking on the phone; it was like being in two dimensions at once.

Mimi ran down the hall with the receiver in her hand, in her excitement forgetting to answer it. She couldn't wait to hold Danny in her arms and tell him how much she loved him. But when she opened the door, Jake and Danny weren't there. She clicked on the phone.

"Hello," she said. Jake was probably hiding somewhere under the stairwell with Danny, who would be laughing so loud the echoes of his laughter would fill the entire hallway. Recently Danny, with his paradoxical interest in language, had informed her that echoes were disintegrating sound.

"Okay, where are you?" she said. She wasn't in the mood for playing right now, but she went along with the game anyway. "Come out, come out, wherever you are," she said, looking for them under the stairwell, but they weren't there. The phone was still ringing but when she clicked it on all she heard was silence.

"Okay, Jake. That's enough! This isn't funny! Talk to me!"

Then, his voice barely audible, there was Jake saying her name over and over again.

"Jake. What is it? Are you okay? Please tell me you're okay!" she commanded.

"Mimi. Danny. Danny had an accident."

"What happened? What happened? Where are you?

Where are you?" Jake told her they were in the emergency room at New York Presbyterian.

"Hurry," he said. "Hurry."

"I'm coming. Tell Danny to wait for me. Tell him Mommy is coming."

Mimi's breasts felt heavy as she ran out the door. Bounding down the stairs, and out across the street, she could swear that, defying all reason, she could feel the old familiar tug of her milk descending.

# The Boy Who Lived
## on a Desert Island

*When Danny was in the hospital, floating in and out of sleep, Mimi made up stories to tell him. She didn't know if he could hear them, and she doubted they would mean anything to him even if he could, but it comforted her to have something to do while she waited by his bedside. This was one of the stories she told him.*

Once there was a boy who lived all by himself on a desert island. The island was made of paper, and all the trees and plants and bushes on it were made of paper, too, except that when the boy would pick the fruits and berries that grew on the trees and bushes, they turned out not to be paper at all. They were as plump and juicy and delicious as any fruit or berry could possibly be. The boy would spend his days walking around the island, looking at all the interesting trees and plants and insects that inhabited it.

One sunny day when he was sitting under a paper palm tree eating a handful of delicious berries that he had just picked off a nearby bush, watching the waves of the ocean crashing against each other onto the shore in a frothy white foam that made him think of whipped cream, the boy noticed a pile of paper lying next to him. There was a paper rock lying on top of the pile of paper, to prevent them from sailing away in the warm breezes that would blow over the ocean onto the island. The boy looked under the pile of paper, and he walked around the palm tree several times, hoping to find a crayon, or a pencil, or a pen—anything he could use to draw with. But there was nothing there except the paper. The boy sat under the tree looking at the pile of paper for a long time, and eventually, not being able to think of anything else to do with it, he just started folding it.

The first thing he made with the paper was an airplane, which he sent flying high up into the sky over the ocean. The boy watched the airplane fly off into the horizon, until he could see it no more. He made dozens of airplanes that day, all of which he sent flying away into the breeze over the ocean until they disappeared from sight. He did the same thing the next day and the day after that and the day after that, but after a while making paper airplanes ceased to amuse him, and so he decided to see what else he could make out of the paper. Before he knew it, he was making all sorts of interesting things by just folding the paper. He made giraffes and dogs and bunnies and horses and a mother duck and a flock of baby ducklings. He made other kinds of animals out of the paper, some of them imaginary animals that he made up himself. He made a dog with wings, and a hippopotamus with the neck of a giraffe, and an alligator with human feet. All day long, the boy amused himself making his little folded animals.

He never ran out of paper. Every morning when he woke up, there was always a fresh pile sitting under the palm tree, waiting for him. And this was how the boy spent his time, until one day a ship came, and took him back to live in New York City, where he wrote a book about his adventure on the island. He called his book *The Amusing Adventures of a Boy Who Lived on a Paper Island*.

After the book was published, when the boy was at Barnes & Noble, sitting behind a table that was piled high with copies of his book, a nice man and woman who looked very much like the parents he had never seen came up to the table and asked him to sign their copy of his book. They asked him if he would mind teaching them how to make things out of paper and he said Sure and he taught them how to make a rabbit and a goose and a flock of geese. The man and the woman liked the boy very much, loved him really, and when they asked him if he would like to come home and live with them, he said that he would, and so they adopted him, and the boy lived happily ever after with his new family.

# A Sample Boy

When Mimi went into Danny's room to tell him lunch was ready, she found him asleep on the floor, under the poster of the periodic table of elements that hung on the wall beside his bed. She stood in the doorway looking at her son: the spray of pimples across his cheeks, the shadow of a mustache above his mouth, the unfinished look of his face made him look like any other teenage boy. His room reeked of sweat and farts and pheromones, reminding her of her brother's room when he was thirteen.

Although it wasn't especially cold, Mimi covered Danny with a quilt, and after gathering up the laundry, she went down to the basement. The washing machines were all in use. She got back into the elevator. The doors slid open at the lobby. A woman pushing a bright orange stroller stepped in, apparently a new client for Norma's day care center next door.

Mimi looked at the child in the stroller and thought of

Danny at that age. The signs had been there already. She recalled with the usual regret how determined she and Jake
had been not to see them. The child looked up at her and
waved his hand and said hi.

"What a handsome boy," Mimi exclaimed. "He has flaxen
hair. I guess that's what is meant by 'flaxen hair.' That's rare,
isn't it? Flaxen hair." Averting her eyes, the woman nodded
and smiled at Mimi politely as she bent down to scoop her
child out of his stroller and into her arms. Mimi, anxious to
escape, blocked the closing door with her foot, and lifting the
blue plastic laundry basket up into her arms, she shoved her
way past the baby carriage, startling the young mother even
more.

She decided to stop off at her mailbox until the elevator
came back down. There was a bill from Con Edison, a bill
from the cable company and a letter from the American Jewish Congress, addressed to Mr. and Mrs. Samuel Borden, the
elderly couple who had lived in Mimi's apartment before she
and Jake had moved there, fourteen years ago.

When Mimi turned around to go back to the elevator, she
was surprised to see her old landlord standing in the lobby.
He was looking up at the recently painted ceiling—a hideous
blend of pink and green and yellow—one of the touches the
new owner had given the building, along with the new boiler,
which allowed him to raise everyone's rent by twenty-three
dollars a month forever.

"Mr. Gotbaum," she said, going over to him, "what are
you doing here?"

"I was in the neighborhood. I thought I would come take
a look at the old place," he said. It had been five years since he
had sold the building and a little longer than that since Mimi

had last seen him. He looked so pale and so thin. Cancer. She hoped it wasn't cancer. Afraid to find out, Mimi just stood there being uncharacteristically silent.

"How is the boy?" Mr. Gotbaum asked. Mr. Gotbaum's affection for Danny remained constant, even after Danny stopped going to the yeshiva. Mimi liked to think that it wasn't just the honor of having held her son during his *bris* that had endeared Danny to her old landlord. She liked to think that there was something else, something that this righteous man (this *tzadik*) appreciated and admired about her son.

Looking at Mr. Gotbaum now, it occurred to Mimi that it wasn't because of his daughter that he never seemed to realize there was anything wrong with Danny; it was really because he didn't live in the real world any more than Danny did. He lived somewhere up in the sky with the God he loved so much. Or maybe it was because he was an immigrant, and he had the blurred vision of an immigrant, living in a country whose language and customs would be forever foreign to him; he couldn't read the signs the way the natives could. She wished that Danny could live in a world filled with immigrants, a world where no one belonged.

"Fine," Mimi said. "He's fine now." Then she told him that Danny had crashed his bike into a tree, going down a steep hill. He and Jake were almost home when the acorn Danny had picked up along the way fell out of his basket, and disobeying Jake, he had turned his bike around and raced down the hill to retrieve it. He had crashed his bike into a tree and had suffered a severe concussion that had left him drifting in and out of consciousness for weeks. "He's going to be okay," Mimi said.

There had been tubes going down Danny's throat and up

his nose, and attached to his arm. The right side of his face had blown up to three times its natural size.

They said that, according to the MRI, her son would be back to "normal" within three months. Mimi paused as she thought about all the days and nights she had spent by the hospital bed, watching Danny breathe, entreating a vaguely imagined, yet cruel and demanding, God to give her back her son, exactly as he had been before the accident. Later, when it became clear that Danny was going to be all right, she hoped that God had not taken her too literally. She hoped He understood that in pleading for her son's life, she had not relinquished her earlier request that Danny be given the chance to live a normal life, like all those lucky children who all those lucky mothers had written books about; children who had been cured by miracle treatments the medical establishment was too arrogant to recognize. Mimi wanted Danny to be one of those children.

"Danny will be graduating high school in five years," Mimi told Mr. Gotbaum.

"That's good," Mr. Gotbaum said, his eyes shifting up to the ceiling again.

Something terrible had happened to her old landlord, she was sure of it.

"How are you, Mr. Gotbaum?" Mimi blurted out. "How is Susan? How is Wendy? Mr. Gotbaum, is everything okay?"

Susan had told Mimi that it was a second marriage for both of them. They had had their families; all their children were married with children of their own; they were in the clear; but they wanted to have a child together and now they were burdened with a girl who at age fourteen still didn't know how to tell time or tie her shoes.

Mimi used to feel guilty whenever she and Susan talked about their children. Danny was making so much progress then. He was going to recover, she was sure of it. Probably, he would always be a little strange. So what? He would have a career—most likely something having to do with science, and one day maybe he would find a girl to marry him, someone odd like him, or maybe someone who had a thing for weird guys. That was eight and a half years ago. Now at thirteen, Danny still couldn't be trusted to go outside by himself; there were days when he didn't say anything except the same things he had said hundreds of times before; he was still incapable of carrying on a simple conversation; he had never had a friend.

"Wendy is gone," Mr. Gotbaum said.

"Gone?" Mimi asked, thinking that she must have misunderstood him. His English was not very good.

"Gone," Mr. Gotbaum repeated.

"Oh . . . " Mimi said. "Mr. Gotbaum."

"She had a heart condition. No one knew."

"I'm so sorry, Mr. Gotbaum."

"There's no one up there," he said pointing up to the ceiling. "An angel. He does this to an angel?"

"Oh, Susan, how is Susan?" Mimi asked.

"Not good."

Mimi said she would like to call his wife and she asked him for their number. He reached into his pocket and found a pen, but he couldn't find anything to write on. Mimi tore a corner off a flyer advertising a couch for sale in apartment 4F and gave it to him.

"This is just for you," Mr. Gotbaum said, explaining that since he sold the building, he had gotten an unlisted number;

the tenants were always calling him, complaining about the new landlord.

"Send Susan my love."

"I have to go. She doesn't like it for me to be away for so long."

Mimi watched him walk out the door and to the corner, where he stood waiting for the light to change. Then, as though he had just remembered something of vital importance, he turned around abruptly, and when he saw Mimi, he rushed back into the building. There was an odd expression on his face, a cross between euphoria and madness. "Do you have a minute?" he asked Mimi.

"Of course."

"I want to tell you something." He was breathing heavily, and Mimi waited for him to catch his breath. And then the words rushed out of his mouth.

"I saw it on the television. They say the universe, it began with one single atom," he said, his eyes widening. "Everything, all the planets, the moon, the sun, the earth, the stars, they say it all started with this thing that you can't even see. Billions of years ago. There's a thing called the Hubble Telescope. They looked through this telescope, and you know what they saw?" he said, putting his hand to his chest. "They saw the universe, there's an end to it. It doesn't go on forever. And it won't go on forever either. One day, everything will end. The earth will get colder and colder and human beings, they won't be able to survive. Everything will be gone. The earth will be gone, all the planets will be gone, the sun will be gone and the stars and the moon and whatever else that is out there will be gone, too. And human beings. Forget it. Human beings will be gone, kaput, like everything else." He stood there for several seconds, not saying anything, trying to catch his breath again, looking at Mimi, the crazed look still in his eyes.

"How old do you think I am?" he asked.

"I don't know, Mr. Gotbaum. I couldn't say."

"Guess."

"I don't know," Mimi said. She figured he was in his eighties. "Maybe in your seventies?"

"I'm going to be eighty-five on my next birthday. Eighty-five years old. I should have been in the ground long ago."

As Mr. Gotbaum went on his way, Mimi wanted to run after him. It made her sad to think of him abandoning his beloved God. The same God who had given him the strength to survive three years in Auschwitz-Birkenau and everything he had witnessed there. She refused to believe that the apocalyptic vision of the world he had painted for her was all he had left to comfort him.

The neurologist had told them they could start taking Danny out for short walks around the neighborhood. It was time to go back to teaching him how to be more independent. One day she and Jake would be dead and then who would there be to take care of their delicate son? Who would there be to love him?

When Jake got home from his daily stint at Starbucks, she would tell him to take Danny to the bodega on the corner to buy a quart of milk. He would trail behind him and prompt him to pick out the milk himself and then he would prompt him to go to the cash register to pay for it by himself. In a couple of weeks, Danny would be going back to school. Mimi would let him walk there by himself. She would trail behind him to make sure he didn't wander off. Bit by bit they would teach him. They would teach him how to cross the street by himself. They would teach him not to talk to strangers and not to touch people. They would teach him to be more independent. And they would be gentle. They would always be gentle.

If only Danny could just go on being Danny, she thought to herself as she unlocked the front door of their apartment. If only he could spend the rest of his life being the sweet, guileless person he was, doing all the things he loved doing. But one day she and Jake were going to die, and leave him all alone, with only the state to take care of him.

Mimi reminded herself she was free now, free to go back to taking care of Danny. The District had finally given her back all the money they owed her. It had taken a solid year of fighting to get them to do it—much more than that, counting all the years before. She couldn't say it had been worth it. Still, she had been right about the money. Teresa Thompson was gone from her at last. The advocate's face, her voice, her ironic smile were all gone. Gone forever. Gone to haunt some other mother, she supposed. But gone from her forever.

Also, a judge had ordered Teresa to give Mimi back everything she had ever paid her. Due to some glitch in the law that allowed her to bypass the statute of limitations, Mimi had sued the advocate in small claims court, and the judge who had ruled in Mimi's favor had reprimanded Teresa for her malfeasance.

In preparing her case, Mimi had discovered that one year the advocate had charged her credit card twice.

Tomorrow she would get to work trying to figure out how Danny could have a good life after she and Jake were dead.

She would find a way to make sure he would be happy. That he would always be happy.

When Mimi went to check up on Danny, he was still sleeping. He was in bed now, lying upside down the way he always did, his head at the foot board, his quilt wrapped around him like a cocoon, the origami Pegasus he had been working on all morning beside him on the pillow. Danny's first week home from the hospital, Mimi had tried doing origami with him, but she didn't have the patience for it. She didn't want to let him out of her sight, so she would sit on his bed copyediting while he sat on the floor making mythical creatures out of kami paper or paper he took out of the printer and cut into little squares.

Copyediting romance novels usually relaxed Mimi. She would mark off choice passages to show Jake when he got home. But this morning she had been way outside the range of comic relief. She had put down the manuscript and decided to sit on Danny's bed and do nothing. That was what everyone was always telling her to do: nothing. And it was nice doing nothing, just sitting there, being with Danny in the mysterious zone of silence that surrounded him.

"What is it? What? What? What?" he kept on asking, as he showed her the origami Pegasus he had just made.

"You know what it is, Danny. Tell me."

"What is it? What? What? What?"

"Remember what we said about asking rhetorical questions."

"Don't ask things you know the answer to!"

"So tell me. What is it?"

"It's Pegasus! Pegasus! Pegasus!"

"And who is Pegasus?"

"Hercules's flying horse! From Greek mythology. Real horses don't fly. It's just imagination."

"That must be nice to be a flying horse."

"How many steps did it take?" he asked.

"Tell me."

"Sixty-nine steps, seventy if you include the last step, which is just showing it."

That was Danny's routine when he finished a model—to report, in the form of a series of questions, what he had made and how many steps it had taken. It was impossible to tell if he was proud of his accomplishment or if he showed it to her out of an impulse as obscure as the one that led him to phrase statements as questions. Nothing about Danny's state of mind was ever obvious. All one could say with certainty about it was that he seemed to like having the same conversation over and over again.

Every now and then he would surprise her with something new, sometimes something so astonishing that it seemed to signal the emergence of a whole new Danny. Like four years ago, when Mimi was in the kitchen making dinner while trying to keep Danny focused on his homework, and out of the blue he had looked up at her and said: "God picked me to be a sample boy," he said. "God picked me to have my own unique point of view. That's what's unique about me—I have my own unique point of view. After I die, God will pick another sample boy to take my place."

Mimi had decided she wouldn't say anything about it to Jake. He would spoil the moment for her with his infuriating rationality. He would say that Danny was probably just repeating something he had heard in a video. But he would be wrong. This was important. It could be the moment they had been waiting for, the first sign of Danny's recovery. She would wait until after everything was okay to tell him about it. Then she would say, See? I knew! But Jake wouldn't mind. He would be so happy. They would both be out of their minds with happiness.

Watching Danny sleep comforted Mimi. During all those years, when at the end of each long day she would be exhausted yet still unable to sleep, she would go into Danny's room and stand in the doorway and look at him. Sometimes she would climb into bed with her son and hug him and he would hug her back. Hugging was something that autistic children were not supposed to do. In all the breaking news reports about the latest cure that friends and relatives would call to tell them to watch, the ultimate proof of a cure, the heartrending affirmation of a life restored, was often the image of a child, previously averse to human touch, hugging his mother for the first time. Before the diagnosis, Mimi had also assumed that autistic children did not like to be touched. But Danny had always craved physical contact, more so than other children, it seemed to her. During those last months before the diagnosis, when her fears about her son had begun to multiply, hugging Danny had been her only comfort.

Mimi wanted to climb into bed with her son now. She knew it was wrong: Danny was thirteen, and technically speaking, practically a man. But what harm could it do? She unraveled the quilt and lay down next to Danny, wrapping her arms around him tightly. Soon she was asleep and dreaming. She dreamt they were flying into the sky on the back of the paper Pegasus. She was sitting behind Danny, who was steering the horse into the clouds, past the sun, past the moon and past the stars. All the while, Danny was talking to her in a foreign language she had never heard before. She couldn't understand any of the words, yet everything he said made perfect sense to her. Soon they were flying to the edge of the universe, where all the planets had gathered together in a circle, as if to greet them, or as if to say good-bye. Mimi held on to her son and rested her head on his shoulder as he steered them out beyond the edge of the universe to where there was nothing, nothing at all.

# The Red Cart

Jake and I started our morning, as we had every morning for the past three days, working together at Starbucks on writing a letter to my doctor at the pain clinic. The purpose of the letter was to refute charges that I was doing something suspicious with the narcotics she had prescribed for my bladder condition. The letter had a subtext (the most important part for me), which was to make the doctor feel ashamed.

Although Jake was helping me, he also despised me, for we were in the middle of a fight that had been going on for weeks. As was so often the case, by now neither of us could remember what the fight was about, but that didn't stop us from hating each other. It was a powerful force, this hatred of ours; it led us by an invisible leash wound tightly around our respective necks and we did whatever it told us to do.

"Why can't you ever learn to keep your big fat mouth shut?" Jake was asking me.

We had come up to the part of the letter where we were

explaining that I had not exactly "threatened" to take my mother's methadone (discovered when I was cleaning out her medicine chest in the aftermath of her recent death), as the duplicitous Dr. Ruttman (always so kind and cordial when we met face-to-face) had put in bold capital letters in her report, but that, in fact, the reason I had told her I was holding on to my mother's methadone was because I wanted to try to convey just how desperate my bladder (that infuriating weight at the center of my body that had tormented me for most of my life) could make me feel. The stash of methadone, combined with the fact that I had tested negative for Percocet, had turned me from a patient with a maddening medical condition into a second-generation drug addict and/or criminal who was scamming the Benjamin Baruch Center for Pain and Palliative Care for narcotics. It hadn't occurred to me to explain that my eighty-year-old mother had been prescribed methadone for back pain—not to wean her off cocaine, which was what the doctor must have assumed.

"Well, I'm keeping it shut now!" I responded. "I'm not saying a word. I won't say a word ever again. Not to you! That's for sure! Not a word! Not a single word!" Jake and I, when we weren't busy rolling around in the mud of our terrible hate, had been trying to figure out what exactly it was I could be suspected of doing, because Dr. Ruttman's charges appeared to contradict each other: On page 4 of her report, which I had read in astonishment on the subway ride back from the clinic the previous week, was written, "intentional dilution of urine suspected," and a few pages after that was written, "diversion possible," which Jake and I learned from the Internet meant that I was suspected of selling the Percocet, instead of taking it.

"If I was diluting my urine, wouldn't that mean I wouldn't want them to know I was taking the Percocet?" I was asking him.

"And if you were selling it on the street, then why would you dilute your urine?"

"Yeah, wouldn't I want it to show up in my urine? I mean I would, theoretically speaking, save at least one pill for myself, you know, for the test." The image of myself standing on a street corner somewhere, whispering to passersby, Percocet! Want Percocet? Got Percocet! appeared to me and I chuckled to myself.

"What's so funny?" Jake asked me.

"I just realized what a respectable person I am."

"Why? Because you're not a drug dealer?"

"Yes. Yet I feel that I am."

"I know what you mean, because I, too, know that you are not a drug dealer and yet somehow I feel that you are," Jake said. "Let's finish this thing."

I wished I could tell the drug addict I had made friends with at the clinic last week what had happened. No doubt he would be able to shed some light on my situation. He had been sitting next to me, at the end of his sad and broken life, with his faded tattoos and his cane and his hacking cough, mumbling to himself as he filled out the questionnaire attached to the clipboard that was handed to all us patients by the surly receptionist upon our arrival at the clinic. I had taught him how to spell "bowel movement."

This is someone who doesn't care about anything, I said to myself as I transcribed his words onto the back of a flyer for eight-dollar shoes that a dejected-looking clown on stilts had handed to me on the corner of 14th Street and Fourth Avenue. "Normal routine: don't have none." "Sleep? Two hours a night—maybe two hours. Tops two hours." "Enjoyment of life: what the fuck does that mean?" He had a nonchalance I admired. What a concept. To have absolutely no expectations. That would be a kind of freedom, wouldn't it?

I was due at the clinic at one thirty, when I was scheduled to pee into a little jar, have the remainder of the pills that Dr. Ruttman had prescribed for me the previous week counted out, and get a prescription for another week's supply of the new drug they had given me—a form of morphine, with many more side effects than the drug I had been previously taking, but presumably with less street value.

I pursed my lips and kissed Jake symbolically on the cheek (for despite everything, I knew that one day we would make up and find our way back to love, and I thought a kiss, premature and insincere though it may be, might give the process a nudge in the right direction) and off I went to go home to print out the letter.

I ran into the exterminator in the elevator. He was a big man with a big red face and a big bald head, every inch of which was covered with beads of sweat—some of them so large they could be more accurately described as bubbles. I told him how happy I was to have run into him. "My apartment is infested with mice!" I said. "I see them crawling out of the stove! It's disgusting!"

"No time," he told me. "Been fumigating for forty-five minutes."

"That's very alliterative of you but you can't do this to me," I told him. "Please. I'm infested with mice! I'm going to call your office." I proceeded to dial the number, which I had stored in my cell phone. "You might as well come with me now. Your office is just going to tell you to go back anyway."

Ignoring me, he escaped with his gigantic canister of poison through the door of the basement apartment, and when he found me waiting there for him eight minutes later, he said, "You win."

"My apartment is on the sixth floor," I told him as I pressed the elevator button. Something told me that one of my neighbors was holding the elevator door open (after years of New York City living, one develops a sixth sense about such things) and I started banging on the door. I prayed that I wasn't going to have to wait forever until someone on the first, second, third, fourth, fifth or sixth floor finished up one of those brotherhood-of-man conversations (Isn't this weather brutal? You look great! Did you lose weight? At least twenty pounds, I bet!) that transpire in the elevators and on the sidewalks of the city.

"How can you go around dressed like that on a day like today?" I asked the exterminator, hoping to divert him with the kind of small talk in which I have always excelled. He was wearing long navy blue pants and a long-sleeved navy blue shirt with MIKE'S EXTERMINATING: JUST SAY NO TO PESTS written above the shirt pocket. "I couldn't bear to wear any kind of sleeves on a day like today, much less long sleeves. And that fabric," I said, grabbing hold of the end of one the shirt tails that had been liberated from the confines of his long, hot pants. "That's a heavy polyester blend. At least they could give you something lighter."

"This is what they give us."

"That's so heartless. Mailmen get to wear those cute little shorts. And so do policemen, don't they? Or is it the UPS

guys? I forget. Yeah, it's the UPS guys. Why not extermina-
tors?"

He shrugged, which involved some effort, considering all
the stuff he was carrying.

"Finally." As the elevator arrived, I asked him, "Don't you
have any water? You should carry around a bottle of water
with you. Put it in the freezer at night and it will stay cold all
day long. That's what I used to do when my son was little."

I felt the familiar sadness creeping up on me. I was thinking about the summers Jake and I used to spend at the beach
with Danny when he was little, before his diagnosis. We
would bury him up to his neck in sand, and Jake, who had
always been so good at finding ways to delight Danny, would
mold octopus arms out of wet sand. My job was to give him
sips of water from the bottle I had put in the freezer the night
before and to scratch the occasional itch that would appear on
his beautiful face. We hadn't started worrying about him yet;
we were still going through the phase of thinking, So what
if he isn't like the other children? Why should he be? We're
weird. He's weird. What else should we expect?

"I did that, but it's all gone," the exterminator told me.

We were friends now. I could relax.

"What's your name?" I asked him. "I'm Mimi."

"Lou. My name is Lou."

I opened the door of my apartment and went off to fetch a
glass of ice water while Lou went off to drop pellets of poison
behind my stove.

"Here," I said, handing the glass to him. "And I'll give
you a bottle to bring with you." I scrambled around in the
havoc of my kitchen cabinets looking for a plastic bottle.
When I found one, I filled another glass with ice and water
and poured it into a funnel, which I held scientifically over

the mouth of the water bottle. It felt good to be performing this simple act of kindness.

"Do you have roaches, too?" Lou asked me.

"Not really. The gel controls them. Do you have any gel? Please use the gel. I hate the spray. I hate the smell, and besides it doesn't work."

"That's because they don't mix it right. The spray works much better than the gel. You just gotta mix it right. Most people don't mix it right. I do. That's what I use in my apartment."

"I prefer the gel."

"I don't have any gel. Besides, like I told you, the spray works better."

"Okay, I believe you. Spray away. And you might as well give me some glue traps. Though they don't work. The little fuckers walk right past them. I used to worry about them being inhumane. The glue traps. But now I don't care. Let them die a slow, wriggly death."

"It's us against them," he said.

"That's life in a nutshell," I responded.

"You can say that again." And with that he was off. This might be the best part of my day, I thought to myself.

The clinic was just twenty blocks away from Jack's 99 Cent Store. Talk about addiction: that's what Jack's, with its profusion of useful and useless things, was for me; so in happy anticipation of the unknown bargains that lay in store for me, I went to fetch my broken cart from the hall closet, where it had sat, among many other broken things, for three years now, waiting to be put out of its misery.

When I got to the clinic, I signed in with the receptionist and she handed me a form and I handed her the envelope containing the letter Jake and I had worked on, which I asked her to give to the head nurse. I sat down in a chair by the window and started filling out the form, cramming the margins with complaints about Dr. Ruttman, but when I was finished with my scribblings and looked at the paper, I thought they resembled the ravings of a drug addict, so I tore up the piece of paper and asked the surly receptionist for another form.

"I just gave you one," she told me.

"Well—yes, I'm sorry, but I made a mistake, could you give me another?"

We hated each other. The week before I had sat there waiting for over two hours, and every time I went up to ask her when I would be seen, she looked at me through the slits of her eyes and said that I would have to wait my turn like everybody else. "You're not the only patient, you know." Those were the same words the head doctor uttered to me forty-five minutes later when I tried to present her with my various theories about why my urine might have tested negative for Percocet.

"No more Percocet for you!" she had said with a smile. She had a name that no one could manage to pronounce and so everyone called her Dr. B.

I told Dr. B. that, according to the results of my last screening, I had tested positive for Percocet.

"That's strange," I said. "I wonder why I tested positive this time, and negative the time before."

"That's because you were taking the Percocet!" Dr. B. exclaimed as she clicked her way out of the room. She was a short, fat woman with a bad complexion who dressed in ill-fitting frilly dresses and stiletto-heeled shoes. She had administered a nerve block to me a month before, a painful procedure that involved sticking an enormous needle into my lower back. I think I insulted her professional pride when I told her that the procedure hadn't worked, that I still felt as though I were being eaten alive from the inside by thousands of tiny bugs, and now she was punishing me for it.

Shortly after my return to my seat, the receptionist called me over and informed me that my health insurance had expired. This seemed to make her happy, and it in turn made me happy to know that her happiness was destined to expire shortly, because I knew with wonderful certainty that my insurance was still active, having just received a notice of recertification in the mail that morning. It felt so good, being without doubt for a change. I dialed the tiny numbers printed on the back of my insurance card, and after explaining the situation to the woman on the other end, I handed the receptionist my cell phone. I could tell from her smug expression that she was giving the insurance lady a hard time and that felt good, too, knowing that I wasn't the only person in the world she treated with contempt.

After a few minutes she beckoned me over with one of her overmanicured claws and I waited on my cell phone with the insurance lady—who turned out to be a great person—until the fax confirming that my insurance was up-to-date came through. We found a common bond in our mutual dislike of the receptionist.

"You could tell, just from that brief conversation with her?" I asked.

"You get to be very quick at picking up signals like that in my business."

"Well, it's a tribute to you that you've managed to stay so nice."

"I try my best," she told me. "We're all in this together. That's what I tell myself every day."

"Me, too!" I said. What a nice woman, I thought as I planted myself back down on my chair and looked around the waiting room. Everyone was white. There was an elderly woman with beauty parlor hair in pearls and two men in business suits and the boy next to me was reading a book about semiotics. There wasn't a single drug addict in the bunch: There was no woman nodding off mumbling into her chest that the doctor refused to renew her presciption for Vicodin because she had tested positive for cocaine; no man in his twenties who looked to be least fifty, his hair in a greasy ponytail, dark circles under his eyes; no skinny woman, reeking of cigarette smoke, with her front teeth missing, dressed in a miniskirt that exposed legs that were covered in black and blue marks—none of my usual crew of fellow patients, in other words.

Then I remembered. This wasn't the poor people insurance day. Monday had been a holiday, and since they were rationing out the painkillers to me one week at a time, I couldn't be scheduled to come in on my regular day, so the clinic had no choice but to put me in with the private health insurance crowd.

I sat in my chair rereading my letter, and in the middle of the third reading, I decided to take matters into my own hands. I made my way through the door to the back, where I planted myself outside the office of Ellen, the nurse who had been so nice to me during my previous visit. I had been sitting in Dr. Ruttman's office in tears, terrified at the thought of my symptoms being left untreated because I was now a person under suspicion. I had demanded that another doctor be summoned, and had been presented with Ellen instead. She wasn't a doctor, but she was the head nurse and such a comfort to me that I was happy Dr. Ruttman hadn't been able to find a doctor to sit in with us. She had held my hand and looked into my eyes and told me that they were going to help me.

"Don't worry, honey," she had reassured me. "We're going to find something that will work for you." What a nice woman, I thought to myself. So unlike everyone else who works here. But now she was saying, "Who does she think she is? Barging in here like she owns the place!" (She was talking about me the way I spoke to my mice—although I spoke much more respectfully to them.)

"What did you expect me to do? Wait all day?" I called out to her. "I have an autistic son and I have to be home for him when he gets back from school!" Lately I had gotten into the habit of using Danny as an excuse for everything.

I have an autistic son, I would write as my excuse when I was called for jury duty; there was a crisis with my autistic son, I would tell my editor when I missed a deadline; and I used Danny as an excuse once when I went to argue a parking ticket as well.

I had always made it a policy to fight my parking tickets, regardless of whether or not I was in the right. It was a game I liked to play with the hearing officers, who never believed my stories about missing street signs or the car not starting or being stuck in the elevator on my way out of my apartment building to move my car. Most of my excuses were things I would make up on the spot, and I would usually take my losses in stride. But since Danny's diagnosis, every ticket had taken on the weight of my monumental grief. Why do they insist on hurting me? I would ask myself. Haven't I been hurt enough already?

There was only one judge, the last one, who ruled in my favor. One of the reasons I prevailed, I think, was because the story I told him happened to be true.

I told him that I had been rushing down the street with my son to get to my car in time to move it, but then he saw the big piece of black tape covering the sign for the W subway line.

"He's very upset that the W line was canceled," I said. "He loves the subway system. He kept on trying to tear off the black tape. And I kept on trying to stop him. My son is autistic, you see, and he wants everything to be the same."

Then forgetting that the reason I was telling the judge this story was to beat the ticket, I went on.

"My son—my son—my son . . . He wouldn't stop trying to pull off the tape. I let go of his hand for a second—I forget why—and he went running to the subway station. I'd never seen him so upset!

"This wasn't the first time he did this," I continued. I was on the verge of tears. "Two months ago he was at the same subway station and he kept on jumping up to try to tear off the tape. Later, when we got home, my husband and I tried to make Danny understand how dangerous what he was doing was.

"We told him he could be arrested. We told him about prison. We told him he could get beaten up in prison. But he kept on insisting that he would refuse to be arrested. He said he would get a get-out-of-jail card. Or he would break out of jail. We kept on telling him that that was fantasy. We kept on telling him stories about what jail was really like. We wanted to frighten him and we didn't stop until we made Danny cry. Danny never cries."

I told the judge that Danny still keeps on trying to rip off the black tape. It's always a battle of wills with us, I told him. I had long ago forgotten who this man was and why I was telling him all this. Then, remembering the ticket, I added that by the time I got back to my car, there was the dreaded flash of orange flapping arrogantly in the breeze.

I could barely talk, my throat ached so much. "That's why I was late. I couldn't get him to budge. He's getting so big—"

The words stuck in my throat. I could tell by the look on the judge's face that I had won him over: The moment of victory I had been waiting for had finally arrived. Here, at last, was a person who understood. I could see my heartbreak reflected in his kind eyes. This made me very uncomfortable.

Holding up his hand, the judge told me to forget about the stupid ticket. I had more important things to worry about. I suppose I must have looked confused, because I *was* confused. He looked me in the eye and told me that mothers like me were heroines as far as he was concerned. "It's important for you to take care of yourself. Think of your son. You have to stay healthy for him."

I decided right then and there that that would be the last time I would use Danny as an excuse for anything and I was sorry now that my resolve had weakened, because Nurse Ellen was stomping out of her office and commanding me to go into the waiting room and sit there, like everyone else. There was such a mean look on her face that I wondered where all the compassion she had shown me last week could have gone. Had it all been just an act? How frightening, I thought to myself; cruelty masked as kindness is cruelty in its most lethal form.

I went back into the waiting room and waited for the time to pass. Finally an hour later. Nurse Ellen came out and beckoned me over to her with a steely nod of her head, her lips pressed together so tightly that all the blood had drained out of them. She handed me a prescription for a week's supply of the new drug, at the same dose.

"Didn't you read my letter?" I asked her.

"It's eight pages long. I don't have time to read an eight-page letter."

"This new drug isn't helping me at all!" I told her, brandishing the prescription form she had just handed me.

"Don't get hysterical. If you get hysterical, I'll call the guards. You'll have to wait until a doctor is available to see you to have the medication adjusted. That's the policy. You can't expect the policy to be changed just to suit you."

The next appointment wasn't for another month and I ran out of the clinic, but not until I told the receptionist what I thought of her.

"The people who come here are in pain and you sit here with that sneer on your face and you're rude. You have a real attitude problem. You should be a token booth clerk or a prison guard, instead of a receptionist in a doctor's office."

"Thank you," she said, looking at me with those standard-issue eyes of hers.

"Don't thank me," I told her. "I'm telling you that there's something wrong with the way you treat people. That you're a morally deficient human being. You shouldn't thank me."

"Thank you."

"Fuck you, bitch," I told her as I made my way out the door

and down the brightly lit corridors of glass-enclosed rooms containing continents of human suffering and human need.

I regretted uttering the words as soon as they left my mouth, for I had been trying to train myself not to overreact to situations like this for quite some time now. Jake and I both had problems dealing with the rudeness of strangers, and one day we had sat at the kitchen table developing a list of rejoinders. For example, in response to people who angrily bark "You're welcome!" when someone fails to thank them for keeping a door open, we would simply say, "You're welcome, too." For the person who orders another person to cover his mouth when he coughs, I wanted to say, "I'm sorry but I have lung cancer, which isn't contagious," but Jake insisted that a flat "I'm sorry" would suffice. We were still working on an effective response for people who don't know—or if they do, they don't care—that it's impudent to order other people to lower their voices in public places (this was a case that really just applied to me, because I was the one with the big loud voice). I agreed with Jake when he told me that "Fuck you" was not the devastating rhetorical device we thought it was when we were teenagers, but the fact of the matter was it was still my favorite phrase in the English language.

My plan now was to walk to Jack's and I was wheeling my one-wheeled cart up Sixth Avenue thinking about man's inhumanity to man when a wall-eyed black woman with a big belly and a big smile approached me. She was wearing a tight red dress that exposed a deflated, stretch-marked cleavage, and she had a friendliness about her that alternately repelled and attracted me. I took her to be the sort of person who has everything figured out because of God or some other spiritual dimension. Still, my experience at the pain clinic had left me feeling hungry for human kindness, so I decided to accept her friendliness at face value.

"I like your cart," she told me. "I've been looking all over for a red cart. I hate the color black. It's so sad and my cart makes me feel sad," she said, pointing to the perfectly lovely, able-bodied black cart she was wheeling. "Red is a happy color and I am a happy person. Do you mind telling me where you got your cart?" she asked, and I proceeded to tell her the story of my cart—how it was supposedly covered by a warranty, but that the company had charged ten dollars and ninety-five cents for shipping a new set of wheels to me and that when the wheels arrived I discovered that it would take an entire factory to attach them to my cart, but I had been holding on to the wheels and the broken cart for five years now—because I had trouble dealing with injustice and defeat. This was one of my issues, I told her. I used the word "issue" because I was sticking with my initial impression that she was a person with a philosophy and I know that people with philosophies are always in the process of dealing with their issues.

"So what I'm trying to tell you is that I don't think this is such a great cart. I wouldn't recommend it," I said.

"It would do just fine for me," she told me. "Yours broke because you carry around too much heavy stuff. You shouldn't do that to yourself. You are one of God's precious children," she added.

"Thank you," I told her sincerely, because at the moment the idea of having some benevolent omnipotent being watching over me appealed to me very much.

"All I care about is the color," she told me. "I don't carry around heavy stuff. I just need it for my business," which she informed me was selling scarves on the corner of 125th Street and Lenox Avenue. She lived in Rego Park, Queens, a good solid white middle-class part of the borough where the median income was sixty thousand dollars a year—that's where her fiancé, a retired lawyer, was from, but Harlem was still in her blood, and she liked doing business there.

"They're still my people. They'll always be my people," she said, concluding her digression. Then she went back to asking me about my cart.

"Okay," I told her, "maybe it will work for you. Anyway, I got it at Jack's. Do you know Jack's?"

"I heard of it, but I've never been there."

"Well, you're in for a real treat. I'm going there now and I'll show you where I got my defective cart."

"Great. And then I'll give you mine. You shouldn't be wheeling around a cart with only one wheel."

"That's awfully nice of you," I told her. "But you don't have to do that," I added, hoping with all my heart that she would give me her cart.

"I want to," she said.

Then we proceeded to introduce ourselves to each other and to tell each other our life stories, starting with our ages and our weights.

I told Renee I was fifty and she told me she thought I looked like I was thirty and she asked me how much I thought she weighed and I told her about one forty, thinking she was at least one sixty, and then she told me about her two sons and their two fathers.

The oldest was nineteen and lived with his father, an African-American who never gave her any money. The kid was a mess, and every now and then she would try to set him straight about life, but besides that, she didn't have much to do with him anymore. Her other son was only five, and was living with her fiancé, the lawyer, a white man who had already set up a college fund for the kid, even though he wasn't his child. Her older son's father, "the black man," she said, hadn't put aside a cent for her nineteen-year-old, but her five-year-old already had fifteen thousand dollars in his name. And then she tried to engage me in a conversation about the superiority of the white race, a line of conversation I had no interest in pursuing.

I didn't tell her about Danny, but I told her that my husband hated me and I told her all about the pain clinic and about my bladder and she told me that she had never found a man who was good for anything, except this last one, but that was only because he had money, and that she had bladder problems, too, that sometimes she peed as often as every half hour, and I told her that sometimes I peed as often as every five minutes and that was why my experience at the pain clinic had left me feeling so devastated.

"It must have been something in your past life," Renee told me, and I told her that this was one thing I hadn't looked into yet.

When we got to Jack's, they were all out of the carts, but then I remembered that the discount luggage store down the street carried the same cart.

"I think they're selling them for five dollars more, even though they're supposedly a discount store," I told her.

"That's nothing," she said. "My man takes good care of me."

I told her I would bring her to the luggage store. I was in one of those moods that my feelings of desperation can lead me to sometimes, where life can seem so meaningless that there doesn't seem much point in forcing myself to spend every minute of every day doing something productive.

Renee told me again that she would give me her black cart if she found a red cart to replace hers, and I told her again that she didn't have to do that, but the fact is I was obsessed with getting that cart, for reasons I will now explain. For one thing, I thought that having a functioning cart would release me from the tyranny of the useless set of wheels that had been lying on the bookshelf next to the computer for the past five years as a reminder that the world is full of broken promises and deceit. For another thing, it would have the advantage of eliminating a source of irritation to Jake, who was always accusing me of being a hoarder and recently had been getting very aggressive about making me throw out things I treasured (the brass coffee table missing its glass top that used to stand beneath the piano, a wicker chair that used to sit in the hallway, blocking the coat closet, my collection of twenty-year-old spices, my collection of Tupperware with mismatched tops, et cetera). Also, I wouldn't have to walk the streets of the city wheeling around a handicapped cart that required great skill and dexterity to maneuver.

But best of all, I loved the idea of some random stranger giving me her cart, just like that. It had a value to me far greater than the cost of the cart itself, for not only would it put the story of my broken cart and all that it represented behind me but I would also have an object that I would treasure for the rest of my life. The cart would be much more than a cart to me; it would be a symbol of the generosity and the potential for goodness that exists in every human heart, and when the time came for its wheels to break, too, as I knew

they would someday, I only hoped that I would have the for-
titude to simply bid it a fond farewell and go out and buy
another one to replace it.

And so, it was with all this in mind that I took Renee
down the street to the discount luggage store on 32nd Street.
My heart sank when I saw that there was no red cart in sight,
although the store manager said that he would look for one
in the back. It was at this point that I decided to take stock of
myself. How likely was it that the merchant would find a red
cart? I asked myself. And how likely was it that this stranger
who believed in the afterlife had any intention of giving me
her cart? And how much more time should I invest in this
venture? And wouldn't it be a sign of mental health—not
to mention self-respect—for me to cut my losses and simply
give up? And so I wished Renee the best of luck and told her
that it was very nice meeting her, and she told me we should
get together sometime and that she would give me her number and I should give her mine and that's what we did.

After an awkward embrace, during which our two carts
collided, I made my way back to Jack's, where the entire time
I was filling my shopping cart with bags of dried chestnuts
for Danny and jars of pickles for Jake and three packages of
Jack's ninety-nine-cent bread, which was still a bargain at a
dollar twenty-nine, and a package of bobby pins to supple-
ment my lifetime supply of bobby pins, a gigantic laundry
bag to add to my impressive collection of laundry bags and
sundry cheeses that were due to expire in less than a week, I
harbored the secret hope that Renee would find the red cart
she had been looking for at the luggage store and that she
would surprise me by leaving her cart in front of the store for
me, and sure enough, as I walked down 32nd Street with my
superfluity of purchases in tow, I could see standing off in the

distance like a figment of my imagination, Renee's practically brand-new black cart waiting for me, and as I got closer to it, I noticed that there was a little piece of paper attached to it—a note for me—I was certain, it was a note for me. Scolding myself for having judged Renee so harshly, I felt a rush of love for her, and it was with a light, repentant heart that I bent down to read the note, which had been impaled on the buckle of one of the pockets (a lovely feature I hadn't noticed until now), and there in the handwriting of a child was written: *This is for you, cheap white bitch.*

The juxtaposition of Renee's note and the gift of her cart made me happy. They seemed to imbue my day with such thematic resonance, such irresistible roundedness, that I decided to leave the coveted cart right there on the curb, with the note attached to it, for curious passersby to look at and wonder about. I couldn't wait to get home to tell Jake all about my day. I would let it unfold exactly as it had, and save the story of the cart for last.

That was the best part of it—the whole experience was so exhilarating that I completely forgot that I hated Jake and that he hated me and even when I remembered the long big hate I didn't feel it anymore and I knew that when I came home to Jake with love in my heart he would forget that he hated me, too, because that was the way it always was with us, it only took one to make the first move and the other would follow.

And so as I worked my way back through the rush-hour crowds at Penn Station, to the A train, I felt happy—happy that Jake was my husband and that together we had created a strange and wonderful creature like Danny; happy that it was summer because now we could take Danny to the beach and make him into an octopus again. I could smell the seaweed and the saltwater and the sun. But then I felt the flood of sadness that would always overtake me whenever Danny emerged out of the sand, his octopus arms disintegrating around him, reminding me that this was ultimately all we were: just sand. But now I told myself: Wake up, Mimi! Is this how you want to be? Seeing misery in every grain of sand? And furthermore, I told myself that it was dishonest and unfair of me to blame Danny's autism for everything, because the darkness that was in me had been there long before he was born.

And then I remembered a time, when Jake and I were first going out, and we were walking down Broadway and I was complaining about something. In response, Jake, out of the blue, turned himself upside down and started walking down the street on his hands.

"This is how we should live our lives!" he told me as his keys, his wallet and all his change spilled out of his pockets and his T-shirt fell over his face. I had known long before this moment that Jake, and only Jake, could give me the peace of mind that had always eluded me, and it made me feel so grateful to hear him put the words "our" and "lives" together in one sentence that I felt I could do anything he told me to do, even be happy.

I was thinking about this and realizing that there existed an eternity in the love that was in my heart for my husband and my son when a man with a briefcase called me a clumsy bitch for accidentally rolling my cart over his foot. My first instinct was to call him a fucking asshole, but I wanted to rise above all that now, and so I simply told him, "I'm sorry, sir, but you see, my cart has only one wheel."

# *Acknowledgments*

The writer Marian Thurm took it upon herself to send my manuscript around, and she refused to give up until she'd found a publisher. If it weren't for Marian, I don't think *Queen for a Day* would have been published. I am also grateful to Marian for helping me navigate the final stages of the publishing process.

Virginia Bones, Joe Olshan's assistant editor at Delphinium Books, recommended my manuscript to Joe, who edited my work with skill, sensitivity and respect. In addition to deciding to publish *Queen for a Day*, Lori Milken gave me valuable guidance. Joan Matthews did a meticulous job of copyediting the manuscript. And whenever I feel unsure about something I have written, I can always rely on Pidge Claener to tell me exactly what she thinks.

By far my harshest critic is my husband, Phillip Margulies, who is also a fiction writer. No one's praise will ever mean as much to me as Phil's. Nor will I ever take anyone's criticism as seriously. Next to his love for our daughter Sammy, our son Benjy and me, Phil's greatest love has always been good writing, and his appreciation is all I have ever needed by way of reassurance that there was value in what I was doing.

I would like to thank the following people for having helped me in my work and in my life: Roland Smiley, Maureen McSwiggan-Hardin, Vicki Sudhalter, Nicole Van Nortwick, Mary Clancy, Marsha Ponce, Ann Slavitt Gordon, Mary Somoza, Margaret Puddington, Meredith Maddon, Sarah Morgridge, Joan Hauser, Luellen Abdoo, Hannah Button, Katelyn Snyder, Becca Jane Rubenfield, Angela Sullivan, Eseosa Aiwerioghene, Michele Aquino, Kat Hooper, Michael Curtis, Sarah Shapiro, Hannah Kantor, Pamela Weinman, Beth Rosaler, Ruth Rosaler, Betsy Jaeger, Jordan Pola, Sami Robbins, Marina Catallozzi, Nancy Elkes and Kinsey Keck.

## ABOUT THE AUTHOR

Maxine Rosaler's fiction and nonfiction have been published in *The Southern Review, Glimmer Train, Witness, Fifth Wednesday, Green Mountains Review, The Baltimore Review* and other literary magazines. She is the recipient of a New York Foundation for the Arts Fellowship for Fiction. Her stories have been cited in editions of *The Best American Short Stories* and *The Best American Essays*. She lives in New York City with her husband, Phillip Margulies.